TOO RICH AND TOO THIN

A BOMBER HANSON MYSTERY

DAVID CHAMPION

ALLEN A. KNOLL, PUBLISHERS
SANTA BARBARA, CA

Allen A. Knoll, Publishers, 200 West Victoria Street,
Santa Barbara, CA 93101
(805) 564-3377
bookinfo@knollpublishers.com

© 2000 by Allen A. Knoll, Publishers
All rights reserved. Published 1999
Printed in the United States of America

First Edition

05 04 03 02 01 00   5 4 3 2 1

Library of Congress Cataloging-in-Publication Data

Champion, David.
  Too rich and too thin : a Bomber Hanson mystery / David Champion.--1st ed.
    p. cm.
  ISBN 1-888310-50-2 (alk. paper)
  1. Hanson, Bomber (Fictitious character)--Fiction. 2. Fathers and sons--Fiction.
Models (Persons)--Fiction. 4. Trials (Murder)--Fiction. 5. California--Fiction. I.

  PS3553.H2649 T6 2000
  813'.54--dc21   00-061544

Text typeface is Caslon Old Face, 12 point
printed on 60-pound Lakewood white, acid free paper
Case bound with Kivar 9, Smyth sewn

Also By David Champion

Phantom Virus
Celebrity Trouble
Nobody Roots for Goliath
The Mountain Massacres
The Snatch

1

High-priced models are as thin as straws. I used to think of them as a little on the slow side—upstairs—as though the straw didn't reach the bottom of the glass.

My idea, anyway. But I'm just a small cheese investigator to the big enchilada trial lawyer Bomber Hanson.

But then Cheryl glided into my modest office as though sliding down a cloud from heaven.

She was the requisite knockout gorgeous, but I could tell by the way her saucy eyes shifted to take everything in, she was not a lassie you were going to put anything over on.

Bonnie Doone, Bomber's secretary, ushered the model in. "Cheryl Darling," she said, and, at first, I thought Bonnie was calling me darling. I should have known better.

It made me feel good to see someone give Bonnie Doone a run for her money in the looks department. Bomber was a sucker for looks, or he wouldn't have employed that airhead. But whenever I remind Bomber that beauty is only skin deep, he says, "That's deep enough for me."

I offered Cheryl a seat in the closet Bomber had designated as my "office" in the one hundred and twenty-year-old Victorian house on Albert Ave. in Angelton, California where we practiced Bomber's profession. Though I can't even think of the word "office" without breaking into a guffaw.

All I could think of at first, with her sitting so close to me, was, *Let me out of here!*—where someone can *see* me with Cheryl Darling. Nobody would believe me otherwise.

She was not really your typical model with the vacuous expression on a column of bones that looked like it was held together by spit and bailing wire. Her visage was not only beautiful, but also intelligent. She had blond hair, with gentle, wavy curls whirling around her head like a feathery crown. She had the face and poise of one who would be at home on a horse. World class dressage, perhaps. Her features were not china doll, but those of a long distance swimmer. She looked like the girl next door because she was the girl next door. Someone you might run into at a drug store soda fountain, when they still *had* soda fountains.

You could only bless a creator who built her, from the blond flowing hair so natural the Clairol folks must have been crying out loud, down to a pair of legs that would have made Michelangelo throw in the chisel.

That was my take on her, anyway. I noticed I had trouble breathing normally while she was talking.

I sallied forth with some artfully crafted pleasantries which, sad to say, I forgot; or more likely, am too embarrassed to remember.

Of course, I knew what she was doing there. The papers were full of it. And the media was milking it for all it was worth:

Aldo diCarlo Died in my Arms and I Bought the Poison

was the screaming headline on the front page of one of those supermarket scandal rags. It was accompanied by a generous photo spread of Cheryl Darling with tears in her eyes, and one with her on the arm of a smiling Aldo. The caption was, *Happier Days*.

It was jingo-journalism at its yellowest, and it didn't seem fair.

I could just see her stewing over what to wear—attractive, but no too attractive so as to belittle the seriousness of the event. Provocative, but not sexpot. Tall and regal, but not towering.

I was never so glad to be tall.

She settled on a shortish raw silk skirt and an ivory colored knit top with shoes to match. The outfit fit, but it didn't cling. Cheryl was warm and friendly, but not flirty.

Bomber *had* to take this case. Regardless of merit. A

vision of such loveliness was not put on this earth to murder anyone.

I'll say this for her—she didn't give me any guff about seeing the big cheese. She was at peace going through the hoops Bomber had set up.

Bomber was my father, and, depending on the day, that is not something I always want to admit. Oh, he's the best trial lawyer anywhere, all right, but the rest of the baggage gets a little heavy at times. Like calling him Bomber. Except for the close affinity the word has to bombast, the appellation is purely chimerical.

He'd been a gung-ho bombardier in Korea. The adrenaline must have been pumping something fierce when he was flying to his first mission. That they were called back due to the armistice he always considered rather unfortunate. So the only bombs he ever got to drop were in the courtroom. And sometimes when he finished, those courtrooms seemed like Hiroshima after the big one.

Cheryl spoke, and it was not the squeaky, giggly voice you'd expect to come out of a Barbie doll, nor the sultry voice you'd expect of a blond bimbo on the silver screen. It was rather a dull monotone—a voice that would not excite a testosterone laden lad in a monastery. I speculated the flat voice was a defense of the body that had been subjected to constant ogling.

"I'm about to be arrested for murder," she said as though reading a grocery list. "You probably saw the story. The tabloids are having a field day with it."

"Tell me your version," I managed to get out without choking.

"Everyone thinks of Aldo diCarlo as a talented designer/entrepreneur," she said. "No better personally, but no worse, than others just like him. He liked to party and have luxurious things. He owned a Rolls *and* a Bentley and used to joke that the Bentley was for slumming, the Rolls for important occasions." I made a mental note to ask her not to pass that tidbit on to Bomber. He was inordinately proud of his Chinese-red Bentley.

"Each of Aldo's four bathrooms cost more that the average house. The materials were all bought from some distant, exotic venue. His house was the size of ten luxury homes—twenty-five average ones. Everywhere you turned, the rooms were dripping with money. He liked ostentation. He had been a poor kid and he made it on his own *chutzpah*."

I tried to figure if she had been in love with him. I couldn't.

"Here are the police facts," she said. "Which aren't in dispute. Aldo died in my arms of cyanide poisoning. It was after a big party at his palatial house in Montelinda. Hundreds of people were there. They didn't all wish him well." Her voice was mellifluous and low. Terribly seductive.

"Someone put the cyanide in something and got it to him."

"How many were still at the party?"

"No guests. They'd all gone home."

"Servants?"

She smiled a half-smile. "Why Mr. Hanson, what a quaint word. There were a couple of caterers cleaning up, I believe."

"Did you see Aldo put anything in his mouth?"

She laughed out loud. "There wasn't anything Aldo didn't put in his mouth. We were starting to call him 'The Mountain.'"

"Who's we?"

"His girls—" she paused a moment as if in self-editing. "His boys."

"Liked both?"

"Afraid so," she sighed.

"But you were the only one left?"

"Yes. I was his favorite," she said without losing her sense of modesty.

"What makes you think the police want to arrest you?"

She looked at me like my elevator didn't reach the top floor. "Because I told them the same thing. No one else was there. I could tell from their reactions they didn't believe me. Maybe there were a half-dozen or so who wouldn't cry at his funeral. But they weren't around when he died."

"So, obviously, there was poison in something he didn't eat until everyone left."

"Everyone but me," she admitted candidly.

"But you've no idea what he ate?"

She shook her head. "There were the pills, of course."

"Pills?"

"He was taking his pills. There were some left on the table. I was in the kitchen, he was in the dining room. I heard him scream for water—I ran in and saw him foaming at the mouth and writhing in pain. I grabbed a glass of water and he downed it in a gulp and I got him more and more. Then he said, 'hold me—.' He was hoarse—he could hardly talk."

Not the accusation of a man who thought she had murdered him, I thought.

I'll admit it. No reason not to: I lost my objectivity. In retrospect, in my meager defense, I think it is better to lose your objectivity over a woman than anything else (if you're a man). Better, for instance, than a dog, cat, or horse, or another man.

In other words, I believed every word that came out of her sensuous mouth.

My judgment was so muddled I made, a fatal mistake.

I took her to see Bomber.

2

Bomber's icy eyes froze my heart to a full stop. Behind his desk, the big cheese was grump city.

I had only intended to show him how gorgeous Cheryl was, because no matter what the merits of a case, if I suggest taking it, he finds dozens of reasons not to—and for me to convince him I have to overcome all his objections.

I could see Cheryl was impressed with Bomber's floor-to-ceiling personally and extravagantly autographed pictures of celebrities; his citations and awards.

Some guys try to be blasé about it, but you can't help but be a bit snowed, if only by the prepondent bulk of encomiams.

Others try to ignore the walls, perhaps on the assumption that Bomber will think less of them if they are too starry-eyed. Cheryl didn't play games. Her eyes bounced wide and she unabashedly turned her head to take in the whole display.

"Impressive," she muttered, and I noticed Bomber blanche, as though she had invaded his privacy. A curious notion when you think of it, but that was Bomber—slap on the wall all those pictures of governors, senators, stars of every stripe and four presidents even, then expect no one will comment on them.

"I'm sorry, Miss..." Bomber groped for her name, but not for very long. "We have certain protocols here, which have been egregiously breached. I hope you'll forgive me, but I have work to do—" he looked at me as if to say, "unlike some slug-gards I could mention who will drop everything for a pretty face."

"I'm so sorry to intrude," she said with bright empathic eyes. "I just want to say that I hope you'll take my case. I'm really desperate. I hear you're the best," she added hastily as though she'd just realized her desperate comment might be misunderstood.

"Yes, well, tell your story to Tod—that's the way we do it here," Bomber said, darting me another of his zinger bullseye glares.

With the nod of overcooked humble pie, I escorted Cheryl back out to our reception area where Bonnie Doone was sitting primly at her desk trying to look busy.

I don't walk outside with all our prospective clients, but Cheryl just seemed as though she would benefit from the reassurance. We stepped out on the front porch of our Victorian house/office. There, with the sun slanting through the monster Araucaria tree in front of the parking lot, Cheryl put her hand lightly on my arm.

"Tod," she said as though we were old friends, "what's going to happen to me?"

"Happen? Maybe nothing. The police need more evidence than what you told me to arrest you."

"Will I go to jail?"

I felt myself giving into a frown, though I tried to fight it. "Let's worry about that later."

"Later? Could they just come and swoop down and throw me in jail?"

My frown was embedded in place. "You'd get a hearing. They have to have solid evidence before they do anything so drastic."

"It's creepy," she said, shuddering.

"What is?"

"The way they are investigating everything about me. It's like my sacred space—my body, everything—is being invaded."

"I'll try to prevent that from happening," I said. It was the voice of Mr. *Gallant*.

"When will you know if Bomber will take my case?"

"I should know either way by tomorrow. Can we have lunch?"

"I'd like that," she said with an encouraging gleam in

her eye. "I hope you'll have good news tomorrow."

I watched Cheryl move down the steps across the small parking lot to her car—a sporty, greenish Lexus. She moved with a tender grace, her body almost liquid inside her beautifully fitted outfit—not so tight she looked like a woman too eager to promote the goods, and not so loose you had no idea what was inside.

She waved to me as she drove off.

Back inside Bonnie Doone unloaded all her boy/girl frustrations on me. I understood it, so I remained blasé.

"Quite a handful for a guy of your, shall I say, *limited* experience," she said. "Would that be tactful? Well, it's accurate enough."

"Thank you," I said.

"Oh, by the way, the Bombardier wants to see you right away—and a word to the unwise—he's not in the peachiest mood. Apparently Miss America didn't light the same fires in him as she did in his most junior associate."

"Jealousy," I sang, "da da-da da da da. *Jealousy.*"

"You wish."

Inside Bomber's office, he could barely look at me. His thick eyebrows seemed to be smoking like the aftermath of July fireworks. He didn't ask me to sit down; that would have been too friendly for his mood. Instead, he launched right in.

"Looks like you need to brush up on your protocol around here. Bonnie can give you lessons if you are indeed as rusty as you just displayed."

"Sorry—"

"A little smitten, are you?"

I blushed.

"Well, let me tell you, it's the worst thing you can do, get a case on an aspiring client."

He didn't have to tell me that. He knew he didn't. But I nodded noncommittally just the same.

"I don't have to remind you the mess you made of things because you fell for that red-headed associate in Pennsylvania."

She only won us the case I recorded in *Nobody Roots for Goliath*, but I didn't argue.

"Okay," Bomber said grudgingly, "let's get it over with."

I summarized the facts as she had presented them as succinctly as I could. All the while I could tell he was seething.

His opinions on the matter, all contrary to mine, were welling up within him. Sometimes it was politic to let Bomber have the floor to get it out of his system. I could see he was gathering steam for the blowout.

"Let me get this straight," Bomber said. "She was the only noncatering employee—you might say the only one who *knew* him—who was with him when he died of cyanide poisoning, and she bought the cyanide—and you want me to take the case?"

"Y-y-yes, sir." The damn stutter was back. All I had to do was look at him and my vocal apparatus went berserk.

"And can you give me one good reason to act so foolhardy after a lifetime of prudence?"

"I-I-I—"

"And don't tell me it's because you're sweet on her." That was Bomber—using quaint, antiquated phrases to belittle the opposition (me). Of course, I didn't *have* a good reason—other than the aforementioned softness of heart. He knew it, I knew it, and it was no good telling him it wouldn't kill him to lose a case once in a while, and in my humble opinion, based on my humbler experience, statistically, this looked like a loser.

"Because I b-b-believe in her," I said, letting the words tumble defensively into electric air.

Bomber got that shocked look on his face as though he discovered he was the only sane one in the nuthouse. Then he nodded that sage all-knowing nod of his that made you want to crawl under the desk. While you were under there, you could consider licking his elevator boots if you were in the humor for it.

"I j-just feel it. I m-mean, D-dad, did you ever j-just

feel a c-case in your gut?"

"When I feel it in my gut, I get indigestion."

I smiled, but I wasn't laughing.

"You *know*, Boy," he was saying, "it's a great defense—someone does something so dumb it's stupid, then they say, 'I couldn't have done that, it would have been too stupid.'"

"He wanted her to b-buy cyanide," I said. "DiCarlo wanted to k-kill the rats that were invading his p-place."

"Lot easier ways to do it," Bomber said.

"Th-that's what he w-wanted. Quicker."

"Tell you himself, did he?"

The blood of embarrassment rushed to my face. "'Course n-not," I admitted. "He's dead."

"Rest my case," Bomber said. "Oh, by the way," he added as an afterthought—"Dinner tonight."

It wasn't so much an invitation as a command. I was touchy about his having a call on my after-work time, and I was about to beg off when he plunged in the sinker:

"Mom's spaghetti."

3

When I arrived at the 'rents house, Bomber was in his study, so I quietly gravitated to the kitchen, where Mom diplomatically asked about my day. I told her.

"A *girl*, Tod? Oh, how wonderful. Could an old woman have a morsel of hope that you might find some common ground with this damsel—and who knows at this juncture—perhaps make a go of it?"

I shrugged. "Though hope springs eternal in the human breast," I said, "this one is up to Bomber."

"Bomber?" she said, cocking an eyebrow as though that were not a high hurdle, or even worth considering. "How so?"

I told her about his refusal to take the case.

"Oh, pshaw," she said. "That's sophistry. I'll handle Bomber. He should be as eager to have grandchildren as I am. She is of childbearing age?" Mom asked with a lifted eyebrow.

"Oh, Mom. A bit premature, wouldn't you say?"

"Premature babies, Confucius say, are better than no babies at all."

Mom told me to call Bomber to the table; she was ready to serve.

I did my duty and was the first one into the dining room.

There are always four chairs and four place settings at Mom and Dad's dining room table when I go to dinner.

There are only three of us. Whether this is in service of symmetry, a tacit expression of a wish that I might have a date, or a memorial to my departed sister, I don't know, nor do I have the temerity to ask.

Sis took a one-way trip into the ocean. The curse of a withered arm and her despair of ever finding a man to love her.

I sat at my designated place, across from the empty shrine. Mom brought in the fruits of her labor and set the plates on the table. The first at Bomber's place, though *he* was yet to make an appearance, the second at mine. She served herself last.

Then Bomber came in. He liked to make an entrance—be the last one at the table. He thought it was his due. I could see the residue of rancor from the office still on his face. If Mom saw it, she chose to ignore it.

He'd hardly picked up his fork when she launched into the topic that was nearest and dearest to her heart.

"Tod tells me he interviewed an attractive supermodel today."

"He did?" Bomber said, then shoveled in the spaghetti as if Mom had commented on the sunny day.

"Yes," she said. "Give you any ideas?"

Bomber stopped his fork in midair. "Yes, it does," he said, "but the ideas it gives me are obviously not the ideas it gives you. We are operating an office devoted to tort law, not a tart dating service."

"Oh, Bomber," she admonished him. "How can you be so reckless with language? I mean, the juxtaposition of tort and tart is cute enough, but do you really want to dismiss one of Tod's all too infrequent opportunities with a flip of the tongue?"

"Tod's social life is no concern of mine, and I won't bother suggesting it is also no concern of yours. I know that's hopeless. But I know what's coming and please understand I do not intend to compromise my principles in the service of match-making."

Mom kept a steady, discerning and judgmental eye on Bomber while he blathered on about principles getting him where he was today. "She's a celebrity," he said. "The victim was a celebrity; the case will be a circus. The last celebrity we defended—what was his name, Boy...?"

"Steven Sh-Shag," I said. It was a case I called *Celebrity Trouble.*

"Yeah," he said. "Nothing but trouble."

"But you won it, didn't you?" Mom said.

"By some miracle, as I recall," Bomber said. "I know miracles do happen, but not that often. This Miss America bought the poison that killed him. She was virtually alone with him when he died, and Tod has a good feeling about her. Well, she's a looker all right, I'll grant that, but I don't fancy every tabloid artist and paparazzi shutter bug camped on the Albert Avenue porch."

"But, Tod," Mom said in frustration. "His future...our grandchildren."

"I didn't get where I am today being guided by frivolous considerations. I take cases on their merits, on some intrinsic, or even extrinsic appeal they have to *me*. Not on some ephemeral, romantic hunch."

Mom didn't take her eyes off him as he exhorted the good fight. In fact, she nodded her approval at every pearl that fell from his lips. It lulled him into a false sense of security.

Then Mom spoke with a quiet penetration, more effective than any bomb from the Bombardier: "Maybe you're wrong this time, Bomber."

Later, I left Mom and Dad to each other. There was a fair dose of quiet seething on Bomber's part as there was in the infrequent moments Mom verbally disagreed with him. It was touching the way Mom went to bat for me, though I didn't expect she would hit any home runs.

In this case, I couldn't tell if Mom felt this one deep down and made the conscious decision to expend some stored capital on it, or if it was just her atavistic zeal to get me married off that caused her to dig in her heels for my side.

I got home to my home on the beach—actually over a garage in a widow's backyard—and went right for the piano—a scarred upright that had seen better days. I picked out some of the notes of my "Suite: Love," that I had written for the red-head, Shauna McKinley, during that Pennsylvania tobacco case I chronicled in *Nobody Roots for Goliath*.

I could feel another composition welling up inside me,

just waiting to burst forth on the music staffs reposing on the upright.

It would be fair of me to admit that due to thoughts of my lunch with Cheryl on the morrow, sleep did not come easily to me that night. Snatches of pretty melodies crowded my head and kept my brain hopping.

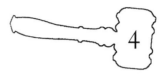

4

Bomber was a good man for holding a grudge. Second to none. And he was a washout at hiding it. Not that he tried.

He certainly wasn't hiding anything that next day in the office. He wasn't at his desk two minutes when Bonnie Doone told me he wanted to see me. She was adroit at conveying Bomber's mood with a twist of her lips, a scrunch of an eye, puffing out her cheeks or rolling her eyeballs. She did all three this morning.

The door to Bomber's office was uncharacteristically open, so as not to waste a moment before tearing into me, I was sure. He keeps the door closed in case some malcontent wants to barge in on him and interrupt his train of thought.

I had been schooled in the precise level of clunking my knock should have—not too soft that he might think it was a mouse scratching the door, nor so loud it scared the wits out of him—"like Gangbusters," was the quaint way he put it.

"Sit down, Boy," he said. "Sit down fast. I don't want to waste another minute on this folly."

I, of course, sat—not in my usual left field position on the love seat on his rogues gallery wall, but in the seat reserved for important folk—right across the desk from him.

He didn't need words to tip me off to his impatience. He was pacing the rug back and forth behind his desk.

"Your mother is giving me no rest on this thing. I know darn well it's a gender matter. If you were married, she wouldn't say boo about this girl—"

He shook his head. "What a sorry mess this is. This is not, I don't have to tell you, a case I would touch with a ten-foot pole. I frankly don't believe Miss Beauty's story. She's pretty enough, I'll give you that, but that can backfire if we get too many women on the jury—or, heaven help us, a woman judge."

I smiled to myself. All this protestation could only mean Mom had convinced him to take the case, if only for his peace of mind.

"As you know, I don't let the distaff dictate my professional decisions. Chaos that day would bring. Her idea—and I'm embarrassed to tell you this—is that it will 'expose you to the opposite sex,' was I believe the charming way she put it. Notice she said *opposite*, not complimentary as she might have. But no matter. And there was no listening to reason on her part. She actually trotted out the old saw about how everyone was entitled to counsel. I reminded her that not everyone was entitled to *my* counsel and if I got in the habit of taking hopeless cases, it wouldn't be long before we'd be on the streets begging for spaghetti ingredients."

I was rather pleased with the direction Bomber's monologue was taking. I wasn't called upon to participate, which kept my stutter down to zero. I didn't stutter in Bomber's presence when he talked, only when *I* talked.

Abruptly, Bomber switched gears. He was going to force me to stutter. "So you said this Sheri Dumpling was some kind of model."

"Cheryl D-Darling."

"Oh, good God, that's even worse. I take it that's not her real name?"

I shook my head. No stuttering.

"Yes, well, I'm relieved to hear that. I don't even want to know what her real name is—it's probably something like Spangler Arlington Brew or something."

I shook my head, but I didn't volunteer.

"So what was she called, her job I mean—clothes horse, model, or what?"

"S-Supermodel."

"Super? Super! What does that mean—like being a super star?"

I nodded.

"Make a lot of money?"

I nodded.

"How much, say?"

"A thousand d-dollars an hour."

Bomber's eyelids shot up as his eyes opened to the world of fashion. He stopped pacing. "That much?"

I nodded.

"Well," he said. "Well, well, well—yes—yes, indeed." He sank to his chair, the wheels of his mind doing flip flops—and why not? "Okay. You want me to take this case—"

I nodded, but he wasn't looking.

"That sounds fair enough to me—a thousand an hour. Perhaps it's time I adjusted my fee. Yes," he said, licking his lips in the most appalling way.

I shot forward in my chair. "B-B-But it c-could take you hundreds of hours."

"Yes, it could," he beamed. I could tell he was hoping this was his out.

"I don't know if she's s-s-saved that much—"

"So let her work some more."

"B-But she's *non grata* with this murder ch-charge. Nobody is using h-her."

"Well, now, son," he said looking me square in the eye. "You wouldn't want me to charge *less* than she does, would you? You'd both lose all respect for me."

"I wouldn't."

"You wouldn't. A thousand an hour for standing around having your picture taken. Unless I miss my guess, hers is a calling that does not overly tax the intellect. What is that worth vis-à-vis a man with intellectual cunning, the persuasive powers to save her life or liberty? Let it be up to her. Ask *her* what she thinks I'm worth."

"Oh, I know she'd agree you're w-worth it. I just d-don't know if she has it. You know these highly p-paid stars aren't often c-careful with their m-money."

He clucked his tongue and said, "That would be too

bad." He meant the opposite.

I shook my head as dolefully as I could.

"Tell you what, Boy. I'm willing to let you handle it—take all the time you want. I'll pay your salary. You charge her anything you want."

The idea sent pure terror down my spine. I was no trial lawyer—we both knew that. It was another of what Bomber charmingly referred to as "the unacceptable alternative," which he loved to pull on hapless clients and employees now and again.

"Okay," he said at last, when I had gasped what I thought was my last breath on the subject. "The grand an hour still sticks. You want to solve the case before I have to get involved, we'll give her your time for nothing. Deal?"

My face broke into such a smothering smile I was embarrassed.

"Deal!" I said without stuttering.

The Four Seasons Vanderbilt on the ocean in Montelinda just down the coast from Angleton, was the kind of place you went if you had bucks, which I didn't.

But I couldn't see taking a thousand dollar an hour supermodel to joints I frequented, albeit infrequently.

I had dreams of Bomber reimbursing me as a business expense—client contact account, but in the light of day I realized it was only a dream.

Whenever I walked in the place I thought the feeling I got was worth the money. Even if this meal was going to set me back about what I netted for a day's work in Bomberland. He didn't believe in spoiling his only son with extravagant salaries— "nepotism is bad enough," he had said, changing his tune somewhat from when he was nagging me to go to law school. It was a more respectable profession to Bomber than writing music, which was my true love.

"What's it like being a supermodel?" I asked Cheryl as soon as we were seated.

She laughed. "Like being a lawyer or investigator or waitress, I suppose. Different for everyone."

"Any common threads?"

"Some, sure. Boredom. The feeling that a robot could do the job. Zero intellectual challenge, and overcompensation for your services. Oh, there's fame and glory to be contended with, too. In our circumscribed circle."

My eyebrow bounced up. "You paint a bleak picture of modeling."

"It *is* bleak."

"Yet you don't seem to fit the mold."

"I don't?"

"No, you're too intelligent, for starters."

"How do you know?"

"Your vocabulary, for one. *Circumscribed?* It's a nice word for one so intellectually challenged."

"I did go to college," she conceded. "They didn't pluck me from grammar school as they seem to nowadays. Twelve, thirteen, fourteen-year-olds. I was over the hill when I started—relatively."

"Didn't seem to hurt you."

"I was lucky," she said.

"Luck? It's luck?"

"Well, sure, a lot of it is," she said. "And I am not just being modest. Face it, how much can we do about our looks? You have what they're after or you don't."

"And not many people do, or they wouldn't pay so much," I said. "Couldn't they broaden their requirements to save a lot of money?"

"Well, but it's like the movies. The public creates the stars. They clamor for certain people—"

"Based on their looks?"

"Exactly. Nothing to do with ability," she said. "Stardom is a quality—I can't explain it. I never had the urge to send the checks back, so I can't pontificate about it."

"Pontificate? Another super-word from a supermodel."

"Oh, stop. You're making me self-conscious."

"How about all those people staring at you? Does that make you self-conscious at all?"

"Certainly," she said. "Indubitably," she added with a wink and a sly smile.

"But I guess that's what being a model *is*, being stared at."

"You get used to it," she shrugged. "In the beginning, I thought, 'Wow these people think I'm beautiful—I'm like a movie star'—Then later you just think, 'Buzz off, you think I'm some kind of freak?'"

"We should all be such freaks," I said.

She smiled so modestly, not like a freak at all, but like a real person. It was, among others, a quality that turned me into mush in her presence.

Mercifully, she was a salad-eater. Unmercifully, a salad here cost as much as a rack of lamb somewhere else.

I, myself, selected from the low-end of the menu—a pastrami sandwich, which turned out to be less tasty than those served at sandwich shops in the less savory part of town. Probably needed more mayonnaise. It was as though they thought class was inversely proportional to the amount of mayonnaise you used. Unlike my model date/client, I considered one of the indisputable products of food and eating to be not only sustenance, fuel, energy and enjoyment, but also the production and maintenance of fat cells.

"Tell me about Aldo diCarlo," I said. "What was he like? What drove him? Who were his friends—and enemies?"

"He was like no one else I ever met," she said fiddling with her lettuce. "What drove him? His poverty, I suppose. He was from a Hell's Kitchen kind of neighborhood and he clawed his way to the top. Is that too cliché?"

"Not if it's true, I guess."

"It's true," she said. "He was in his way, insatiable. He could never get enough of anything—cars, houses, antiques, women, men—honors, standing ovations at shows. Someone always had to time his ovations and other couturiers'—his had to be the longest or he thought he failed."

"How did you meet him?"

"The model agency sent me to him. They sent a bunch of girls to him and he picked the ones he wanted for his runway show."

"What's that?"

"When designers bring out a new line—spring, fall— they have shows for the press and big buyers to hype the product. Models wear the clothes and walk the plank with everybody staring at them. They call it a runway…"

"Oh. He kept use…employing you?"

"Yes, he did. I made out quite handsomely from Aldo diCarlo designs."

"Will that end with his death?"

"Oh, yes."

"So you had nothing to gain with him dead—" I said.

"Oh, no," she said so dutifully that I resolved to stop asking leading questions with puffball answers I wanted to hear. I'd have been thrown out of the court for such foolishness.

"How well did you know Aldo diCarlo personally?"

"Well," she said. If she had gotten used to all the folks staring at her, I had not.

"Were you…" I was going to say "intimate," but it stuck in my throat… "an item?"

She smiled. "Nice choice," she said. I wonder if she knew that I wanted her to deny it. She didn't. It was in the papers, anyway.

"An item," she said, "yes, I guess you could say that. For a short while."

"How short?" I asked, pain lingering in my chest.

"A year or so," she said. "That was long for Aldo. His appetites were voracious."

"Many women?"

"Scads. I don't know, but I might have won the longevity prize."

"What ended it?"

"He did. A younger girl."

"You aren't exactly old," I protested.

"No, but there *are* younger. I may have qualified for the long in tooth prize, too."

"Really? I can't believe…" I wanted to ask her how old she was, but I'd find out soon enough. I think the tabloids put her in her mid-thirties. Aldo was almost sixty when he went to glory, as they say in the Salvation Army.

"What can you tell me about your replacement— besides, she was young? How young, by the way?"

"Would you believe sixteen?"

"No—"

She nodded. "It was like he was waiting for the bell to ring, putting her past the statutory limit."

I cocked an eyebrow, asking her for more.

"A pretty thing," she said, "as you can imagine. Plain girls were not in Aldo's line of fire."

"Were you angry?"

"At first, I suppose. Hurt. Though if I had been honest with myself, I'd have said it was inevitable all along. But what girl is honest with herself about men?"

"Hope springs eternal—?"

"Does it ever."

"So when did this, ah, dumping of you happen?"

"Oh, a year ago or so. Actually, thirteen months and nine days, if you want to be specific."

"That's pretty specific," I said. "Hurt more than you are letting on?"

"I'm letting on," she said.

"So the police are going to say you did it to spite him—to give him his recompense for getting rid of you."

"Well, the timing is wrong. I might have felt it a year ago, but you know what they say about time healing all wounds."

"But you were still friendly?"

"Oh, yes. He kept using me as a model too. Gave me a high-priced exclusive contract when we were..." she groped for the word, "close."

"Why were you the last one at his party?"

"I don't know. I had nowhere to go. I've always been a night person. He asked me to stay. He said he was lonely."

"What happened to the sixteen-year-old?"

"Didn't last."

"How long?"

"Six—seven months."

"What happened?"

"He found a boy in the sewing room that appealed to

23

him more."

"Oh, dear."

"Aldo always said he had too much love inside him to limit it to one person, or even to one sex."

"And you put up with it?"

"I'm afraid I did."

"Why?"

"Ah, there it is, the quintessential, unanswerable question: why? A lot of flip quips come to mind, like 'Damned if I know,' or 'You tell me.' But who can explain the heart? The closest I've ever heard is the saying, 'Reason of the heart knows no reason at all.' What can I tell you? He was charming. For our time together he was attentive, responsive, loving. His attention flattered me. In spite of my quote fame and knockout salary, I am just an insecure girl underneath, looking for validation. Aldo gave it to me."

"And yet you bought the cyanide that killed him?"

"Apparently."

"You mean you might not have?"

"I bought him cyanide to kill rats. He was a madman about rats—vermin of any kind. I'd say he had a cleanliness fetish. Anyway, as far as I know that was used to kill rats. The poison that killed him could have come from someone else."

"Whoa—maybe you should have been a lawyer."

"In this fix I should have been anything other than a diCarlo model."

"You didn't have any fights the night he died?"

"No, he was on top of the world. His show that afternoon had broken his standing record for standing ovations—sixteen minutes and thirty-three seconds was, I believe, the official time. His creations were startling, original and beloved all at the same time—no mean feat in this business."

"Where was his—boyfriend?"

"Upstairs in bed. Aldo had been in there with him earlier in the evening—"

"How do you know?"

"Aldo told me."

"He *did*?" That seemed a little odd to me, and I said so.

"We were pals," she said, shrugging her stunning shoulders.

"So tell me again about the death scene."

"He was at his long dining room table. He took five or six pills every night—for hypertension, for mania and depression, for blood pressure, I don't know what all. I was in the kitchen, just ready to leave when I heard this screaming. I darted out, found him at the dining room table clutching his throat, gagging and screaming for water. I went to get it—"

"Yes," I said. "You told me. You think he'd been taking his pills?"

"There were three left on the table. Unless his dose had been lowered, he took two or three of them—one of them must have had the cyanide in it."

"Was he drinking coffee or anything?"

"Yes, I guess it could have been in the coffee."

"Did you get it for him?"

"No, he got it from the caterers."

"No household help?"

"Yes, but this was such a huge party, he farmed it out."

"How many people?"

"Hundreds."

"His house is that big?"

"Bigger," she said. "Want to see it?"

"Can you get me in?"

"Sure," she said with a wry smile. "I have a key."

6

Cheryl Darling and I drove up tree sheltered streets to where the houses ended and the national park began. We were in my piece of junk which passes for a car to the unsophisticated. Cheryl, who was accustomed to high life and plush vehicles, was a good sport and made believe she didn't notice.

"There it is," she said pointing up to the top of the hill at a place that looked like the White House. Only it seemed a little larger. And it was up a higher hill.

We got to a wrought iron gate. In the center was Aldo diCarlo's symbol: an A in a circle

incorporating the first and last letters of his name, Cheryl told me. She told me the code for opening the gate, and I reached out to finger the keypad. The gate rolled open with an ominous sound befitting the weight of the gate and the late owner of the house.

We snaked up the driveway which had more curves than the late Marilyn Monroe and took roughly the time of a New York to Paris run on the Concord.

And then we were there—the scene of the crime. Cheryl used her key to open the front door. There were remnants of the police sealing the place, but they seemed to be an insignificant part of history now.

The inside of the palace knocked the wind out of me. I still can't think of it without experiencing shortness of breath.

Murder is no respecter of turf. You might expect they'd all happen in the poor and squalid sectors, but not so. There are as many venues for murder as there are motives, and the rich are not immune to jealousy, hate, retribution, greed, passion, and a dozen other emotions.

Aldo diCarlo's place was one of those Montelinda mansions you hear about and see pictures of in the slick magazines but never get to visit. Bomber could live in one of these estates, where you drive half a mile from the street to an eight car garage, where there is enough grass to zap the water supply for several fair municipalities, where the house puts you more in mind of a Ritz Carlton Hotel than of a single family dwelling.

I always wondered about the psychology behind a domicile of this size. Where did the buyer/builder/investor get his ideas of how many bedrooms and bathrooms he might need—of how large the rooms should be? What was large enough and was anything too large? Why not, for example, have a living room the size of Montpellier, Vermont? There could be smaller areas, sunken I hope, where you could have a conversation with someone, should that become necessary—conversation pits you could call them. Conversation held there would be in the pits, not necessarily the pits.

Everything about the place seemed to be just a bit more than the grandest place heretofore. As though Aldo diCarlo had measured the tallest ceiling in any residence and added a foot, and squeezed in more square footage to be the champion of livable area. How he could live in such vast, vacuous spaces I couldn't tell, but it certainly put my apartment in perspective. It was smaller than the walk-in closet in one of his guest bedrooms.

"You think anyone resented this display of ostentatious wealth?" I asked Cheryl.

"Sure," she said. "Jealousy is as American as apple pie."

"Any idea who?"

"My guess is everybody."

"What can you tell me about his last night?"

"The party? Like all his parties, Aldo always did everything in grand style—food, drink, dope, swarming waiters, boys and girls. He always strove for a different theme, a different look. This time it was orchids. There were a thousand white orchids all over the place, orchid leis for everyone, two huge orchestras, fortune tellers, magicians, masseuses, even an acupuncturist. I've never seen anything like it. I hear it cost him a quarter of a million dollars, but I wouldn't know. And, as usual, the noise level grew more deafening as the evening wore on."

"Were you here alone?"

"I had a date of sorts. He crashed early."

"Who?"

"A friend, really."

"Is he a...steady...friend?" I asked the question, I admit, more for personal than professional information.

"Off and on. His...goals and mine don't coincide at this point."

"So he went home early?"

"Went to sleep is more like it. A buddy of his took him home."

"What are your friend and his buddy's names?"

"Freddie Haajib and Billy Pasternak."

"Association with the deceased?"

"Billy did his photography. Freddie was just my date."

"Animosity?"

"A stretch."

"Who had it?"

"Phew," she said. "Where to start? Every girl he ever dumped, I suppose."

"Including you?"

She bobbed her head. "The police think so."

"You had no flare up or anything?"

"No. We'd settled into being more or less friends."

"More or less?"

She shrugged. "Sometimes more, sometimes less."

"For the party?"

"Oh, the party—Aldo was all by himself at the party. He had just come off the biggest triumph of his life. I don't think any of us can relate to it. He was simply on top of the world."

"Step on bodies to get there?"

"Well, I expect, a few."

"Like who?"

"There was the little designer who claimed Aldo stole his designs."

"Did he?"

"Wouldn't be surprised."

"What was his name?"

She giggled. "Aldo called him Pussy. Isn't that a crack up?"

"Nickname, I hope."

"I hope," she said. "Aldo got it from Gertrude Stein. It's what she called Alice B. Toklas. His real name was Jeffrey Xavier."

"You'll tell me where I can find this guy?"

"Oh, don't worry, I won't keep anything from you."

"Any exes in the male contingent?"

"Not sure. Aldo wasn't so open about those relationships. One of his early plusses was, people thought, 'Here is a dress designer who actually *likes* women.'"

"Do you think he did?"

"Yes," she said. "In his way."

"And what was that?"

"It's kind of a mystery, really. May I give it some thought before I sound more perceptive than I actually am?"

While I was trying to formulate a clever response that did not come to me, a tall, spare, forbidding looking man took possession of the room. There was no mistaking his expression; it was not one of kind hospitality. He looked like one of those cinema English butlers with the stiff upper lip and a proprietary interest in the place.

Maybe he intended it. I made a note to ask about Aldo's will.

"Ah, Miss Darling," the spook said. "Do you think it seemly for you to be returning here—under the circumstances? And with a guest?"

"Well, Gaiters, meet my 'guest.' This is Tod Hanson, Gaiters."

"Pleased to make your acquaintance, sir."

From his accent, I'd say Gaiters was more cockney in his origins than he was a good mimic of the upper crust.

"Tod is my attorney."

"Very good, Madame." Gaiters said. "Prudent in your predicament, I'd say."

"Kind of you, Gaiters," she said with a sarcasm buried so deep I don't think he caught it.

"Yes, well, the police have told me not to allow visitors."

"I'm hardly a visitor, Gaiters," she said with a teasing smile.

"Yes, ma'am. All the same, I'm going to have to ask you and your friend to leave—" Was I wrong, or did he raise a dubious eyebrow when he said, 'your friend'?

"And of course, I shall have to report this unexpected intrusion to the police."

"You do that, Gaiters," she said. "Whatever is in your heart."

"Yes, Madame," he said with a bow, then followed us to the door—just to make sure.

"Where did Gaiters get that name?" I asked Cheryl Darling as we wound back down the driveway to civilization.

"Oh, I don't know—suitably pretentious, don't you think? I always have to fight from calling him Garters. I don't know why."

"Another part of the leg, I guess." I said. "What's his story?"

"Gaiters? I don't know, really. He's always been there it seems—like before there was a Gaiters, there was no Aldo."

"What did he do, play butler?"

"Yes. He just ran the household. Aldo couldn't move without him."

"Is there a Mrs. Gaiters?"

"Oh my, no. Gaiters is married to his job."

"Did he run the party?" I asked. "The final one?"

"Oh, yes. All the parties."

"So he *was* there when Aldo died?"

"No, Gaiters was very particular about his bedtime. Over the years, I guess he'd gained more and more power over Aldo. Had his way in many areas. Oh, he always had a good sense about what he could get away with and what he couldn't. I always thought he knew when to stop pushing. Midnight was his limit—if he had to be up by six to get everything going. Quite an undertaking just keeping a property like Aldo's afloat. 'I turn into a pumpkin at midnight, sir,' he used to say. 'And I'd be of absolutely no use to *any*body if I were a pumpkin.' I used to call him Pumpkin."

"To his face?"

"Oh, yes."

"Did he like that?"

"Not much. Gaiters was not noted for his humor."

"What was he noted for?"

"His efficiency," she said. "His seeming responsiveness to Aldo's every wish."

"You say *seeming?*"

"That was one of the stumbling blocks between us. I always doubted Gaiter's altruism. He knew it. He didn't like it. Thought I was out to get him."

"Were you?"

She considered that for a moment. "It crossed my mind, but only fleetingly. He was Aldo's, after all, and if he pleased Aldo, it was no skin off my derriere."

And, I thought, what a needless sacrifice that would be. I said, instead, "Any reason Gaiters would want to pop old Aldo himself?"

"None that I can think of. He seemed to have it pretty good. Lived in his own cottage in back. Had his run of the place when Aldo was abroad, or in New York or wherever."

"He didn't go with him?"

"No, I don't think Aldo could have taken *that* much of

him. He was an efficient manager, but he wasn't Mr. Personality."

"Did you see him at the party?"

"Oh, yes. He's always a presence. Butlers, traditionally, try to blend into the background. Somehow, Gaiters never did. He was always hovering like a surveillance helicopter or a turkey vulture."

"Notice anything unusual about him at the fatal party?"

She shook her head. "I can't see Gaiters doing anything to rock the boat. Unless he stood to inherit everything, it wouldn't make any sense."

"And what do you think, in their darkest moments, the police think is your motive?"

"Jealousy, a broken heart."

"But you were still friends?"

"Yesss," she said slowly, and I didn't press it. Bomber would later say I was so smitten, I lost my objectivity. I took comfort in the realization that Mom would approve.

"Want to see my place?" I blurted out.

She waited, I thought, a touch too long to answer, but when she did, she made up for it with enthusiasm. "I'd *love* to!"

It was not far in distance from Aldo diCarlo's mansion in the hills of Montelinda, to my apartment on the waters edge. No, the difference was in the style, substance, and size.

"Isn't this cute?" Cheryl said when we drove behind the cutesy, cottagy front house to the parking pad in the back, which served as a stable for my vintage vehicle.

I understand the etiquette on going upstairs is the woman first, and it's reversed going down. This is so if the woman falls, the man can catch her. Or so is the received wisdom on the matter. So I let Cheryl go first and was glad I did. There was a momentary joust for position on the small landing at the top of the stairs and as was inevitable, we had some brushing physical contact that I found not at all unpleasant.

When I opened the door and thumbed on the light, Cheryl said, "Oh, this is just adorable." Coming from her, it was sure delicious hyperbole. Adorable was a bit of a stretch. Even cute would border on exaggeration. I did straighten up the place in the hope that she might be persuaded to come up, but I'm afraid to qualify as adorable, a major redecoration would have to take place. This was an eventuality that was forestalled by the meager salary Bomber paid me, which was in keeping with the most stringent rules of economy. For as Bomber would point out on those infrequent occasions when I had the nerve to bring it up, I was being paid exponentially more than I could ever expect to be as a classical composer.

So I had a bed—made—with pillows thrown against the wall in the conceit that was to double as sitting furniture. I never sat on it; it was too uncomfortable.

"Oooo," she said. "You have a *piano*. Do you play?"

"A little," I said, sheepishly.

"Oh, would you play for me? I'd love to hear you play."

I'd like to report that it took some coaxing to get me to the keyboard, but that would have wanted a certain accuracy. She sat on the bed. "Play," she said and in retrospect, I'm not sure she meant the piano.

I started heavy on the romantics—Schuman (*Traumeri*), Rachmaninoff ("Prelude in C-sharp Minor"), some Liszt ("Variations on a Theme of Paganini") to show off, and settled into a veritable Chopin recital (Preludes, Etudes, and "The Military Polinaise").

Cheryl Darling seemed to be enthralled. She was certainly extravagant in her praise; when I let it slip that I, myself, had written some music, she said, "No, really? Would you play some for me, please?"

Why, I reasoned, make her coax me? So, I trotted out the works I had done for other cases I'd worked on.

"Do you mean you write music for each case?"

"Oh, not every one. Sometimes there's no inspiration. Nothing clicks. But when I have the slightest impetus, I do something. Like "Phantom Virus" and "Suite: Love"."

"Tell me about this "Suite: Love", what a super title.

Were you in love?"

I must have blushed, for she quickly added, "Well, don't tell me if you don't want to. Was it a girl?"

That put me on the spot. If I told her no, she'd have thought it was a boy—I said, "Well..."

"Can you tell me anything?"

Why not?—she didn't seem to want to let it go.

"Very complex," I said, mysteriously. "She was a lawyer who worked for us on the case, then was bribed by the enemy."

Then she asked me all about my compositions, right down to the instrumentation, and almost begged me to play them for her after I demurred. She seemed to listen with a solid attentiveness. Her praise was washing over me like a mighty stream.

We talked about music far into the night, and I was amazed at how knowledgeable she was. I was astonished at the insight she demonstrated with her ability to connect my thoughts of the cases with the musical elements.

So, I invited her to an upcoming concert by the Hungarian pianist, Radu Lupu, and she said, "Why, thank you, Tod. I'd love to."

7

Needless to say, I was a little bleary-eyed the next morning when Bomber accosted me in the the reception where Miss Airhead of Zip Zip hung out.

He looked at Bonnie Doone, then at me, and I began to tremble at the thought of him unloading all in front of her.

It was a great sigh of relief expelled when he punctured my anxiety with, "Come into my office, Boy, and give me the lowdown on the superbabe." Though I wasn't keen on his characterization of a human being, it was preferable to having Bonnie Doone audit the whole conversation.

In his office, Bomber, as always, skirted the issue. I don't know if he was sensitive to my stutter (only when talking to him) or he was shy about familial relationships—he certainly was when Sis drove off the pier. I had to be the strong one in that situation. Whatever the reason, Bomber didn't always hit me with both barrels. This was one of the times he played the reluctant debutante and slid into his inquiry as though he couldn't care less.

"So, not that I've any right to pry—with our arrangement with Superwoman—but if you need a consultation and are worried about the cost, I give the first consultation free."

"Thanks," I said. I'm often able to get out one or two words without a stutter. Beyond that, it's a crap shot.

Bomber seemed a trifle disappointed I wasn't asking for his advice, even though it was free. So he slid into an offer of his own: "I, ah, suppose, since you are handling this *pro bono publico* so to speak, I should keep my own counsel, so to, ah, speak."

He looked at me through a bushy set of eyebrows, his head tilted down in that semisuperior, professional air.

"So," he tried again, "just tell me if you don't want any advice from me."

"Oh, no," I tried to protest, but my delivery was lame, at best. "I'm always h-happy for your a-ad-advice."

"What's your modus operandi so far?"

"I've b-been questioning Cheryl."

He nodded and even his simple nods made me feel inferior. "Anything else?"

"N-no-o. We've had the case less than twenty-four hours."

"A word to the wise," he said. "Start talking to others. The client, no matter how personally attractive to you, may not tell the whole story."

The advice was unnecessary, already realized, but annoying just the same. I felt the blood flare up in the back of my neck. How many times, I wondered, would I be suspected of placing personal considerations before the case—and ultimately, the client herself?

But it was wisdom I couldn't ignore—no matter the inherent predisposition that no advice from a father was worth a darn.

Gaiters, diCarlo's butler, seemed the ideal place to start. He was in town, and there was no one closer to the victim for as many years.

He answered the door with maximum disdain. I smiled my most engaging smile, which turned out to be not engaging enough.

"I'm afraid, sir, I am expected in town in ten minutes and it won't be possible."

"Another time, then."

"Why should I?"

I gave him the Bomber alternative. "Well, we *could* subpoena you. Not as convenient for you perhaps—along with the stigma that you didn't want to cooperate."

"Oh, but I have cooperated with the police. I recognize

them as the authority in this country." The superior air was choking me.

Of course, strictly speaking, there was no charge against our client yet, and we couldn't legitimately use that subpoena blackmail. My hope was Gaiters was not that sophisticated. It must have worked, for he did agree to see me later that afternoon.

When I returned, Gaiters opened the door to the main house before I knocked. That threw me.

I followed him into the house where he indicated a seat in a conversation pit all done up like a set on a modern Hollywood movie.

He sat, folded his hands across his lap with cultivated hauteur, and said, "Yes, sir." It wasn't exactly a question, but I took it as his opening gambit.

Gaiters was surely the inspiration for the phrase *Persona non Grata*, for the feeling was bred in his bones. His nose was a scabbard, forged in the toughest steel. I do not speak metaphysically, for I was convinced that if he looked at me crosseyed, I'd be decapitated.

On closer look, Gaiters' skin had started to sag and the flesh hung from his face like last summer's leaves. His posture was still good and he held his head like one of those puppets on a stick. Gaiters' demeanor was neither ambivalent nor ambiguous. He was not suffering me gladly.

"How would you like me to address you?" I began, thinking California informality might loosen him up. "Do you have a first name?"

"Just Gaiters, sir."

"Is that your first name?"

"Surname, sir," he said.

Gaiters' answers were not forthcoming. He answered just as briefly as he could, as though he'd mastered the art of the witness—never volunteer anything. It was a frustrating experience.

"How long did you work for Aldo?"

He eyed me as though I had committed a sacrilege. The throngs of the designer's public may refer to him by his first name, his logo may incorporate the first and last letters of his first name, but that was no call for an upstart like myself to call him Aldo.

"I have been in the employ of *Mr.* diCarlo," Gaiters intoned with maximum severity, "for twenty-seven years."

"I suppose in that time you got a feel for his passions and prejudices, his friends and enemies?"

"Some, sir."

"What can you tell me about his enemies?"

"I wouldn't presume to characterize any person as an enemy."

"No one who might wish him harm?"

"Cheryl Darling obviously wished him harm."

"Why do you say that?"

He looked surprised. "I should think it were obvious, sir. The circumstances of Mr. diCarlo's death..."

"What were they?"

Again the butler's eyebrows arched like a cat on edge. "Certainly you are aware, sir, of the pills. The painful cyanide death. That Cheryl Darling was attending him when he died. How she alone of his acquaintances was with him at the time of his death."

"But I should think you would be the one to arrange his pills."

"Arrange? I had the prescriptions filled. Mr. diCarlo put them in place himself. Obviously, someone altered one or more of the pills."

"All right, who was at the party that might have wished Aldo dead?"

"I don't know why anyone would have wished him dead—except a woman scorned."

"So who was here in the last few days before Al...*Mr.*

diCarlo's death that wasn't at the party?"

"No one, sir."

"You would have seen *everyone*?"

"Oh yes, sir. Mr. diCarlo didn't ever answer the door himself."

"Could someone have come in without your knowledge?"

"No, sir. Security was very tight."

"If Aldo had wanted to see someone—a secret lover, perhaps?"

"Mr. diCarlo had no secret lovers," he said with a haughty hoist of his razor proboscis.

"Had no secrets from you?"

"No."

"If you knew, they wouldn't be secrets, would they?"

"Mr. diCarlo was not a secretive man. To hide things you must think they should be hidden. Aldo diCarlo thought he could do no wrong."

Did I detect some sour grapes in that? In the spirit of getting more info, I let it go. But I couldn't resist asking, "Do you think he could do no wrong?"

"Hyperbole, of course, sir. But he was a good man, as men go—"

"Was he loved by all?"

"I know of no enemies, if that's what you mean."

That wasn't what I meant, and I wasn't happy being backed into the dental profession. Getting anything from Gaiters was too much like pulling teeth. Mine. I tried another tack: "If you had to name a dozen or so people that were close to Aldo, who would they be?"

"Close in what sense, sir?"

I looked at Gaiters, trying to convey my frustration with his dancing tactics. He returned the look with one of his own: bland and nonplussed.

"In *any* sense," I said. "Personal, romantic, business."

Gaiters sat back, looking for all the world like a man inconvenienced beyond his capacity for patience. Then, without fanfare, he began: "His last girlfriend, as you might call her, was Wissie Murray." He blanched—"An unfortunate name, Wissie; but she was young—"

"How young?"

Gaiters turned up his nose. "I hesitate to say lest my late employer appear in a less favorable light than called for. Sixteen, I believe, sir."

"And how old was Mr. diCarlo?"

"Fifty-eight, sir."

"I heard there was a young man in the sewing room. Hispanic, I believe."

"That would be Lupe. Eduardo Guadalupe Espinal."

"Romance?"

"I really couldn't say, sir."

"Any...suspicions?"

"No, sir," he said. "Not my place, sir."

"Ex-partners?"

"Long time ago, sir." he said. "There was an early financial arrangement with some Las Vegas money."

"Specifically?"

"I don't have that information, sir."

"Any romance there?"

"Oh, sir. I would doubt that. Though, of course, I have no knowledge."

"Did you yourself ever have a romantic interest in your employer?"

"That is a terrible suggestion, and I will do you the courtesy of ignoring it."

It was my turn to turn a suspicious and, I hoped, supercilious eye toward Gaiters. "Anyone angered by his success?"

"I would imagine, sir, that would be only natural."

"Names?"

"One of his designers had some disagreement over who

should get credit for some of Mr. diCarlo's successes." I could see he was pausing for effect. Then he said, "The failures were never in dispute."

"There were failures?"

"Always, sir. Aldo diCarlo enjoyed unprecedented success and acclamation, but there were occasional slips."

"Anyone else?"

"Not that I can think of, sir."

"How many of them were at the last party?"

"All of them."

My eyebrows went through the twelve-foot-high ceilings.

"Mr. diCarlo was not one to hold a grudge. And everyone *loved* his parties."

"And you left the party when?"

"Midnight, sir."

"How many were still in the house then?"

"All of them, I believe. Not many left Mr. diCarlo's parties early."

"Except you?"

He glared at me as though I had accused him of some malfeasance. "That is correct," he said.

"How difficult would it have been to crash the party?"

"I screened all visitors."

"Could you miss a crasher who wanted to hide out in the house?"

"Unlikely."

"After you left the party? Could someone crash?"

"Unlikely," he said, firmly. "Crashers usually come earlier."

Unless they have murder in their hearts and knew you went to bed at the stroke of twelve, I thought, but decided against saying it.

"Oh, by the way," I said, "who did the catering?"

"That would be Queen Millie," he said.

"Queen Millie? That was her name?"

Gaiters shrugged. "Mr. diCarlo doted on her. She did all his parties."

"You, I take it, were not as enamored?"

"Not my place, sir."

"But, if pressed, how would you rate her?"

He seemed to sniff the air. "She used illegals, I would say."

"She used undocumented Mexicans?"

"Exclusively," he said. "Cost her less, but Mr. diCarlo was not a beneficiary of the savings."

"Where can I find Queen Millie?"

"In the phonebook, I expect," Gaiters said.

Gaiters showed me out. He seemed vastly relieved to see me go.

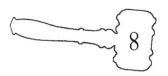

8

Queen Millie was all and more than her name implied. I went to see her in her westside house—west of the freeway, that was. The lower rent district. The house was simple stucco on the outside. She greeted me effusively, and I could see why Aldo took to her. She had a bubbling way about her. She was on the heavy side—if I weren't trying to be tactful, I might call her fat. But jolly, and I liked her immediately. She wore a flowing, flower-spotted granny dress that any self-respecting granny would have given to Goodwill.

She invited me in to sit in her dark living room, which was furnished from the Victorian era. I commented. She said, "This was my grandmother's stuff. It ain't much, but it's home." She was not a woman who used "ain't" by mistake.

"Your name is really Queen Millie?"

"What's in a name?" she asked before forcing some tea on me. "My daddy always called me 'princess,' but I figured I outgrew that moniker, both in years and size, so when I went into the catering biz, I bumped it up to Queen Millie. Catchy, don't you think?"

"Very," I said, approvingly. "How was Aldo to work for?"

"A peach," she said. "I loved him. I'll miss him, I know that."

"Do a lot of work for him?"

"All his parties. Like two to three a month. He loved parties—a caterer's dream."

"Same people work for you for all the parties?"

"Oh," she said, looking distracted. "It's a high turn-over biz."

"Mexicans?"

"*Si, señor*," she said.

"Do you remember who worked at Aldo's the night he died?"

"Sure," she said. "I keep beautiful records. My teachers always praised my penmanship. I was always very organized, too. I made a list for the police and, of course, I kept a copy."

She got up and moved to an old-fashioned desk that had a door that pulled down to make a writing table. Like a homing pigeon landing on home base, she put her hand in a cubicle and withdrew a list. In homage to her neatness, she lifted the writing table to cover the desk and returned to where I sat in a stuffy stuffed chair and handed me the list.

I glanced at it and said, "No gringos?"

She shook her head severely. "The Mexicans do all the work here. The gringos have had it too good for generations. Lazy."

"And more expensive?"

She waved that off as she settled back into her chair. "I'd pay it. I prefer Hispanics."

"They have papers?"

"Ah, *papers!* Do you know what you're talking about?" She got agitated and her words were speeding forth rapidly. "First of all, those Mexicans who *have* papers are just as lazy as the gringos. On welfare, most of 'em. You take away the undocumented workers from California and the whole place would sink to its knees. Nobody else is willing to do the dirty work."

I counted eight names on the list.

"Who of these were there when Aldo died?"

"The ones marked with little checks on the left."

I squinted at the neat little checks beside two names: Rosa Gonzales and María Hermosillo. "Where can I find them?"

Queen Millie waved a hand as though she were dismissing a servant. "Disappeared—according to the police. They were here some weeks ago. Wanted to question them."

"Where should I look for them?"

She shrugged. "Mexico, I suppose."

"Big place."

"Yes, isn't it..." she trailed off as though there were nothing to be done. "Their last address is there. But they come and go all the time."

"Anybody on this list know Aldo in any way besides through your catering?"

"I'd be very surprised."

"You notice anything different about Aldo that night?"

She thought a moment. "Well, it was a party celebrating his biggest triumph. The reception for his line was, I understand, astonishing. I suspect he had to be pretty pleased with that—yet..." She didn't finish the thought.

"Yet he wasn't happy?"

"Oh, I couldn't say that. I don't believe I've ever seen Aldo *un*happy. And I don't believe we mere mortals can understand feelings like that—public acclaim of that magnitude. There's bound to be a letdown. I know in my little business when I get a lot of praise I immediately start worrying about the next gig. Can I keep it up? Maybe it is pure projection, but I sensed some of that. But then, I imagine he was exhausted—an emotional letdown—all of that. Even so, he was just as charming as ever to me and the staff. They *loved* him. He was the *best* tipper."

"See any arguments—anything suspicious?"

She shook her head.

"What time did you leave?"

"About one-thirty."

"And the last girls left when?"

"Two-thirtyish. They put three on their cards and I didn't quibble. What they went through—seeing that ugly death and all was worth another half hour."

"Did you talk to Aldo before you left?"

"Yeah."

"Notice anything?"

"Anything? He was feeling no pain, if that's what you mean."

It wasn't, but that was good enough for now. I thanked her and left her my card. "If anything else occurs to you," I said, demonstrating that she was not the only one who could speak in incomplete sentences.

*   *   *

The last known address for Rosa Gonzales and María Hermosillo was only a couple of blocks from Queen Millie, so I swung by to check it out.

A sullen lad in residence told me Rosa and María didn't live there anymore and he had no idea where they were.

"Go back to Mexico?" I asked and the slight beat that preceded his answer made me suspicious.

"I don't know," he said.

"Know anybody who might know?"

He shook his head. His pose was set in *cemento*.

"No friends, relatives—co-workers?"

He threw up his shoulders. "*No sé*," he said.

I gave him my card. "If you remember anything," I said, "give me a call."

My only remaining question was, would my card hit the trash before I was in the car or slightly thereafter?

9

Bomber went through the roof when he heard Mom had invited Cheryl Darling to dinner.

I was in his office—the Rogue's Gallery Mausoleum—and if he'd put on a performance like this for a jury, he'd be jailed for overacting. His arms were flailing everywhere, his platform shoes were trembling.

"Jesus Jenny, Boy, we don't entertain clients in our home," Bomber said with galloping decibels. "Least of all, those accused of murder!"

"N-n-not yet," I stammered.

"Any day now," he predicted. "Web Grainger three, our wastrel District Attorney, is itching to be back in the headlines—you can feel it in a two-mile radius around the courthouse. He'll do one of his dog and pony shows for the grand jury any day now."

"Will they l-l-lock her up?" I stammered.

"You bet. Murder one—no escape. So if we just put your mother off for the nonce," he said, almost pleading.

I said nothing. Bomber knew I didn't want to put it off.

"Your mother is getting unreasonably uppity about this—talks about the presumption of innocence as though she were Blackstone himself."

Mom was as far as I imagined you could get from an uppity wife, but apparently she was holding her ground on this one.

"I *told* her you were an adult and as such you would surely resent this meddling in your life, but she wouldn't come to reason. You've got to talk to her, Tod, the predicament is unnerving. She says you don't have a home for entertaining and I counter that there are plenty of restaurants around."

"What d-did she say t-to that?"

He shot a hand out at me through unfriendly air. "Some blather about the warmth of a home—stability. Blah, blah, you can't feel commitment in a restaurant. I swear she's already planning the wedding and picking a china pattern for you and you just met the girl! *Talk* to her. I let her talk me into taking the case, but this is way over the edge."

It was, for all intents and purposes, an idyllic family dinner. Mom had trotted out all the best china and silver that she got as wedding gifts and had so little opportunity to use. Bomber was not ordinarily what you'd call gregarious, the wall full of pictures in his office notwithstanding.

Mom even had flowers in the center of the table—a nice year-round *melange* of sunny Angelton specialities. She was her own hospitable self, sharpening the focus of the conversation on Cheryl, our guest. The only surprise of the evening came from Bomber who seemed suddenly to have developed a serious case on Cheryl. I found his abject reversal amusing at first, then annoying. It was almost as though he were competing with me for her attention.

For her part, Cheryl was the model guest—model. She expressed an interest in all the Hansons and everything Hanson, and complimented the cuisine of the house with lavish sincerity. Her handling of the heretofore grumpy Bomber was nothing short of masterful. She lavished on him her special thousand-dollar-an-hour smile, and watched him with those gorgeous eyes as though he were the only person in the room.

Cheryl sat at the place that was always set up as a memorial to Sis. Dinner, exquisitely prepared by Mom and impeccably served, was, for me, shrouded in clever conversational quips by the reluctant debutante himself, Mr. Bomber Hanson, attorney at law—the same guy who came to this dinner under fierce protest—the man who railed against mixing business with personal pleasure.

Dessert was Mom's astonishing lime chiffon pie that takes her hours to make, what with swirling the bowl of filling around in ice cubes, fabricating an unusually delicate crust, and a soft meringue/cream topping that is just sublime. Eating the lime pie was an experience after which heaven would be an anti-climax.

After the pie was more subsumed than consumed, Bomber startled me by inviting Cheryl into his study.

We always sat in the living room after dinner. Bomber's study was sacrosanct, as though unauthorized persons would forever sully the premises. It was, of course, a much more intimate space than the living room.

Cheryl accepted with pleasure. She, too, to my chagrin, reveled in Bomber's attentions. I consoled myself with the belief that that was just polite under the circumstances.

"I call it a study," Bomber said, leading the way into his book-lined hide-away. I followed Cheryl like a lap dog, which may or may not be a step up from a hang dog.

"Lawyers have their libraries, but ministers call their offices studies. Connotes deep thought—I always wanted to be a deep-thinking minister. Fire and brimstone," he beamed. "What do you think?"

"I think you'd make a perfectly marvelous minister," Cheryl said, putty in his hands. I rolled my eyes but no one saw it. Mom was in the kitchen cleaning up.

Bomber settled in behind his desk and pointed Cheryl to the chair directly facing him. I sat off to the side against the wall where I could observe even the nuances of expressions on the faces of the principals. She was all eyes and ears, he was a pig in clover, reliving some long gone youth. And it was working. He looked nineteen years old in that guise, and she looked adorable.

"Modeling must be a fascinating profession," Bomber said, expansive with the hands.

I'm sure I smirked at that double-edged boffo contradiction. Hadn't Bomber told me it was an insufferably boring job for mental deficients?

"It has its moments," she allowed. Then added, "When you go beyond the obvious."

"Oh?"

"There is more to it, I guess, than meets the eye."

"Oh? Like what?"

"A whole raft of enterprises make up fashion modeling. First, there are the different types—editorial for print work, magazines, catalogs, et cetera. Runway—for fashion shows. Advertising—TV, commercials, billboards. Then there's the agencies that schedule and really control the girls."

"Control them?" Bomber asked. "How?"

"They do the bookings. The girls are getting younger. There are all kinds of men out there, so when you bring a twelve-year-old girl on board you have to keep a constant eye on her. Agencies set up housing where they have supervision. It keeps the girls relatively safe."

"*Relatively?*"

She shrugged.

"Who pays?"

"Oh, the girls pay. Four to five hundred a week to share an apartment in New York with ten other girls. It's horrendous."

"Where does a guy like Aldo diCarlo fit into all this?"

"He's a fashion designer. One of the top three, I'd say. He has a lot of power, gets a lot of control. Gets the girls he wants—some of them exclusively."

"Is that good for the girls?"

"A good agency will see that it is. If a top model is tied up exclusively, she's going to be handsomely compensated."

"Like a thousand dollars an hour?"

She smiled.

"Were you exclusively Aldo's?"

"No. I'd never sign an exclusive contract. Fortunately, I didn't have to. I always had work."

"Did that make Aldo angry?"

"Oh, it wounded his pride a little, but he got over it."

"So who signs exclusive contracts?"

"Girls who don't want to work too much, who fear uncertainty. Those who have self-doubts and like the sinecure of steady, certain employment and income."

"The designer has complete control, doesn't he? I mean,

if he has a falling out with someone he can just refuse to use her—"

"Yes, but he has to keep paying her."

"But if someone isn't seen and just grows old in the job—I assume there is a limited number of years a model is marketable?"

"Sure, but it expands—depending on the model and the product. Some models can work well into their forties—fifties even."

"But not many."

"True."

"So what scenarios can you give me—pure fantasy is fine—why *any* one would have *any* reason, no matter how remote, to pop old Aldo?"

"Oh, Aldo was a super-star celebrity. It can go to your head. I heard he had some business partners and backers that he shucked when he made it. Also, people are always accusing you of stealing their designs. Then there are the long lines of jilted lovers."

"Of which you are one, I believe?"

"Yes and no. Nobody likes to be dumped, but when I'm honest with myself, I was ready."

"How about competitors?"

Cheryl Darling thought a moment. "Well, certainly, the competition is fierce—brutal at times, but it's never risen to the level of murder."

"If it had this time, who do you think...?"

"I can't, really. I'd love to finger somebody, don't think I haven't thought about it. I just can't come up with anything. He was rich, he was successful, he was a good-time Charlie. He loved with his whole being and when it was time for you to be over, he let you down easy—still loved you, blah, blah, just in the interest of his genius, time to fry more fish."

"Did you feel you were stiffed by him?"

She looked at Bomber out of the respectful corner of her eye. "What a perceptive question," she said. "I suppose as soon as anyone—" she lifted her hands and wriggled two fingers of each, "'Makes it,' they start to question everything. You have all these riches, all this adulation—and you started from ground zero with nothing but your looks, which you inherited, you didn't have to work for them. But suddenly you're queen of the ball and before you know it, little things crop up that make you question if you're getting a fair deal or not."

"What kind of things?"

"Hours, venues, travel, who you had to work with—maybe a model grated on you or a photographer irked you. Travel. Maybe you didn't feel like going to Belize for Christmas. You can always find something to gripe about."

"How do you handle it?" Bomber asked her.

"Different ways. Some become prima donnas. Show up late for work. Drink—take drugs. Others go with the flow and realize they have a pretty good thing going. But it's human nature to want to improve your lot, and after you have everything, how do you do it?"

"Aldo had everything too, didn't he?"

She nodded.

"And you?"

She nodded again, but the reaction time was longer. Bomber didn't miss that.

"So what *more* did you want?"

She took a breath in the time it took her to consider whether or not she should answer that. The call came down to answering, but it was a close one.

"Control," she said. "In spite of the huge salary and the adulation, fame, whatever you call it, there is the feeling you are being controlled—not always in ways you like. When you are near the top, you get a yen to control your own destiny."

"How do you do that?" Bomber asked. "In your business, I mean?"

"The Agency controls your destiny—more so when you are starting out, but even to an extent after you've made it. Of course, if you are willing to sign an exclusive with somebody, the agency role fades—they take a chunk of your fees and are on their merry way. But you need them again when the contract runs out."

"An agency can make or break a model?"

"Well, in a way. But it's subtle. They, finally, do the booking. Photographers too can also choose their models. That's often a power play in itself."

"So what do you do about it?"

She laughed. "Exactly! With photographers, you try to kiss up to them."

"Nocturnally?" Bomber asked, vaguely.

"Sometimes," she said. "Some do—some don't have to. Some photographers prefer the other gender."

I didn't ask her what her experience was. But I thought about it.

"And the agency powers? What do you do about that?"

"Well," she said slowly, drawing out the els. "If you are big enough, you can try to start your own agency."

"You ever consider that?" Bomber asked.

"Maybe," she said coyly.

"If," Bomber said—"only *if* of course, you had your own agency, would you have control over Aldo?"

"With my models—in a way. But you don't make a go of an agency by angering designers."

"Did Aldo approve of this move? Your agency," he said, assuming she had admitted it.

"I didn't tell him," she said.

I could see Bomber had many more questions to ask. I myself could think of about a thousand, but it was getting late, he didn't want to make it sound like a courtroom rehearsal, so he wrapped up the evening with some small chitchat.

Flirty, to be sure.

I couldn't help but wonder if Bomber was going to send Cheryl a bill for one thousand dollars an hour.

10

I was eagerly looking forward to my date with Cheryl for Radu Lupu's piano recital Friday night. It was that day Webster Arlington Grainger III, district attorney of Weller county, decided to indict and arrest Cheryl Darling for the first degree murder of Aldo Cabrisi diCarlo. But not without the full force of the Angelton press corps, as well as the Los Angeles media—replete with TV cameras, cables underfoot, lights overhead, the whole shebang.

Bomber and I were there, of course. "Yes, I'd be glad to comment," Bomber said when a young, comely reporter thrust a microphone in his face. "Webster Arlington Grainger three has just upstaged the Ringling Brothers. He's not so much a district attorney as a circus master. If he paid more attention to prosecuting cases of merit—which this one obviously is not—and spent less time currying press as a schlockmeister circusmaster, he might have a better conviction record."

I cringed, off-screen of course. Webster Arlington Grainger III was not the kind of man who was able to laugh at that. It certainly wasn't calculated to make my obligatory visit to the D.A. a piece of cake.

Standing beside Cheryl Darling while she was being arrested and fingerprinted had to be among the hardest things I ever did. It was a gargantuan effort on my part to keep from blubbering right in front of the cops. Cheryl's stiff upper lip and the gleaming tear in the corner of her stoic eye didn't help matters.

The troops at the jailhouse were ga ga over their celebrity prisoner—falling all over themselves to be gracious and gallant. That was comforting.

I made my best empty assurances that we would do all

in our power to get her out. She patted the back of my hand and said, "That's okay, Tod. They already told me first degree murder wasn't bailable. As is so often the case, I think the fear was worse than the reality."

"That's very large-spirited," I said.

"I know I didn't do it. Seventeen eyewitnesses swearing I did wouldn't change that. I have total faith in you, Tod. I'll manage." She took my face in her hands and kissed my trembling lips. I gasped and caught my tears before they cascaded down my front and threatened to drown us both.

I had work to do. I must have looked back umpteen times after leaving her, until all I could see was a bored guard leafing through a grimy tabloid with Cheryl Darling on the cover. The headline said:

Cheryl Darling, Supermodel, Supermurderess?

I didn't feel like doing much after I left Cheryl. But duty didn't only call, it pressed.

So I took it on myself to visit the D.A. of our home county, the polished, umpteenth generation something, Webster Arlington Grainger III, whom Bomber had begun referring to as "three," then after a pungent pause he'd add, "on a scale of ten."

Everything D.A. Webster Grainger three did, he did with a grim determination—whether jogging to keep his body electorate-friendly, or prosecuting cases for the great state of California, it was all serious business.

Natch, Bomber got under Web's skin when he made fun of him—which was depressingly often. You never knew when a friend in the bureaucracy might come in handy—but Bomber burned those bridges.

You-know-who was the sole member of the reclamation squad, and you can imagine how little good it did for me to try to turn the grim D.A. into the Jolly Green Giant.

Everyone else called the D.A. Web. This was California,

after all. I called him Mr. Grainger. He never corrected me.

I had barely sat down in his fancy decorator office before he unloaded on me.

"You can tell that father of yours for me I don't appreciate his berating me to the press. I don't appreciate it at *all!*"

I'd be surprised if Bomber didn't already know that. "Sometimes Bomber gets carried away in defense of a client. Always what he does is his best judgment about what's good for the client."

Webster held up both hands to push himself away from that argument.

"Please," he said. "I've heard that so often it makes me want to vomit. Your father is a showoff, pure and simple. He doesn't think, he just jabs—like a punch drunk fighter."

I didn't argue. It was in our interests that Webster Grainger underrate his opponent.

"It's so unprofessional!" Webster said. "We have enough trouble being taken seriously in this little tourist trap as it is, I don't know why he wants to go and belittle my efforts. It belittles him as well."

"That's just Bomber, Mr. Grainger. He doesn't mean anything by it."

"It's grandstanding for the press," Webster pouted. "He'd never get away with that in court."

"Maybe that's why he does it. Could both sides be a little guilty of using the press? Not uncommon these days," I said. "I guess you know I've come for your file on California v. Cheryl Darling?"

He nodded as though it were the nuisance it surely was to him, and that nod told me his opinion: if it weren't for the law compelling him to do so, Bomber could kiss him where he couldn't see without a mirror.

So I swung into my impassioned plea for him to let her out of jail, pending the trial.

"She is certainly no threat to society. You and I both know men do the murdering, not women…"

"Not exclusively," he corrected me. "No. Woman's lib has had the curious fringe benefit of giving us more murderesses. Perhaps it's all those movie ads with pretty women holding guns."

"This was poison," I reminded him.

"Yes—a *woman's* method."

"Well, Aldo diCarlo had a lot of women. Boys, too."

"I'm well acquainted," he said, eying a file on his desk that I thought was destined for Bomber, via me.

"I'm sure you're also acquainted with the defendant's celebrated reputation—as well as her universally acclaimed beauty. I don't think there's a place on this earth she would be able to live unrecognized. The risk of her flight is virtually nonexistent."

"*Virtually?*" he said, cocking an eyebrow.

"Totally," I said, brazenly. "Set the bail at whatever you want. She can raise it. Hook her up electronically—just don't subject such a tender, sensitive soul to the indignities of the jail-house."

"That's a very sweet rendition," Webster said, "and I don't blame you. If I were younger and unmarried—" he paused and I had that sinking feeling he was working up to one of his funnies— "or one or the other, I'd be throwing my bedroll right in there with you. But there are certain laws in this state that I have sworn to uphold. Keeping murderers off the street in one of my high priorities."

You couldn't accuse Webster Arlington Grainger III of not speaking like a bureaucrat. It was bred in the bone.

"Well, here's the file. After Bomber reads it, I expect he'll want to plead."

"Bomber? Plea Bargain?" I said, astonished. "When has he ever done that? 'I'm not a horse trader,' he says, 'I'm an advocate. The best! You want to cop a plea, you don't need me—you can get by with one of those cheap lawyers.'"

"When you see the file," he said, handing it to me with that smug grin he had patterned, "maybe you'll change your mind."

I raised an eyebrow of my own. "Then I expect you'll want to throw the book at her?"

"Well…" he paused, "of course."

"But?"

"But nothing, if that's what he wants." He was back to petulance at the thought of mixing with Bomber. "I just thought since she's a celebrity and all, you'd want to save her face—"

"By admitting she murdered her boss?"

"Extenuating circumstances."

"What are they?"

"I'll leave that up to her resourceful defense counsel."

Ordinarily, I would act as a delivery boy and ferry the file of the case from the D.A. to Bomber without reading it. Bomber did the hearing as he did all the court work.

This time I went right out on the expansive court house lawn planted with palm trees and other giants that had stood the test of time and now, a century later, provided generous shade and dappled patterns on the luxuriant green carpet of tough but tender grass.

I was surrounded by homeless people, men and women, now, some in animated conversations drinking from the bottles concealed in brown paper bags, as though anyone were fooled into thinking the bag covered a milk carton. Some others were docile and apart from the revelers. They all seemed to know what limits their boisterousness could take before they were hauled in by Angelton's finest on charges of drunk and disorderly and disturbing the peace.

I settled in on a bench on the edge of the lawn to read the file. I began, a young man of hope and promise, but gradually became mired in despair.

There were, indeed, some unpleasant surprises.

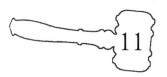

Radu Lupu looks like an angry, furry hippie, but his piano playing is sublime. The sensual experience is not enhanced by looking at him, so one might be better off keeping the eyes shut for the duration.

I couldn't help (not taking my own advice) contrasting Mr. Lupu's appearance with that of the missing Cheryl Darling. I didn't try to sell Cheryl's ticket to someone else. I couldn't bear the thought of some overweight guy with booze on his breath spilling over the armrests into my space—probably start snoring as soon as Radu Lupu started playing.

Or worse still, a pretty young woman who sat as prim and perfect as a—well, a model. I'd probably lose it before anyone started snoring. So I had the luxury of an empty seat beside me, into which I projected my vision of Cheryl.

Listening to these piano prodigies I often had pangs of jealousy when I compared their playing to my own. Radu Lupu transcended that envy. I like to think it's because his playing was in a higher, untouchable realm; but it could have been his peculiar looks.

At the intermission, a spook snuck up behind me. I turned with a start to see Gaiters' nose slicing down his face.

"Oh, Gaiters, you scared me," I said.

"Sorry, sir," he said without the feel of any kind of apology.

"You a fan of classical music?" I asked.

"Indeed, sir. Very much, indeed. And you, sir?"

"Oh, yes," I said. I decided to go no further. I was shocked he addressed me in the first place.

"I just wanted to tell you, sir, due to your involvement in matters, that the authorities have the right person in jail."

"Oh?" I said, arching an eyebrow. "Have you some evidence?"

He held up a hand like a traffic cop. "I am not at liberty to go into detail. I am merely imparting the intelligence to save you unnecessary bother."

I looked him in the eye, as though a hard stare would rattle the info out of him. It didn't work.

Naturally, Gaiters' shared intelligence ruined the rest of the concert for me.

The I-know-something-but-I-can't-tell-you-what school of intrigue was childish. I only wish I could have ignored it.

"Jesus Jenny, Boy!" Bomber said the next morning after he'd had time to digest the California v. Cheryl Darling file. It had given him heartburn. He'd called me into his office with the time honored method he used when his dander was up—way up: by shouting across Bonnie Doone's office from his. "Boy! Get in here!"

"I take it Miss Model of ought ought did not find it in her heart to *share* this intelligence with you before Gopher Grainger nosed it out?"

I shook my head dolefully. He grunted.

"She needs a primer in full disclosure to your counsel, and a good dose of your lawyer is your friend, little girl."

I couldn't disagree so I said nothing.

"She pulls this again, she's on a shopping spree."

"Excuse m-me?"

"She'll be shopping for another attorney."

I knew Bomber wanted to put the fear of God in Cheryl, my darling, but she wasn't handy, so he put it in me instead.

"Now you want me to take my introductory lecture to her down at the jailhouse at a thou the hour, or do you want to deliver it yourself—at slightly reduced rates I suspect..."

It was, as they say, a no-brainer.

Then he threw me one of his Tod-testers that he reveled in at my expense:

"Tell you what, Boy, I'll go to see her in the slammer gratis. *Pro bono publico*. Say the word."

The word I said was "No."

He knew I would. He smiled. I knew he would.

The woman's lockup for Weller county was on the outskirts where the mountain began to get serious about rising.

There was little growth other than the natural chaparral around it, as if to prevent any escapees from hiding in the bushes. Sort of an Alcatraz on land.

From the look of the clientele on the inside, it was largely homeless women and some druggies, and it was evident that feminism had not yet made women as vicious as men.

Visitor rooms in all the jails I'd ever visited were like chambers from hell. The stark-barren school. Strictly no frills.

My delicate flower among the thorns stood out even in the drab prison garb. My heart ached to see her there, and I didn't want to think about the burden I'd taken on to get her out.

Cheryl Darling, I noticed, had a comforting equanimity about her. She looked much less bothered about her surroundings than I did. Perhaps that was the hallmark of a great model—a seemingly effortless adaptation to any surroundings. Like she'd been hired to model some clothes in jail.

"How are you?" I asked—in a burst of creative conversation.

She smiled. "Believe it or not, Tod, I'm fine. Oh, I might rather be in Philadelphia, as W.C. Fields might have said, but it's an interesting experience—talking to all these poor women. Most of them have had it pretty rotten. And everybody treats me like a celebrity, which I'm not comfortable with. Excessive deference always makes me uneasy—especially in *this* situation."

I found that clearing my throat came in handy as a signal to myself that objectivity should come to the fore. So, I cleared my throat and said, "The D.A. has given us his file—that's his case against you."

"Oh," she said. "What's in it?"

"Yes, that's the, ah, disturbing thing. Bomber was kind of angry because, well, he felt you hadn't told him everything."

She looked at me kind of funny. Inquiring, she cocked her head. "What didn't I tell you?"

"The will, for instance."

"The will?"

"Aldo's will, leaving you five million of his estate—"

"Oh, but that's history. He's written another one since," she said. "That was his schtick with all his girls...and boys, I suppose. He'd put his girlfriend in for five mil while he was taking the last one out. I was replaced long ago by Wissie and I suppose she's been replaced by Lupe."

I studied Cheryl's face to see if I could detect any hokum there. I couldn't. Either she believed what she said, or she was such a good actress no juror would know the difference.

I nodded slowly. "That may be," I said, "but the will leaving you five million was still in force when he died. This lawyer—what's his name...Orban Pillburn, is it? He's going to testify that the new will was drawn up and Aldo was going to sign it the morning after he died."

Cheryl sank back into her iron chair. "I didn't know that," she muttered, and I tried to read her despair. Was it because she knew the knowledge was so incriminating, or because it cut into her alibis—like (1) She didn't kill Aldo, but this made her look like she had or (2) she killed him and this was oppressive evidence she hadn't counted on?

"Well," I said, struggling to put a happy face on it, "the good news is at least you are five million richer—" Then I paused as my own reality set in. "That is, unless you are convicted. There is a law, of course, that says you can't benefit from your own crime."

She shook her head under the weight of it all. "Believe me, Tod, this is a shock. Aldo must have gotten negligent in his old age. It's not like him to be sloppy with details. Certainly Bomber doesn't think Aldo took me into his confidence and said, 'Cheryl, I'm cutting you out of my will tomorrow. The only way you can stop it is to kill me'? You may not believe this, but even if I'd known any of this, money just isn't important to me. I had a healthy upper middle class childhood—wanted for nothing and before I even graduated from college, I was making more than doctors—I won't say lawyers," she smirked. "I have *never* felt like I didn't have enough money. Fears of destitution never hounded me. I mean, five million? What is that—two to three years work time?"

"More," I offered, low key, "when you consider inheritance is tax free."

She waved her hand as though that were a boring detail.

"And we must be prepared for the prosecution to say your peak earning years were past and five million—let's just say to the average juror—might come in handy."

She shook her head. "Money, no, it just never was a consideration. I'll inherit more than that from my father."

"Can we verify that? Will he testify to that?"

"Sure. Ask him."

I looked into Cheryl Darling's sweet, guileless eyes, and I was aching to believe her. How, I wondered, did all those hardboiled guys manage to stay *un*involved with women like this? Then I decided mine was a unique case. There *were* no other women like this.

"Cheryl," I said. "Think now, if you will, please—what else about your relationship with Aldo could be a surprise? Anything, no matter how remote you think it might be."

She shook her head. "I've thought, believe me. I have ample time to think in here. The obvious evidence is against me, I know that. I also know I didn't kill Aldo, though I don't doubt more fantasies can be cooked up that make me look like Lizzie Borden. But I'm sure the same kind of things could be drawn from any of his associations."

"Well, how about that? Can you give us some ideas of why someone else would do it and why?"

She pursed her lovely lips and twitched her head once as

though she were deflecting a fly.

"Aldo was eccentric, acquisitive, demanding, exacting, but underneath it all, he was a pussycat: lovable, a devoted lover, just uncertain enough to be endearing. One on one with Aldo and you had his full concentration. He would look at you like there was no one else in the world. I'll never forget those hot eyes boring, boring right through my skull. They said, 'You're mine, all mine, and nobody else in the world matters to me.'"

I absorbed that lovely rendition and paused before I threw away my next question. "I see in the file you were married?"

"Ah, yes," she sighed. "The indiscretions of youth. It didn't take."

"What was he like—your husband?"

"Handsome, tall, dark, debonair. Rich. Sophisticated, fun while it lasted, which wasn't very long."

"How long?" Each question I asked her about her personal life was like a dagger plunged into my heart.

"Maybe a year. Maybe less."

"What went wrong?"

"Well...in addition to those aforementioned happy adjectives, he was controlling, even sadistic. Jealous to the point of insanity and as faithful to my memory and person as a jack rabbit. Other than that," she shrugged, "he was just like the boy next door, I guess."

In a parting gesture, I touched her hand and told her to keep thinking about more incriminating surprises and any memories that might tie Aldo's murder to someone else.

"I will," she said, and I had the feeling she was making a marriage vow.

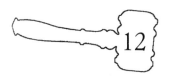

12

Bomber had asked me if I wanted to represent Cheryl Darling at the preliminary hearing—against the charge of murder in the first degree, with malice aforethought and all that charming verbiage.

I demurred, as they say down at the courthouse. Though I realized I'd be saving Cheryl a grand an hour, in the long run it could have been much more expensive.

The cameras were everywhere as we walked into the courthouse with Cheryl Darling, super-*super*model—and I'll say this for her—she sure knew how to walk—but I guess that was part of her stock in trade. She strode with a slight sway connoting supreme confidence. All eyes were glued to her. She betrayed no annoyance at all the attention. Perhaps the only one unhappy about the attention she got was Bomber, who was more accustomed to having it lavished on him.

Cheryl Darling was garbed in a straight ankle length black skirt and a teal silk shirt. Bomber had won the battle to allow her to wear street clothes instead of prison garb by agreeing the attire would be simple, not flashy. Bomber reasoned that even judges could be prejudiced by seeing a defendant as a prisoner.

As luck (bad) would have it, we drew a woman judge. Estelle Emory who was, unhappily, no match for Cheryl Darling in the looks department. "Short and dumpy," was the charming way Bomber characterized her. "Emory Board," he called her— "She grates on my nerves. We can kiss goodbye any advantage we might have gotten from an all-American red-blooded male judge who has maintained in his heart—no matter how hardened it had otherwise become—a soft place for a beautiful woman."

"Naturally, we wouldn't w-want or expect any

favoritism," I communicated to Bomber.

"Naturally," he said, with reverse spin only he can give to words.

D. A. Web was methodical and he offered us no surprises at the hearing. Not that he had to. Nor should he show more of his hand than he needed to to set the case for trial.

After we all settled before the judge, Web got right to it.

The nerdy clerk who sold Cheryl the cyanide was the first Judas. Yes, he sold the poison to Cheryl, he had the date and invoice—a couple of weeks before Aldo died. Yes, he was sure.

"How can you be sure it was she?" The district attorney asked, smugly satisfied with his clever question.

The nerd, a schoolboy with his face reddened with a crush, grinned from ear to ear as he looked squarely at Cheryl Darling. "She's *famous!*" he virtually shouted—"and *so* beautiful. I'd never forget her face." That was good for a laugh all around, except for Judge Estelle Emory. When I glanced her way, she didn't seem to find it amusing. Bad sign for our side.

The coroner told us Aldo died of cyanide poisoning.

The cops ponied up the same gruel that their buddy, the D.A., wanted to hear. The call came from Cheryl Darling, and she was there alone when they arrived. There were three pills on the table in front of the victim.

"Not too bad," Bomber said to Cheryl at the break. "Flight is evidence of guilt, and you didn't fly."

I'm not sure that cheered Cheryl up. It didn't do much for me. Though Cheryl was in stoic good form, I could see the reality sinking in. How would any of us feel to be on trial for murder? Not what you'd call a weekend amusement.

After the break, lawyer Orban Pillburn took the stand. He was in the last stages of middle age, prematurely distinguished looking, and sure of himself. The kind of guy who'd been getting away with excessive fees all his professional life. He was fastidiously dressed, and there wasn't a hair out of place. In short, he was one of Bomber's favorite targets.

Bomber doesn't usually ask any questions at a preliminary hearing—there's no need to show our hand—it is solely to see what they have and for the judge to determine if there is enough evidence of the charged crime to bind the defendant over for trial.

But after hearing attorney Pillburn rattle on with information Bomber thought might mislead a careless judge, he felt some clarification was demanded.

The D.A. seemed surprised when Bomber asked to cross-examine attorney Pillburn. He used his eyes as he would to convey his opponent's desperation in taking this absurd step, but it seemed lost on Judge Emory. She knew better.

"Attorney Pillburn," Bomber began, standing tall in his elevator shoes, "you testified you wrote all of Aldo diCarlo's wills. Is that correct?"

"That's as far as I know. Aldo never indicated he had any other wills."

"But he could have?"

"I suppose."

"So maybe you weren't the only person to write wills for Aldo diCarlo?"

"Anything's possible."

"Now you also said the defendant—Cheryl Darling— was being cut out of a will with one you were preparing for Aldo's signature the day after he died. Correct?"

"Yes."

"How did Cheryl Darling react when you told her she was being cut out?"

"I didn't tell her," he said smugly. "That would be unprofessional."

"Just so," Bomber said. "Congratulations on your ethics. So who told Cheryl Darling she had been—or rather, was about to be cut out of Aldo's will?"

"I don't know," Pillburn said.

"You don't know if anyone *did* tell her?"

"No."

"Did you tell Cheryl Darling she was in the prior will? The one you were rewriting?"

"No, I didn't. That's not my place." Attorney Pillburn looked down at Bomber. "You're familiar with the attorney/client privilege?"

"Well, yes, thank you for asking. That tidbit *is* in my meager fund of knowledge; but fear not, I'm always happy to learn about the law from my betters. And while you are instructing me about the attorney/client privilege and such, perhaps you could enlighten me on another matter. Did anything you said on direct examination in any way suggest—or should be construed to mean this defendant had *any* knowledge whatsoever of any of the contents of Aldo diCarlo's wills—so far as you know?"

"No. I didn't tell her, or anyone else—the only person besides myself who knew the contents was Aldo himself."

"Do you have a secretary?"

"Yes, I do."

"She types the wills? This one in particular?"

"Well...yes."

"Do you have any reason to believe she would tell anyone else?"

"Certainly not." Orban Pillburn was angered at the suggestion. "She's been with me for twenty-three years and in that time has never breached a confidence."

"That's good to hear. So you agree that your testimony does not in any way indicate Cheryl Darling had any knowledge of the contents of various wills you concocted?"

"Objection," the D.A. said. "Asked and answered. I also object to Bomber's editorial phrase—the word 'concocted,' specifically."

"Do you have any idea what the district attorney hoped to legitimately accomplish through your testimony?"

"Oh my goodness, Your Honor," Web was on his feet. "I object to this unprofessional behavior. Bomber obviously thinks he is prejudicing a jury instead of grandstanding before a learned judge."

"Sustained," she said resolutely. I wondered if I had really seen her at that moment, preening just a bit.

"I stand corrected," Bomber said. I'd rarely seen him

squander that bogus humble pie favorite before a judge. That was strictly a jury ploy.

"Just one more thing, Attorney Pillburn. Did the district attorney ask you to connect your testimony to Cheryl Darling?"

"I don't understand."

"Yes—did the district attorney ask you to connect your testimony about Aldo diCarlo's will to Cheryl Darling— through someone who might have told her?"

His eyes closed halfway as though he were trying to remember an obscure fact. "Well…"

"He did, didn't he?"

"It might have come up."

"But you couldn't connect it, could you?"

"No."

"Cheryl Darling was never in your office when either will was mentioned?"

"No."

"And you never told her?"

"Certainly not."

Bomber was finished and the judge excused Orban Pillburn while Bomber made a helpless gesture with both arms. "Your honor," he said. "I must respectfully implore you to quash this indictment. Not only is there reasonable doubt—which I understand the jury must pass on, and I am proud to tell you I came by that intelligence without the aid of lawyer Pillburn."

"Oh, Bomber…" the D.A. said sotto voce.

"Not only reasonable doubt, but total, unqualified doubt. What does the district attorney have? Cheryl Darling bought cyanide. Aldo diCarlo died of cyanide poisoning while she was in the house, which was the size of our Grand Hotel— she could have been half a mile from him when he took the poison and still have been in the same house. Then we have this fanciful last witness who was changing Aldo's will, yet again, apparently. Nothing new in that—I believe he'd been through a dozen revisions with his famous client. But where, Your Honor, is the testimony that the defendant knew *anything* about it? It doesn't exist, Your Honor and I submit that is a fatal flaw in their case, and the indictment should be quashed and Cheryl Darling released immediately from custody."

Judge Estelle Emory dropped her eyes to some papers on her judge's bench. D.A. Webster Grainger stood up to clutter the silence.

"Your Honor is well aware this is a *preliminary* hearing, not a trial. Probable cause is all we must establish, and I submit we have. Naturally, we will have to flesh in these details when we go to trial, but I can assure you we can and will do so in order to meet—at the proper time—our burden of proof."

The judge seemed to breathe a sigh of relief. I figured she thought the evidence was a little thin, but she didn't have it in her heart to give up her shot at a highly publicized celebrity trial.

Besides, supermodel defendant, Cheryl Darling, was just too damn thin. Emory Board bound Cheryl Darling over for trial.

Before the prison matron led Cheryl back to jail, she asked Bomber, "How does it look?"

"They don't have a hell of a lot. May take more than that to get a jury over the reasonable doubt hump. Of course, he'll beef up his case in the meantime, just as we will keep digging for a solution. It would be nice if Tod could turn over some other dude who done it—a plausible scenario for what actually happened and why. We don't know much yet," Bomber said, "but one thing we do know—"

"What's that?"

"That there is a lot more to know about the victim, and Tod's going to find it. It's all up to Tod," Bomber said, putting me on an impossible spot.

But Cheryl just smiled and *winked* at me. "I have," she said, "unlimited faith in him."

I wished I shared it.

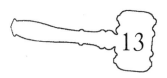

13

From Cheryl Darling I got a list of Aldo diCarlo's amours known to her. She admitted there were perhaps hundreds of casual encounters she didn't know about, but her list was a starting point.

I decided to start with the model that replaced Cheryl Darling.

After a lot of aggravation and telephonic pursuit, I got an appointment to meet Wissie Murray, the sixteen-year-old supermodel sensation. She wanted me to understand she had no interest in talking about Aldo diCarlo because, she said, "I have nothing good to say about him." But I prevailed—in a matter of speaking, *viz.* I would get a few minutes of her time before a runway show she was doing in Beverly Hills, because that evening she was off to Paris in a never-ending swirl of acclaim.

So I drove to Beverly Hills, and found my way backstage in an oven that passed for a communal dressing room, where a flock of models were applying makeup, which I saw as an assault of redundancy.

Wissie Murray was so painfully thin she put me in mind of an empty straw. Her face was beautiful in a befuddled sort of way—like you might find on any teenage girl who had lost her way and didn't want anyone to know. She had piles of blond hair which looked like too much head on a beer.

It was an odd get-up for a model, but Wissie got away with it. It was like a trademark. It made her look like a sophisticate from the wrong side of the tracks. She was a down home girl in the big city.

Before I had a chance to open my mouth, a woman swooped down on us. She put me in mind of a vulture intent on picking my bones clean.

"Wissie, who *is* this?" She asked.

"Oh, Mom," she said, leaving no doubt about her exasperation at the tight supervision.

"Who are you?" she said. She was a good-looking woman herself—more than twice Wissie's age—but not much more. Still statuesque and modely.

I told her who I was. "I just have a few questions," I said.

"Impossible!" she snapped. "She has a runway show to do in a few minutes. Her mind has to be clear. I can't allow any distractions."

"Oh, Mom," Wissie said. "I'm sixteen years old."

"So I've heard, though the way you act, I sometimes have my doubts."

"Well, I'm making a good living for both of us, don't you think you can treat me like an adult just this once?"

Wissie's mom glared at her daughter with a ferocity that would have melted most lesser mortals. "Look what happened when I treated you like an adult." If her look wouldn't knock you over, the tone of her voice would. "I'll treat you like an adult when you act like one. I think we've had quite enough of Aldo diCarlo. Now run along, Mr. Hanson, perhaps another time."

"Sure," I said. "No problem. I drove over one hundred miles to get here, but sure, another time. I'll just drive on back there and get a little subpoena and you can both drive up there instead—at my convenience. Be a shame if it cut into the Paris trip."

Mom was fuming. "Is that blackmail, Mr. Hanson?"

"Gosh, I hope not," I said. "Just reality, I guess." I shrugged. "You decide. I'll take a few minutes now or we can spend a day or so in Angelton."

I think I saw blue smoke puff out of Mom's nose *and* ears as she stormed off in a huff. Bomber's subpoena trick had never worked better.

Wissie seemed amused. "Bravo," she said under her breath. I think the plaudits were for me putting one over on her mother, rather than any eagerness to talk to me. Mom stood at the far end of the room with her arms folded across her chest. Her eyes never left us, and I could feel the blue smoke coursing down my shirt front.

I tried to warm her up. "Where did your name, Wissie, come from?" I asked.

"It's Wilhemina," she said, shrugging at the hopelessness of it all. "Wilhemina was a famous model my mother admired. Mom was a model, too. Gilda Murray—maybe you heard of her. Can't do much with Wilhemina, can you? Wilhemina C. Murray—C. for Clarkson, my grandmother's maiden. Can't do anything with that unless you want to sound like a boy. Now that I'm a model, Wilhemina would be confusing. Like you don't want two of them. Anyway, in school, someone called me Wil C. when we were into nicknames, I don't remember exactly. Wil C. became Wissie and it just stuck like old gum to the bottom of your sneakers."

"How long have you been a model?"

"Two years," then added hastily, "I made it too quickly. Early fame has a way of shutting off your brain."

"What was your relationship with Aldo diCarlo?"

"Relationship," she said with a dull flutter. "That is the question. I'd have to say 'close' for awhile. Then…" she looked away as one who had not come to praise Caesar. "Pfft—" she snapped her fingers to convey the loss.

"Why?" I asked.

She shrugged. "Who knows? Maybe relationships are meant to be short."

"Another woman?"

She didn't answer.

"Perhaps you and another man?"

She shook her head slowly. "The answer is in there somewhere, but the players are not in the sequence you imagine."

"Meaning?"

"Lupe from the sewing room. That's Aldo di Carlo—

AC/DC."

I didn't let on I knew that. "Did you know Cheryl Darling?"

She looked at me as though I were crazy. "Of course I knew her," she said. "I took Aldo from her."

"She angry?"

"Wasn't too happy."

"The two of you get into it over him?"

"Yeah. A bit. She called me a couple of choice names. It wasn't pleasant, and I'm trying to forget the whole thing."

"But I imagine Cheryl must have resented you…"

"I imagine," she shrugged.

"Aldo diCarlo apparently had many and various loves—how do you account for it?"

"He was upfront. He said he had so much love to give that he couldn't think of bestowing it on only one person."

"I'm sure you all thought that you'd be the one to stick?"

"I was that dumb. I can't speak for the others—I'm just a kid. But I have been modeling for over two years already." The way she said it sounded like a lifetime.

"Know any reason why any of them would want to kill him?"

"Sure, we all had reasons," she wrinkled her cute little nose. "With Aldo it was always love/hate, but only Cheryl Darling had the guts to do it."

"Really?" I asked. "Weren't you *all* at the final party?"

"Not when he died."

The activity in the dressing room seemed to suddenly speed up to an alarming pace. Makeup complete, the models started throwing off skimpy skin coverings that guarded their modesty from the heathen.

Just as suddenly, I felt I was in a palace of purience with gorgeous, almost-naked women all around me. The trick for me was to see as much as I could without anyone knowing I was looking. I adopted a deadpan, bored look and would shift my gaze from innocuous place to innocuous place, and pass my eyes over the good stuff as though it were an inconvenient nuisance in between.

Floor—girls—ceiling. Girls. The mirrors helped. Girls, gorgeous girls in all states of undress, throwing clothes off, sliding them on.

There in the middle of all this frenetic activity stood a delicate little man. He was the vortex of the storm. His arms were moving in seven directions at once, and his head swiveled to take in as many focal points.

"Who's that?" I asked Wissie.

"That's Jeffrey Xavier," she said with an indulgent smile, "the whirling dervish. Head honcho of this show."

"That the position Aldo would have been in had it been his show?"

She nodded. "But *totally* different," she said.

"How different?"

"I don't know where to start. I always thought Aldo liked women, Jeffrey is just a flagrant fruit. Aldo liked women—wanted to make them beautiful—because he liked to look at them, plus it was good business. Whatever. Sometimes you feel like you are just a stick being draped with the designer's latest ego trip. Some of these guys kind of hate women and make us look silly."

"Like today?"

Wissie wrinkled her nose. "Whatever," she said.

"Do the clothes affect you in any way?"

"Well, yeah," she said, "but it better not. You see all these girls on the runway—if you watch their faces they're all blank deadpan. Honestly, we don't always know the difference. It's like I just do my job and they pay me plenty."

"But you liked Aldo's designs?"

"Yeah, because I liked Aldo. I thought he liked women—till he left me for a guy."

"Can you tell me a little about the affair itself?" I blushed asking have a question. But I soon learned one did not have to blush in the presence of sixteen year olds.

"He was a lousy lover if that's what you mean. It was like he wanted to conquer me, but once that was accomplished, he seemed to lose interest—no wonder, it turns out he likes boys."

"You didn't know that?"

"I didn't know anything. The famous designer wanted me. *Me!* My career was assured."

"How long did it last?"

"Pft," she said, misunderstanding me, "five minutes."

"Five…I mean, how long did you date him?"

"Six months or so. He'd make this big show in public—like we were long lost lovers, all kissey-poo. But when it came time for a payoff, he was nowheresville."

"Maybe he just wanted people to think he was heterosexual," I said.

"Maybe," she said. "I mean he never asked me to keep my mouth shut or anything. It was just…weird!"

"When did you find out Aldo was…bisexual?"

"He left me for a *guy!* Then I began hearing things about other guys."

"How did your mother take it?"

She pursed her lips and shook her head. "Not good. I thought she'd *die* when she found out, she carried on so. 'Mother!' I said, 'I'm sixteen years old. I've been earning my keep for two years! I can take care of myself.'"

"Think she was jealous?"

"Well, I guess—she was something. My mother is a *gorgeous* woman. She was *the* top model in her day—I should only hope to live up to her."

"So what was the problem—the age difference?"

"I never knew exactly. She said I'd probably get AIDS and I should be tested. She knew he went with boys."

"Were you tested?"

"Yeah. I didn't have it."

"Think Aldo did?"

"Don't know—didn't give it to me if he did."

"Wissie!" Someone with a walkie-talkie headset and clipboard shouted. "You're on—" Mother hen took that as a signal to come and hover over her chick, checking her dress, hair, makeup, primping here and there.

Wissie fluttered her fingers at me in a goodbye wave and positioned herself in a small line at the stage entrance.

I don't know why I had the suspicion she was holding something back from me. But as she said, she was just a kid.

But, oh, what a kid.

I slipped out into the back of the audience, where I stood in the back to watch the show. The models were a grim lot, like slot players in Las Vegas. Here the gamble may have been nothing more than falling off the runway.

Then Wissie Murray came out in her waves of funk. A dress so bizarre I can't imagine anyone buying it. But I could imagine it getting press for the designer.

Wissie had a lot of poise for a sixteen-year-old.

Maybe too much.

*   *   *

There was thunderous applause when the fashion show ended and Jeffrey Xavier came out on stage with his models for a curtain call.

The girls dwarfed him as he smiled modestly and held up his hands, palms out, to quiet the throng of well-wishers.

When he'd finally achieved a semblance of order, he spoke with a voice as squeaky and tenuous as his stature. His inflection smacked of the Bronx.

"Thank you, thank you, thank you—I 'preciate…thank you…very much. I jus wanta say, in addition to thanking the girls for a simply scrumptious performance, that dis here is my memorial service to the daddy of us all, Aldo Cabrisi di*Carlo!*"

There was the obligatory roar from the audience. When it subsided, Jeffrey said extravagantly, "Those of us who strive ta be creative wid fashion owe it all to Aldo diCarlo. I myself had my tutelage under 'im—" There was scattered tittering at the double entendre. "We owe 'im enormous gratitude which we can nevah repay."

When he reluctantly left the crowd as if to seek his gravitational home backstage, Jeffrey was flushed with the adrenalin of huge success.

I followed him back there, dodging the multitudes like an accomplished running back. No one seemed to want to leave.

In the back, in the inner sanctum of the feminine beauty machine, well-wishers, retainers, and sycophants closed in on Jeffrey. I figured I had as much chance of penetrating them as I had in breaching the Great Wall of China with a pea shooter. Patience and perseverance paid, however, and at the the tiniest breach opened, into which I ceremoniously inserted myself.

The thing I noticed about the chitchat was if one was complaining, one could talk indefinitely, laying out all the facets of the perceived failure; but compliments were compressed to the soul of wit. For as Mark Twain observed, "I don't like people to praise my work—it is never enough."

And so it was the praisers said their truncated pieces and moved on, finally leaving me facing the beaming and exhausted couturier, Jeffrey Xavier.

I introduced myself. He looked like he couldn't place the name.

"Our firm represents Cheryl Darling," I said. "I wondered if you'd be good enough to help us by answering some questions?"

"Oh," he said, "well, yah. Certainly," he looked over my shoulder in search of more compliments. "'bout what?"

"Aldo diCarlo, Cheryl Darling. Suspicions."

"Well, I'd be honored to tell a the little I know—it, ah, just isn't convenient right now. Could ya come back, ah, some other time?"

"When?"

"Well, ah, I dunno. Things been so hectic, and now dere's da post show letdown."

"Tomorrow all right?"

"May—be...gimme a call."

"You were his protégé, weren't you?"

"Well, datsa matter of interpretation."

"What's yours?"

"Look, I really doan have no time right now, why doan you gimme a call?"

"Where?"

"Oh, we're in da book," he said, his wrists limping before my eyes as he flitted off into the sunset.

14

Señor Guadalupe from the sewing room was docile. He put me in mind of a thinly stuffed, furry animal. A Persian kitten, perhaps.

He saw me willingly into the grungy house he shared with one hundred other people. Maybe that estimate is too high, but not from the look of the place. It was in the old town part of a town not too far from Angelton geographically. Economically was another story.

Lupe's *casa* abutted a three-story apartment building that dominated the block. The *casa* was *pequeña* with six cars, by actual count, parked on the front lawn. Three or four of them had wheels.

Inside, the furniture all looked like it had been reclaimed from the junkyard. I was afraid to sit for fear of contacting St. Vitus' Dance at the least. But the options were worse, so I sat. I must have looked like a prim schoolmarm, passed over in the marital Derby.

Kids of all ages appeared and disappeared in the room while we were talking.

From the other rooms came sounds of TV game shows, laughter, anger, half-hearted disciplining. Odors of deep frying were about the place, and I pictured crispy tacos wrapped around shredded lettuce, tomato, cheese, and stringy meat.

I tried, without appearing insensitive or snobbish, to contrast Lupe's hovel. "This is an adjustment for you...after being in the big house with Aldo?" I asked.

He flashed a killer smile that put me in mind of one of those movie pretty boys who sells tickets by the carload. Then he gave his shoulder a flip. "It don't matter to me none where I hang out. I been everywhere—*Jeffe's* palace and under the freeway." (He pronounced it Heffe). "It don't change you none."

"Who was *Jeffe?*"

"That's Aldo. Calling him *Jeffe* is Spanish for boss."

Lupe's English wasn't perfect but it was effective. There was a touch of south-of-the-border accent that lent a charm to his unthreatening, but not really feminine, bearing.

"How long did you know Aldo?"

"You mean a lover, or total?" He was without guile.

"Both—"

"I sew for him in the shop maybe a year or more before he notice me. Then, maybe six month, eight month more he pick me out. Say I'm a beautiful boy—stuff like that."

"How'd it make you feel?"

"Good, man. A Mex wetback don't get that stuff every-day. Next thing I know I'm moving into the biggest mansion you ever saw in your life."

"How was living there?"

"Cool. Anything I wanted, anytime I wanted it. A stuck-up butler who had to dance when I whistled."

"Did you whistle?"

He smiled. "Sometime."

"How'd he like it?"

"Not much. It was like he didn't want me around the place if Aldo wasn't there. When Aldo was there, Gaiters, kiss my butt."

Like the word "stuff," "butt" is not exactly what Lupe used here, but you get the picture.

"How'd the butler treat you when you were alone?"

"He ignore me," he shrugged. "Gaiters always try to make us think he's better than us, but I know better."

"Were you still sewing for Aldo?"

"No. He had me quit so I'd be available for him any time he wanted. Still paid my salary, though."

"How often did he... 'want' you?"

"Sometimes three or four times a day. Other times—*nada.*"

"Not at all, you mean?"

"Yeah."

"Did you know why the difference?"

"Nah. I could take it either way."

"Did he have…I mean, did you know of any other romantic involvements Aldo had while you were living there?"

"Oh, he had lots."

"Boys or girls?"

"Both."

"Jealous?"

"Oh, yeah." Then he seemed to think better of it—as though it might have incriminated him. "That jealous stuff never lasted. I was his favorite."

"How do you know?" I asked carefully.

He wasn't angry. He shrugged again— "He told me."

"So people came in and out with Aldo while you were living with him?"

"Yeah."

"Know any of 'em?"

"Nah—I seen guys. I don't know where they came from or where they went and I don't care. He's gone and I'm sorry."

"Ever feel like killing him?"

"Nah, I had him to the end. It was good, man."

"What if you had lost him?"

He thought a moment, then shook his head. "Nah. Talk to some of the rejects. It's the losers who murder, not the winners." He was proud of his status of last in the long line of Aldo's amours.

"Were you at the party?"

"The last one? Of course. I was Aldo's date."

I don't know why that word stunned me. I always considered myself broadminded, but hearing it paraded around with such pride surprised me.

"Were you there when he died?"

"No." He laughed. "Aldo wore me out before the party, so I left early and went upstairs to bed. I tried to get Aldo to come too, but you couldn't keep him down." His brow furrowed as though he were discovering the irony. "But someone finally *did* keep him down—for good."

"Any idea who? Or why?"

"I'd have to say Cheryl Darling would be the one," he said. "She was there. I hear she bought the poison."

It was all so pat, I thought. She bought the cyanide. She was there when he died of cyanide poisoning.

"Any idea why she would hang around? After she allegedly gave him a poison pill, why not clear out of there?"

"I don't know," he shrugged. "Maybe she wanted to be sure it worked."

"Why would she want him dead? Why now?"

"Beats me. But a woman pushed aside for someone else she won't never forget it."

"But there were a lot of women, weren't there?"

"Some," he shrugged. "More boys, I think."

"How would you characterize your relationship with Aldo?" I asked.

"Characterize? What's to characterize? We were lovers," he shrugged as though that told the whole story.

"What else did you do together?"

"He took me on trips."

"Where?"

"To Vegas, mostly."

"Vegas? As in Las Vegas gambling?"

"Yeah. He liked that stuff. He was a Vegas hound. The worse the odds, the better he liked it."

"Did he ever win?"

"Win?" He looked at me as though I were some kind of naïf. "You don't win in Vegas. Not in the long run. He'd win and lose—overall, he'd lose."

"A lot?"

"What's a lot to a guy with Aldo's bucks? A lot to me is a hundred bucks. I don't think a hundred thousand was a lot to Aldo."

"He lost that much?"

"Sometimes, maybe. I wasn't counting."

"Ever complain of losses?"

"Nah. That Aldo was one rich puppy. He could have anything he wanted. Sometimes I thought he was too rich."

"Why?"

"All the fun of the game was out of him. He always looking for something to thrill him—new excitements. I don't think Vegas did it for him in the long run. Every big success in fashion seemed to make Jeffe more restless. Like he expected more, or something. Like he could never be satisfied."

"Did you satisfy him?"

"Sometimes, yeah, but it was short-lived, you know. In the big picture, I expect I was only a toy."

"Did that bother you?"

"Not especially. He was a toy, too."

A rich one, I thought. "Did you ever argue with Aldo?"

He looked at me warily. "What's to argue about? He gave me anything I wanted."

"Such as?"

"Hey, I wasn't after anything. He bought me some nice stuff—clothes, jewelry—this gold bracelet—" he held up his arm to show me some substantial tonnage of gold.

"He ever confide in you—his inner thoughts—fears— people he didn't trust or feared? Anything?"

"We didn't talk heavy stuff, man. Happy talk is what we were into. I told you we were toys. Toys bring joys."

"And others were toys, too?" I asked Lupe.

"Oh, yeah. Everyone was a toy to Aldo. He was the king."

Somebody got tired of being played with.

15

"What are you waiting for?" Bomber asked when I told him about Aldo's gambling. "It's on to Lost Wages for you—" At first I thought he was talking about me working for nothing, which was only slightly less than I was making now.

"Check with that supermodel first. See what she knows about his gambling. I take it it didn't come up in your conversation with her?"

"No."

"It may be nothing. But find out how much he lost, did he pay all his debts, was he caught up on his losses, was he a cheerful loser—any mob connection? Could he have been laundering money for the mob or for himself? Maybe he imported his own cocaine—drug deals get messy sometimes. Could be Cheryl Darling is complicit in some illicit enterprise of his— working both ends, perhaps. Up to you to straighten it all out. Say," he said, the thought just hitting him, "can you get one of those free hotel rooms?"

"Those are for the b-big gamblers."

"So tell them you're a high-roller."

"Want to b-bankroll my stake?"

He waved his hand at me to emphasize how ridiculous the notion was.

Cheryl couldn't help much. On the prison phone she told me, "I wasn't into Vegas. I only went with him once when we had a shoot there for *Vogue*. He gambled far into the night, but I didn't pay much attention. It didn't seem out of the ordinary."

Las Vegas from the air was a revelation to me. The kitschy skyline of miniature Manhattan was new since I'd been there years ago. There was a camp pyramid, too.

Under the circumstances, I don't think I should mention the real name of the hotel where I did the bulk of my investigation. Suffice it to say, it was one of the older, original establishments that dotted the sparse main street back when it was founded by some of the less savory characters the immigration pool had to offer. The hotel was a venerable institution known more for its history than its glitz. It was a "people place" where they afforded suitable deference, you might say fawning, to its celebrity clientele.

For simple identification I shall call it the Venerable Hotel.

I rented a car at the airport and drove to the Venerable. I walked by a bank of slot machines to get to the front desk. It was not that glamorous a place by current standards, but I guess to Aldo diCarlo, it was home. I'd booked the room for one night only. I could always extend it if I had to—there seemed to be twenty million hotel rooms in town after the last building boom.

I checked in and threw my small bag into the room, finessing the bellboy to save money. Then I strolled the game rooms where I saw a lot of grim gamblers hard at work perfecting the craft of losing money.

There was no question of me playing any of the games. Bomber would have apoplexy if he saw x dollars for gambling on my petty cash sheet. So I tried to look like a savvy gambler without actually gambling. It was no mean feat. I sauntered the floor looking for friendly forces. A lot of the faces looked embalmed, and I tried to picture where these people would be working had there been no dens of iniquity in the desert. Ushers in a movie house (while they still had them), waiters in some subterranean, sunless room. Any place they could maintain their waxy pallor. No lifeguards or college professors.

I was surprised at how many people were gambling before noon. And drinking, too. If you lost enough money, they gave you free drinks. And if you won, they'd give you free drinks to help you lose. Even at 11:30 a.m.

I was standing watching a 21 game with a salt-of-the-earth couple and a dealer who looked as though she had been kicked into middle age, and wasn't that happy about it. This fellow came up to me and asked if he could help me.

Though I recognized the move-on hustle when I heard it, I surprised him and said, "Maybe you can." I introduced myself, and he stuck out his hand as if in a serious business transaction. "Red McDuff."

"Been here long?"

Generously, he offered me a sliver of a smile. "Not long," he said. "Going on eighteen years. You?"

"Half hour, maybe," I said jovially—as jovially, that is, as you can be with the feeling of *persona non grata* creeping up your back.

"Aldo Cabrisi diCarlo," I said up front. "Know him?"

Now his look changed to curiosity.

"What if I did?"

"Consider a few questions?"

"Such as?"

"Our client—we're lawyers," I said hastily, "but hear me out before you throw me out. Then you can tell all the lawyer jokes you want."

A grim smile told me I'd bought a short reprieve.

"We are defending Cheryl Darling…" I paused to look for recognition—I found it, but added anyway: "the supermodel."

"No kidding. My kid wants to be a model."

"Great!" I enthused. "I'll get her an autographed picture."

"Would you?"

"Sure. Piece of cake."

"So you think she's innocent?"

"I know she is—"

"How do you know? Doesn't look good to me."

Those cavalier, easily purchased judgments hit me in my gut like a sledgehammer. "Feel it in my bones." I said. "What can I tell you? You ever see Aldo diCarlo here?"

"Sure, all the time."

"Lose a lot of money?"

"Don't they all?"

"An unusual amount?"

"What's unusual? It's all relative."

"Ever have any troubles with him?"

"Nah. He was a standup guy."

"Any trouble collecting?"

"Never heard of any."

He looked at his watch.

"Lunchtime?" I asked.

"Yeah—"

"Take you?"

"Got to wait for my replacement—okay, there he is." He signaled to a heavyset man in a maroon jacket just like his.

We went to a restaurant in the hotel. On the way, Red told me he was a pit boss. "I supervise dealers, see that everything goes okay."

When we were seated at the table he said, "Cheryl Darling, geez, no kidding. Wait till I tell Tiffany that. Sure you can get her an autographed picture?"

"Sure."

"To Tiffany—a model-to-be, or something like that?"

"No problem," I said.

After more small talk, we ordered. I asked, "How would you characterize Aldo diCarlo as a gambler?"

"Characterize?"

"Yeah. Good sport, sore loser, generous tipper, laid back, compulsive—"

"Yeah, sure. I guess all of those at one time or another. So what's your angle? He abused her and had it coming?"

"Would that be believable?"

"Not to me. Everybody liked Aldo."

"What did they like about him?"

"He was a fun guy. And he was a great tipper. Win or lose, it didn't matter none to him—very generous," Red said.

"Lived life to the fullest, you know. I always had the idea he was trying to keep his life full of excitement."

"Did he succeed?"

"He'd had so much success, it was hard to follow. Success only seemed to make him want more success—bigger and better success."

"That's why he gambled?"

"Maybe. What else is there after you have everything? Beating the odds in Vegas would be quite a triumph."

"Since no one has done it?"

"Not over the long term. There've been some big winners, but the only way to keep the win is to go home. The more you play, the more you lose. It's just built into the system."

"Did he ever win big?"

"Sure."

"Go home?"

"Not in a million years. Not Aldo. He was a guy who liked the chase more than the win."

"Know anyone I should talk to? Get a different slant, maybe—any enemies he might have made here?"

Red scratched his neck. "Don't think there were enemies, but, sure, I can give you some names."

"Anyone in management?"

"Walter Shelbourne was his man, if I'm not mistaken."

"His man?"

"When we had celebrities like Aldo, someone was assigned to see he was taken care of. You know, had everything comped—his favorite drinks—a suite at the top—saw to it he never wanted for anything. Free booze flowed here. I won't say it impairs a gambler's judgment, but I've never seen it make anyone any smarter," Red said, and would you believe—he winked at me?

"Aldo drank a little, did he?"

He closed one eye and opened the other wide. "You might say that," he said.

"Ever think he was—well, not in as much control of his

judgment as he might have been?"

"A fair statement," he said.

"But you can't think of anyone who'd want to kill him?"

He looked at me a long time as though considering placing a fat bet.

"Talk to Walter Shelbourne," he said.

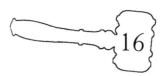

16

I called Bomber and told him my news. "Everybody said Aldo was a standup guy—the model Vegas denizen. Big tipper, happy-go-lucky, they all miss him."

Bomber listened with admirable patience, then he said, "I did a little checking of my own. That hotel you're at, the one Aldo patronized exclusively, is one of the originals in Vegas. One of the *least* glamorous, I'm told; was there anyone more glamour conscious than Aldo? Why wasn't he betting the ranch over at some of those posh, new numbers? Why not at least check it out?"

"He was comfortable here. Like an old shoe."

I used to stutter when I talked to Bomber on the phone. Then I read that people didn't stutter on the phone. That was news to me. Then I got to thinking about it. Maybe my problem was I visualized him when I talked to him on the phone, and if I stopped visualizing so vividly, perhaps the stuttering would go away. And in time, it did. Now if I could only overcome the in-person terrors, I'd be on my way to normalcy.

"Ah, he sure was comfortable there." Bomber mused. "But why?"

"He'd been coming here for years. Before those fancies were built. They fawned over him. He was their boy. Salesmanship. They made him feel important."

"Yes and do you know who *they* were?"

"The hotel?"

"The mob," he said. "Organized crime. Now ask yourself why is this rich, famous couturier pandering to the mob?"

"I don't know that he was pandering. Maybe they're friends because he's Italian."

"Um hm," Bomber said, "and tse tse flies give buttermilk."

"So, what do you think?"

"Me?" he boomed. "I'm not there, you are. Ferret it out, my boy. Use your noodle."

"I was ready to come back," I said meekly.

"So you were," he said. "Take all the time you want. There's more to this case than meets the eye, and we've got to know what it is, or your chickie's going to the guillotine. Now stop lollygagging and get to work. Results!"

How charmingly he put things.

It was, as they say, no piece of cake to get in to see Walter Sherbourne, who was billed as vice president, gaming relations. As near as I could glean, that was a euphemism for customer relations, public relations and high roller relations.

Unfortunately, I didn't seem to fit any of those categories. I certainly wasn't a high roller, or even a customer, and I wasn't from the media whose favor he might have curried. So I played it by ear and presented myself to Sherbourne's secretary —steadfast as the keeper of the gate. She was a presentable woman, this Jennifer Norton. No Cheryl Darling supermodel, but PR guys didn't hire dogs. He was booked solid all day, didn't have a minute for me, and didn't know when he would. Tomorrow was also jammed with appointments.

"Busy man," I said, straining to hold the sarcasm to the barest minimum.

"The busiest," she said, smiling as those Vegas dancers do, sturdy, consistent, as if to no one in particular.

"What about dinner?" I said.

"Oh, he's having dinner with the mayor."

"I meant you," I said, leveling a passable smile of my own in her direction.

Was she flattered or flustered? She fussed with some pencils and note cards on her desk before answering. But she finally allowed as she might be able to work it in.

We went to a place in North Vegas, away from the tourists. Simple yellow table cloths where the food was as sturdy as her smile, and the prices were down to earth, for which I blessed her.

It was a PR dinner. I got her story—not too different from a zillion others up and down the strip. Some sadness in childhood, disappointment in love—her sole attempt at prolonging the species was aborted at the behest of the abusive father; the entire transaction without the imprimaturs of church or state.

She didn't know much about Aldo diCarlo, she said and I didn't try to squeeze her. He had seemed to be pals with Walter Sherbourne, her boss, and she'd had a secretary's intuition that the relationship was deeper than a high roller one, but she had absolutely nothing to go on.

I laid it out about our poor, innocent client who seemed to me the victim of too pat circumstances.

Jennifer seemed sympathetic, and when we wrapped up the evening with a chaste hug, she promised to do her best to get me in to see Mr. Sherbourne—as she referred to him—in the morning.

She was as good as her word. I only had to cool my heels about ninety minutes until he agreed to give me—"Five minutes, no longer." And those were his greeting words to me, though he was on his feet to deliver them.

"I appreciate it," I said, not wishing to squander my time on overdoing the pleasantries.

Walter Sherbourne was a tallish man whose skin had been drowned in tanning lotion. He wore an open neck shirt with a couple rows of gold chains between them and the hair beneath. Lots of it. He was proud, I could tell. Made him feel virile, no mean feat at his stage of the game, which I pegged at post social security. So there was some reason he was hanging onto the old grindstone.

I proffered the introductory intelligence. "Defending Cheryl Darling, supermodel, in the murder of Aldo diCarlo, who I understand was a regular here. I just wondered if you could tell me anything about Aldo's relationship with the hotel that might help us solve the case."

Sherbourne's mouth was tight, his eyes were steely. He

spoke elliptically, which given the time constraints, wasn't all bad. Unfortunately, he didn't reveal anything.

"You understand…business. Unfortunate for all…a standup guy. Devastated."

I wondered how more often I'd be able to listen to Aldo referred to as a standup guy without losing it. He obviously wasn't standing up any longer.

"Not anxious…connection to the hotel…News, you know. Happy place…games…fun…what's the song?…'Don't nobody give me no bad news.'"

"Was Aldo a friend of yours?"

"Friend? Yeah, friend, I guess. Back a few years. Wasn't nothing then. Making hats or something. Love to help more…not our responsibility."

"What can you tell me about him personally—I mean with others? Did he have any enemies you know of? Any run-ins with people?"

Walter Sherbourne shook his head. "Nah."

"Can't think of any disagreement he might have had with anyone?"

"Not here. Aldo was a sport. Left a lot of dough here. Miss that."

"How much…dough?"

"Not at liberty…"

"More than a million?"

"Over the years? Way more."

"How much more?"

"Way more."

"Many millions?"

"Not at liberty," he said, fanning out his arms like a bird wanting to get the heck out of there.

"Was there any relationship with anyone here besides the gambling?"

"What we do here…gamble."

"Anything else?"

Did I see a flush of anger shoot up his neck? "Check the

door," he said and I thought he meant for me to go through it. "Says gaming relations—VP—all I know, all I know."

"You've been here many years?"

He nodded with a curt reluctance, as though that were no badge of honor, but he couldn't escape admitting it, "Thirty-seven."

"Do you keep records on high rollers like Aldo diCarlo that go back to the beginning?"

"Possible."

"See them?"

"Impossible."

"Aldo have any markers?"

I could see he was getting impatient. He wasn't answering the question, so I asked one I knew would be final— "Does this hotel have any crime connections? Could Aldo have been hooked in some way—drugs, prostitution, money laundering?"

Walter Sherbourne stood up, a deliberate action, as though he were a hod carrier lifting a load. But he didn't fool me. Inside, he felt like he'd been shot out of a cannon.

"Time's up," he said with a grim smile and he showed me the door.

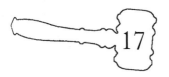

17

I walked across the street and down a bit until I came to another "original" hotel-gambling palace, which must, I'm afraid, also remain nameless.

The new mayor, who used to defend the mob with a vengeance, may say people find organized crime glamorous, and nobody comes to Vegas to find mickey mouse stowed behind a rock. My own comfort level with those hoodlums is sub-basement.

I stopped at the door in front of an eager looking, but underemployed, bellboy who looked seasonably long in the tooth.

"Been here long?" I asked, fishing in my pocket for some heavy tip money.

"Nah," he said. "Thirty-two years."

I wondered if he ever aspired to advance beyond bellboy, but then I realized he could well have worked his way up from dishwasher or janitor.

A car pulled up and he went to the trunk as though he were on automatic pilot. He grabbed a bag that seemed the size he was and threw it unceremoniously on a cart. There, a second tip magnet would deal with it.

He was built like a jockey and had begun his profession before luggage was limited by number rather than weight. It was the ingenious customer outsmarting the air carrier. Two bags only? No sweat. We'll make each the size of a small plane.

I gave the jockey a ten and when he glanced at it, he said, "Thanks," and pocketed it, in that order. I immediately realized it was not enough. He didn't seem to question my motives, as though people came off the streets all the time and handed him tens. I'd have made it twenty, but I could hear

Bomber looking at my petty cash reports (yes, believe it or not, he does) and screaming, "Twenty dollars! Half that would have been generous."

"I'm writing a book," I told the bellhop, not far from the truth, "and I'm looking for lore on the hotel across the street. Know any?"

I wish I could say my news excited him. "Nah," he said, but made no gesture to return my tenner.

"Know anybody who does?"

"Nah," he said, displaying once again the depth and breadth of his vocabulary. He walked off, leaving me with his impression I was just another sucker from the corn country. I was in the midst of despair when another bellman, younger and more padded, appeared. He looked at me and said, "You want someone who knows some history?"

"Yeah," I said. "Know anybody?"

"Could be," he said, his eyes shifting to the same pocket that had produced the ten for his information-deprived cohort. Suddenly, I panicked. Would another ten do it? It hadn't last time. I had in that pocket a five, some ones, a ten, and a twenty. I had no illusions about the five and the ones buying anything useful, so Bomber be damned, I gave him the twenty.

"Kinky," he said. "Hangs out by the pool."

"Does he like to talk?"

The bellman grinned. "Nothing better," he said.

I made my way through the lobby pockmarked with slot machines and a battalion of middle Americans dressed for trouble, then out to the pool.

If you fancied sunshine, this was definitely the place to be. Of course, ninety-nine plus percent of the visitors were inside, sheltered from the constant brightness, basking in the recycled freshness of the air conditioning behemoth.

The few exceptions were strewn around and in the pool. It looked to me like a couple of women tourists whose husbands were inside losing the farm, who might have been more self-conscious about their bodies. Especially in the presence of what looked like a handful of dancers whose endowments were no more modest than they were at sharing them.

One man sat under an umbrella, smoking a cigar that put me in mind of a baseball bat. Gray hair—with tight curls matting the top of his head. He had a knocked up nose that only a mother could love and a pair of spectacles made especially for him by the Coca-Cola Bottling Co. Through them, his eyes were on the dancers, not the tourists.

He wore a pair of denim blue swimming trunks that I'll venture never got wet. He wore a white filigree shirt with all the buttons open down the front—a little too lacy for my taste.

"Are you the man called Kinky?" I asked, facing him with my most disarming smile.

He gave me the grin he would to any patsy. "That's for my hair, not my sex habits. So, who wants to know?" he asked, not unfriendly.

"Tod Hanson," I said.

"Yeah?" he said with surprising interest. "Bomber Hanson's kid?"

"Afraid so."

"Well, I'll be damned." He took my hand and pumped it. "Take a load off—" he waved me to the chaise lounge next to his. I flopped down on it and felt the dry desert heat wash over me like a blowtorch.

"That's some hotshot lawyer," he said with admiration. "Could have used a guy like that once or twice myself."

"Oh?" I raised an eyebrow; he waved a hand of dismissal.

"Yeah," he said. "hard as it is for some people to believe nowadays, this town wasn't built out of no Catholic church poor box. Wasn't all goodness and mercy neither."

"Get a little rough, did it?"

"You could say that. You know the boys. 'Boys will be boys,' I always say."

"Serve any time?"

"Some," he said, taking a deep puff on the baseball bat

and blowing some world-class smoke rings. "Your dad coulda got me off. But that was a long time ago. 'Can't make omelettes without you bust a coupla eggs,' I always say."

I didn't tell him my dad would not have taken his case. Mobsters turned him off.

"Know anything about a boy named Aldo Cabrisi diCarlo?"

"The fairy designer?" he said. "I heard of him. Liked to play the rivals across the street."

"Know why?"

"Heard some rumors. What's your interest?"

"Bomber is defending Cheryl Darling, the model they have in the slammer—"

"Think she did it?"

"Not me."

"Ticked he dumped her for a guy, no doubt?"

"But he didn't. Dumped her for a girl first. That one he dumped for a guy. All happened about a year before he got whacked," I said, trying to adopt his vernacular.

"Aldo Cabrisi diCarlo," he said. "To each his own. Myself, I prefer..." (here he mentioned some rather crude designations of parts unique to the female).

"So how long have you been in town?"

"Pushing sixty—"

"No kidding. You've seen it all then."

"Pretty much, yeah."

"I guess you know where the bodies are buried, as they say."

"Yeah, could be," he said. "And the closer I come to being one of them buried bodies, the more I think about it. But I'm not anxious to join them, so I'm not about to ask for it, if you know what I mean—" he was looking at me through an especially large smoke ring.

"Aldo's dead—"

"Yeah, but some other's are alive. More or less."

"They'd harm you—at your age?"

"Oh boy, are you naïve."

"Granted," I admitted. "But surely you can tell me something about Aldo diCarlo that won't get you in any trouble."

"Surely not," he said, waving his cigar at me as though he wanted me to go away. Then, inexplicably, without warning, he opened up.

"You know, that Cheryl is a looker. Man, did I look at her in them magazines. I smell a bum rap, but I got no proof. Nothing. You here trying to tie him to the mob, you got a bunch of rumors and suppositions, no hard facts. But you want a reason for the mob wasting him, you got your work cut out for you. Aldo was, by all accounts, a—"

"Standup guy," I finished the sentence for him. He looked surprised.

"Yeah," he said. "You took the words right out of my mouth. But," he waved the cigar again, "not surprising. He was well thought of in these parts."

"Well thought of all over," I said. "But someone didn't think too well of him. Got any ideas?"

"Nah." He reflected for a moment. "But you never know when a guy's crossed a guy. Maybe he hasn't been suitably grateful for a favor."

"Justifies murder?"

"Could to some."

"Can you give me an example?"

"Take a guy like Aldo. What was he, some punk making hats at a department store in New York? Hundred fifty bucks a week, maybe. Some guy's wife takes a shine to his hats. Gets her husband to bankroll a larger operation. Maybe he asks a favor that is not granted because this punk hat maker is outgrowing his britches, if you get what I mean."

I got it. "That happen?"

"Hey, I got no idea. Pure speculation. You asked for an example—I give you one."

"Ever hear of Walter Sherbourne?"

"Yeah, I heard of him."

"Any questionable associations—with Aldo—or anybody?"

"Walter Sherbourne is a stooge. He won't tell you anything. Scared of his shadow."

"For good reason?"

Kinky laughed. "Yeah, his shadow's tougher'n he is."

There was a message for me when I returned to my hotel room. It wasn't a telephone message, or a written note, nor was it a subtle rearrangement of the furniture.

As I usually do, when I stay in a hotel room for more than one night, I hung my clothes in the closet and put my underwear and socks and shirts in the drawers.

When I went to hang up my pants in the closet, I saw something so bizarre, it didn't register with me right away. My clothes were hanging neatly on the hangers, as I had left them, but they were sliced in neat ribbons of consistent width, as though someone wanted to make a well-tailored scarecrow.

No piece of clothing was out of place, there were just more pieces.

I checked the drawers. Same thing—ribboned underwear, ribboned socks, ribboned, shirts—all neatly refolded to their original configuration.

That was the message. If someone wanted to scare me they could have done it a lot easier.

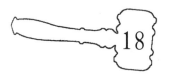

18

I changed hotels. Whoever got to me in the last one had a key and/or the collusion of the staff. So in an effort to prevent my ribboned clothes from becoming little squares of clot (I might even start a new style of sliced clothing) I moved a couple blocks away and registered as Randy Grant from Kansas City. The clerk said, "we aren't in Kansas anymore, eh, Mr. Grant?" and I laughed like that was the funniest thing I'd ever heard in my life.

There should come a time in every case where things start to fall into place—or perhaps fall apart, or at least start to make some sense. Not this time. I had a lot of ideas but none of them seemed to lead anywhere.

Even though I was in a new hotel, I couldn't sleep for fear of someone breaking in.

I lay in bed in the dark trying to clear my mind by mentally sketching the themes and motifs for my Cheryl Darling music piece, as yet untitled. I drifted off into sleep with snatches of song eluding my brain.

I was jarred awake by the insistent *brring* of the telephone by my bed. In that brief state of consciousness, I cursed Bomber for interrupting my sleep. I groped in the dark for the phone and when my hand settled around it, I navigated the receiver to my ear and grumbled my sleepiest, "Hello," in the hope of tipping Bomber off to my not appreciating this kind of nocturnal interruption, which from the sound of my groggy voice, he would surely recognize as bordering on major trauma.

"Tod Hanson," a whisky voice I didn't recognize came through the earpiece.

"Hmm," I hummed in response to the man or woman, I couldn't tell which.

"I can help you," the voice said, and I was leaning toward female.

"Who is this?" I asked.

"What I have is more important that who I am." I got the impression she was whispering to me from under the covers of her bed.

"I'm listening," I said.

"Not on the phone," she said.

"Where?"

"Here."

"Where is here?" I asked getting just a little perturbed at her mystery, but not willing to turn my back on any lead.

"My place," she said without telling me where it was.

"Nine o'clock be okay?"

"No. You have to come now."

"Now? It's two in the morning."

"I can tell time," she growled. "I can't risk meeting you in the daylight. I don't want what happened to your clothes to happen to me."

My grogginess was lifting. "How do you know about that? And *how* did you find me?"

I heard a low chortle through the earpiece. "This is a small town and I know everyone in it."

"Where are you?"

"I'm not giving that away unless you commit to come."

I didn't have to ponder long. I was being jarred awake by this hoarse, whispery voice in the darkness.

"Okay," I said, and she gave me the address.

"And come *now*, and make sure you're not followed," she said. "You come in the daylight, I can't vouch for your safety."

Convincing. I threw on my only clothes that had not been cut to ribbons in my last venue, and threw some cold water on my face and said one name as I made my groggy way to my car.

"Cheryl." I checked my rearviews and the periphery and

saw no signs of a tail.

Mystery woman's condo was not far from the center of things. One of those stucco conglomerates that acted as an homage to *España*.

The paths were lit with low voltage knee-high lights. It was not a lot of light, but enough to get you where you were going. The place was nicely planted and must have taken an ocean of unseen water to keep it flourishing.

I found her door and knocked lightly. No light emanated from the windows.

She opened the door—just a crack first—then released a security chain, enough for me to come into her unlit cave. I made her out to be a lump of clay, unmolded in any discernible shape. She closed the door as soon as I stepped inside. There seemed to be a nightlight on somewhere, I couldn't tell where.

She had on a baggy house dress, spotted with daisies and chocolate, the universal elixir. She wore, I was sure, nothing underneath. She had come to the point where there was nothing to hide—and long past caring about holding anything up.

We went into the living room where the lights were so low, I thought I was at the movies.

My first thought was she wasn't the full quid, as they say in Australia, but in my own plainspeak I'd call her just plain nuts.

Her condo was a repository for anything that had touched her life along its merry way. She had so many pictures on the wall I was transported back to Bomber's office. Hers didn't go floor to ceiling like Bomber's, but there were some you had to get on your knees to see.

In the dim light, I saw pictures of what must have been her in her prime. She had been a rare beauty. I tried to see her that way now, but I didn't have that much imagination. I saw only a puffy, chunky woman, crushed by the sadness of time. Her youth and beauty and effervescence all gone to seed.

The way she looked at me, like I was an object of some deep, forgotten sensuality, haunted and repulsed me. She invited me to sit on the couch with her.

"I appreciate the offer," I said, smiling lightly, "but I am taken."

"*Taken?*" she said and giggled as though that were a quaint and antiquated notion. "Oh my, which century are you from?"

"I'm here for information," I reminded her, trying to be all business. "That *was* the enticement."

"Oh, a man of principle," she said, smiling with a pixie smile which was dwarfed by her body. As though I was the most amusing anachronism.

"How did you find me?" I asked, when I settled into a single wing back chair, while she sat solo on the couch.

"Small town," she said, waving me off. "Everybody knows everything."

"Why all this secrecy?"

"Small town. Everybody knows everything," she repeated. "I don't want to wind up like my ex—"

"Ex? What happened to your ex—?"

She looked at me as though to see if I were really that naïve. "What happened to him? Exactly! That's what you're trying to find out."

The light bulb was going on—full on. "Aldo?"

She nodded rather morosely, I thought. I didn't know if her mood was governed by his tragic demise, or the state of their marriage.

"You're *Mrs.* diCarlo?"

"I guess I still am. We never really got a divorce."

"And you know who killed him?"

"Sh!" she said, looking around the room.

My eyes were adjusting and I saw the magnitude of the goods she had accumulated. And none of the furniture seemed to go with the rest of it.

"Do you have any evidence?"

She patted the seat beside her on the love seat. "Sit here," she said.

105

I shook my head.

"We won't have to shout," she whispered.

"I can hear you," I said.

"Old-fashioned chivalry?" she said as a plea. "It died an unlamented death. Why? Ask Aldo—but he's dead. So why should I have a revival? Why resuscitate the old? Because the old doesn't know she's old—a ruse she can keep up if she stays away from mirrors. I took them all out of my house, so I need punks like you to remind me I'm old. Well, I got news for you—Cheryl Darling will be old some day and so will you. Look at me—almost sixty years old. I'm ashamed to admit I'm making a shameless play for you and I could be your mother. Shame," she said and began to whimper. "Disgrace!" she said and cried the full Niagara.

By this time I was convinced I was caught in the undercurrents of a first class funny farm and could think only of my safe and sane exit. To be polite, I asked some questions.

"How long were you married?"

"To which one?"

"More than one?"

She nodded as though her mind were far away.

"To Aldo?"

"We lived together perhaps a year. Possibly more, possibly less. It's difficult to remember."

"The marriage was..." I paused, "consummated?"

"Oh," she said. "Oh." Then she said nothing while I looked at her puffy face in an attempt to mind read.

"I think Aldo liked women then. Maybe he didn't know about boys, maybe he was repressing it. Maybe he thought it was to his advantage to camouflage it. But, yes, he was very courtly for awhile. Gallant. Especially before the wedding."

"Then?"

"He got the pigeon and seemed to lose interest. Like with Aldo, the thrill was in the chase. The conquest. I wasn't bad looking in those days if I do say so myself." She tossed her head in the direction of the wall of pictures. "See for yourself," she sighed—the weight of the world was pressing in on her. "But good looking or not, I'm convinced Aldo wouldn't have wanted me if I hadn't been married to the one man in the world Aldo owed big time. Aldo didn't really want me. Neither did Franco by then, but his pride was hurt."

I waited for her to tell me who Franco was, but she hadn't even told me her first name.

"Mrs. diCarlo," I said, "would you mind telling me who Franco is and what his connection is to Aldo?"

She didn't say anything. Perhaps she was cogitating whether or not she could trust me.

"You don't know?" she said.

"I don't even know your first name," I said.

"Oh," she said. Then, after another pregnant pause she said, "Ursula. It's Ursula."

"Nice," I said. "Who is Franco?"

"My first husband."

"Yes." I thought I was encouraging her.

"You *really* don't know?"

"Well, I know we never had a president with that name. How would I know him?"

"He owns half of Vegas. The hotel you stayed in until they chopped your clothes like so much lettuce."

In spite of myself, it was starting to sink in. But some things still didn't make sense. "How long ago did this happen?"

"Thirty-five years ago."

"Are you telling me this Franco would hold a grudge thirty-five years? Have you been afraid to turn your lights on for thirty-five years?"

"Silly boy," she said, taking a long look at me. "You don't know the crime families, do you? This is a Mafia town. Grudges don't last only thirty-five years, they are passed down through the generations."

"He's holding a grudge thirty-five years because you left him for Aldo? After, you say, Franco was tired of you?"

"But you don't understand—or you're naïve—"

107

"Or both," I volunteered.

"Yes. Aldo was nobody. He did some freaky hats around town. I liked his hats. I liked the attention they got me. I liked Aldo. I didn't know he was AC/DC. Probably didn't even know what it was in those days. There was still such a thing as reticence and privacy then."

"So?"

"Oh, yes. I begged Franco to bankroll Aldo in the dress designing business. He wanted no part of that. You can imagine the fun his rivals would have with *that*. Loan sharking, gambling, drugs, numbers, prostitution, and dresses." She shook her head. "But I didn't let up. Aldo was *so* talented, I told him. The stake he needed was peanuts in the scheme of things. So I wore him down and he gave Aldo his start, and the rest is history."

"But why would Aldo want to woo you from Franco?"

"I told you—the thrill of the chase. It's like people buying stuff they collect and never opening the boxes. Aldo didn't seem to register what he was doing was a slap in the face and totally ungrateful. Aldo was pretty self-centered. He made a go of his designing business, paid Franco back, but Franco expected to continue as a silent partner. That was the deal, he said It would have paid off handsomely, but Aldo reneged—*and* took Franco's wife in the bargain." She seemed almost bemused by it by now.

"Why didn't Franco do something then? It's thirty-five *years!*"

"What, and admit he'd invested in *dresses?* He'd have been laughed out of town."

"An anonymous hit?"

"No such thing in this town. People find out."

"So you think Franco could have done this?"

She nodded circumspectly.

"Were you at his last party?"

"Oh, no," she said. "I don't travel anymore. But I could have gone. There's no animosity."

"Did Franco go?"

"Goodness, no. He would never…" she broke off then backed up. "But he could have sent someone."

"Know who?"

"Doesn't matter," she said shaking her head. "*Any*body could get lost at Aldo's parties. Just in the house. He built it to be bigger than Franco's, you know."

"I didn't."

"No, if Franco wanted to get him, he'd get him."

"Think he did?"

"I can't think of anything else."

"But the Mafia," I said doubtfully. "A well-placed bullet or two, but *poison?*" I shook my head. "Not their style."

She smiled a wry smile. "Maybe they're changing," she said, patting the seat beside her. "Now come on," she said, as though I owed it to her.

"How can I talk to Franco?"

"Try that, Mr. Tod Hanson, and you won't hear the answers."

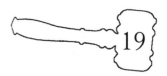

19

When I left the forlorn widow in the darkness of her cluttered lair, I raced back to my hotel room and dove into bed. I will confess to looking over my shoulder at every step, behind the door and under the bed before I did the diving.

But by that time, my heart was pounding so heavily, I couldn't sleep. I didn't have much luck sketching in my mind an ominous section for my Cheryl piece either.

I was out of bed at first light. I gulped what passed for a breakfast, I believe, though I have no memory of it.

I didn't expect Walter Sherbourne's secretary to be in much before eight-thirty or nine, but I went over there anyway, perhaps in a perverse effort to see if Ursula diCarlo's paranoia had any basis in fact. Of course, if they'd cut my clothes to ribbons, the sight of me might inspire them to do that to me. Needless to say, I kept my eye out for threatening behavior by anyone, including the dogs I saw on the way into the hotel/casino.

I went to the office area and found it empty. I walked surreptitiously through the gaming area, keeping alert for what I now perceived as the enemy. I went outside in search of the employee parking lot, afraid to ask anyone where it was. I strolled around the back of the hotel and through a parking structure as though I knew where I was going. Soon, a stream of cars came in and parked in a special section. I went out facing the oncoming traffic, which I had judged to be employees as opposed to hotel guests. They came in a side street behind the hotel. I walked in the desert heat, already doing us dirt so early in the day. I tried to be inconspicuous because even at that early hour, there weren't many people walking on the street. My modus operandi was to glance at the oncoming cars without making eye contact until I found who I was looking for. Then I would make eye contact and signal for her to stop so I could hop in the car. I realized this could be risky for her as well as me.

Then I saw her coming towards me in one of those cars not unlike my own, a car that shouldn't feel out of place in a junkyard. I signaled quickly for her to stop. There were no cars behind her so I thought it was relatively safe. She smiled in recognition and stopped, unlocking the door for me to hop in.

"What a surprise," she said. "Need a ride?"

"No," I said. "Thanks for stopping. My case is heating up." I looked at her. Could I trust her? She looked innocent—she also looked like the job was important to her and she might not fancy taking any undue risks. Then I decided *I* had to take the risk.

"I had a chat with Franco's ex-wife last night."

She stiffened suddenly. "Where did you find her?"

"She called me up."

"I hear she's crazy."

"Ever meet her?"

She shook her head and drove past the parking garage entry. She was looking out the windows of her car warily.

"Think I could meet him? Franco?"

She shook her head with some vigor. "No, I.... He's a recluse, you know. Very rich, but very strange. I don't think he'd talk to the president of the United States if he showed up. We *never* see him."

"So what's his story?"

She turned visibly nervous. "I don't think...I mean...I shouldn't be talking to you about...Franco's *very* strange about these things."

"Can you just tell me where to find his secretary?"

"If I did," she whispered, though we were alone in her car, "I'd be in intensive care and you'd be in the morgue—probably unrecognizable. Please get out of the car here—" she had driven me out of the heart of things without me realizing it. "*Please.* I like my job. I *need* my job—please—"

I couldn't argue with her. I heaved a sigh of bereavement and said, "Okay. Where am I? How do I get back?"

"It's only three or four blocks," she said, "but if I were you, I wouldn't go back. Go on home, whatever you'd learn from him is not worth the risk."

I don't know why I didn't listen to her.

It was noticeably hotter when I got out of Jennifer's air-conditioned car. Even the heaps had to be air-conditioned in Las Vegas. I slogged down the street in the direction of town—having faith she had told me correctly.

I found the hotel and looked for my pal with the aspiring model daughter. It was just before nine a.m. and the faithful were already in place like wax dummies in front of their slot machines, propped on their elbows at twenty-one and sending their roots through the floor by the roulette table.

I looked around for my pit boss.

The term, pit boss, warmed my heart. He or she was like a supervisor of a bunch of dealers, all feeding from his (or her) pit, I suppose.

Maybe it was just a place to promote a burnt out dealer. And maybe they were like pit bulls, ready to tear limb from limb anyone they sensed was an enemy.

My friend, Red, had turned into a wary pit bull when he saw me approach him in his pit.

"Hi, Red," I said with a heartiness that should have reminded him of what one great guy I was. It didn't.

Sotto voce he said, "Sorry, you're person not grata around here. Can't talk—"

"Okay, just tell me where to find Franco, or his secretary."

Red's eyes narrowed. "No can do," he said.

"Why?"

"Look, you're a good guy, but you're a little naïve. There are cameras all over this place. Now do us both a favor and find another casino."

I nodded as though I understood more than I did.

"Why don't you explain it all to me at your break. I'll wait."

"No."

"I'll follow you home if I have to. I don't mean anyone any harm. I'm just after information."

"The wrong kind."

"Why wrong? I don't believe anyone here is connected with Aldo's death. But there are a lot of mysteries—questions the answers of which might help us defend an innocent girl."

"What if she isn't innocent?"

"That's for the jury to decide."

He shook his head.

"Look," I said. "You can always excuse talking to me as a ploy to get rid of me. Answer a few questions—harmless, non-incriminating questions, to be sure. We spring Cheryl Darling and we'll fly her out here to *meet* your daughter—"

His eyes lit up like a Saks Fifth Avenue window at Christmas. Then he furrowed his brow. "Ten-fifteen," he said. "Back entrance. Now make yourself scarce."

I took his advice and strolled back to see Kinky at the pool across the street. I stopped into the hotel haberdashery and sported myself to a sporty outfit on the expense account. Socks, underwear, white pants and a blue and white stripped shirt. I asked the clerk if the clothes were bulletproof. He didn't get it. I carried the old stuff in a bag which I later realized made me look like a shlump. I always admired those characters who could blithely toss their belongings in the nearest trash can. That wasn't me.

Out back Kinky was in the same chair, working the same kind of cigar and ogling a different set of feminine charms. I don't know why at that moment I thought, to paraphrase Siggy Freud— "Sometimes a cigar is more than a cigar."

I smelled that cigar smoke as soon as I had opened the door to the pool area. It hit me like a typhoon in its pungent intensity.

Kinky's baseball bat cigar was an effective insect inhibitor. Not that the Las Vegas chamber of commerce could afford to allow insects.

"That's quite a cigar," I said, realizing I wasn't telling him anything he didn't know.

Kinky took the bat out of his mouth, held it sideways and inspected it for fleas. "That it is," he said. "That it is. I get a lot of enjoyment out of smoking cigs," he said.

"Not afraid of dying young?"

"Too late," he said. "You get to be my age, what's left to enjoy? I like my cigars and I like looking at the girls. So that's how I spend my days. I can smoke the cigars. With the girls, all I can do is look."

I slid into the plastic chair next to him. He eyed my plastic bag. "What you got in the sack?"

"Just some old clothes," I said. "I'm going to drop them off at the Salvation Army."

Kinky nodded dubiously. "Very charitable," he muttered.

"I'm here for another slice of your wisdom," I said, "about things Las Vegas."

He stared straight ahead at a few young girls—hotel guests, I guessed. It was a little too early for the nocturnal dancers. The girls in question were, I thought, a little too young to look at.

"Got an interesting phone call in the middle of the night."

"Interesting," he said, not questioning my choice of words, but rather, a dull and flat statement denoting the opposite. I wasn't dissuaded.

"Whisky voice telling me she could help me."

He nodded. "Ursula," he muttered. "She's crazier'n a bedbug."

"So you wouldn't put too much stock in anything she said?"

"Nuts," he said. "I just can't think of a nicer word for her."

"So I should disregard anything she says as pure fantasy?"

114

"I didn't say that," he said, taking his cigar out of his mouth and inspecting it for I don't know what.

"Was she married to Aldo diCarlo?"

He nodded slowly, as though reluctant to reinforce her.

"*And* to Franco?"

Was I wrong, or did I notice him stiffen a tad? "That's the rumor," he said, trying to be cool.

"How did they do?"

"Do?"

"Yeah, were they a fun couple, or what?"

"What."

"Were they..." I started to repeat.

He silenced me by interposing the cigar between us. "You gave me an option."

"Oh, they weren't a fun couple."

"You met her," he said through a cocked eyebrow.

"Well, now..."

"Yeah," he said. "She was a looker, I'll tell you. Smashing. Gorgeous." He clucked his tongue on his teeth at the wonder of it all.

"Problems?—The marriage?"

"No better, no worse than all marriages, I guess. Low spot was when Aldo took the blushing bride. Aldo! Whose tastes ran to pretty boys!"

"Why do you think...?"

"The chase, the challenge."

"Gets you into trouble sometimes," I offered.

"Yeah, this time I guess it did."

"Think Franco had him offed?" I said in language I hoped he'd understand.

There was a long silence.

"Any idea?" I pressed, but gently.

"I'm not at liberty to say," he said, chomping down on his cigar.

A pair of twenty-year-old fems came on the scene. Maybe dancers, maybe not. Kinky shifted his attention. The way he worked his cigar in his mouth told me that it was definitely more than a cigar.

"So what I hear you saying is it is not out of the realm of possibility that Franco had Aldo wasted?"

"I didn't say nothing," he said.

"You know where I can find Franco?"

"Never heard of him," Kinky said.

On my way back across the street to meet Red the pit boss, it was sinking in that Franco was a figure to be reckoned with. For some reason I had not yet built up sufficient fear. Mafia types were not in my experience. Just people like you and me, who loved their families, enjoyed, as I do, a good dish of pasta, washed their hands— et cetera.

Wrong.

I was waiting at the back door of the anonymous hotel wondering if Red would show, when he came out looking like a white boy in a black ghetto after midnight. He hustled briskly away from the hotel and I followed.

"I got to be crazy," he said. "Am I really risking my life for a few minutes of pleasure for my daughter?"

"Oh, I don't think I'm asking anything life-threatening. Naturally, I'm going to ask how to get in touch with Franco—"

"And just as naturally, I'm going to tell you I don't know—and I don't. I'm a peon here and that's fine with me. I don't need much, but I do want to stay alive."

"So there *is* a real danger?"

"You bet."

"Know Ursula, Franco's ex?"

"Know of her."

"And?"

"Word is, she's loony."

"Convenient?" I asked. "Passing the word Ursula's a loony so no one will pay attention to what she says?"

He shrugged. "Possible."

"But if everyone's so innocent, why?"

"You don't understand anything, do you?"

"Maybe not. But the one thing that bugs me is if there was such animosity, why did Aldo come back here all these years to gamble? I mean, why didn't he go somewhere else?"

"Hm," he said quietly. "Good question. Don't think it hasn't been asked around these tables." He looked over his shoulder. We were out back walking away from the hotel. "Couple of theories been kicked around. One is it was Aldo's way of paying his debt to Franco—a debt that he wouldn't or couldn't acknowledge. Bringing the money home to where it rightfully belonged." He stopped as though considering the likelihood.

"What's the second?"

"Ah, the second, yes. That's more complex. Probably need a psychiatrist to validate the idea. That is that Aldo was, I don't want to say mentally unbalanced, but let's just say a little off-center. I don't think I'd get any argument from anyone who knew him."

"And?" I prodded.

"And he got his thrills taunting Franco. Throwing it in his face, so to speak. 'I'm rich and famous on my own now and I can afford to throw all this money at you and what are you going to do about it?'"

"Like he was goading him into killing him?"

Red nodded carefully, as though he weren't quite convinced.

"If he was, do you think he got his wish?"

"I don't know. Around here, we learn to think anything is possible."

"A thirty-five year grudge?"

"Piece of cake. I could tell you stories that would set your hair on end—which I won't for obvious reasons."

I decided to hit him broadside: "Where does Franco hang out?"

"Nobody knows, really. A hideaway in Mexico sometimes, penthouse in New York. Has a place in the Hamptons. Montelinda up by Angelton, California. He's very secretive about his movements. Nobody knows except his entourage."

"What's that?"

"The guys who go with him. Bodyguards, flunkies, yes-men. Assistants."

"He have any contacts at the hotel? A secretary, liaison or something?"

"Walter Sherbourne is as close as anyone comes, I guess."

"Been there," I said. "Not too forthcoming."

Red shrugged, a what-can-I-tell-you? gesture.

"Well," he said, looking at his watch, "time's up. Don't forget, you get Cheryl Darling off, you fly her out to see my Tiffany—with the autographed picture?"

It was a cheap enough promise to make.

He asked me to let him return to work alone while I walked two more blocks in the other direction.

It was the least I could do.

20

When Jennifer Norton saw me coming back to her little alcove outside Walter Sherbourne's office, she looked like she wanted to crawl under the desk. There was nothing quite like the welcome I was getting in these parts.

"May I have three minutes with Mr. Sherbourne?" I asked, all business, as though we were semiperfect strangers.

"Please have a seat," she said, following suit, "and I'll ask him." When she got up to let herself into the inner sanctum I saw she really was a presentable woman, and I wondered if she had ever been called upon to present herself to Walter Sherbourne.

She returned after what I thought was an eternity, and I could tell the news was not rollicking. She was frowning. "He will see you for three minutes maximum," she said. "I'm to time it." She looked worried.

"When?" I said.

"Now," she said, indicating with a turn of her head that I'd better move; the clock was already ticking.

I entered the big man's lair after a gentle knock and a grumbled, "Come in."

He was at his desk, didn't get up this time and his demeanor gave me to understand he was not overjoyed to see me.

"Three minutes," he underscored my offer.

"Yes sir," I said. "Franco—the elusive owner here, your boss, I conjecture. How can I talk to him?"

"You can't."

"Maybe only another three minutes?"

He shook his head sternly. "Franco is a man obsessed with his privacy."

"Know when he was in Montelinda last?"

The lips tightened. The head jerked to the side once. "If I did, you'd be the last person I'd tell."

"Why so?"

"Because you are obviously trying to hang Aldo's murder on Franco, or someone close to him. The notion is so ridiculous it doesn't warrant any of our time— including yours."

"So there was no bad feeling because Franco staked Aldo, then when Aldo made it, he cut out Franco?"

"Nobody cuts Franco out if he doesn't want to be cut out."

"Oh," I said with eyebrows at a skeptical high. "Same go for Aldo taking Franco's wife?"

A curt nod this time. If he had a recording system in his office, he wasn't doing much for it.

He looked at his watch. "I have only enough time left to tell you to go home. There are powerful people here who cherish their anonymity and who will go to *any* length to maintain their privacy."

"So perhaps it is in Franco's best interest to talk to me," I said with a hopefulness that signaled I didn't get it.

He stared a hole through me big enough to drive a Mack truck through. Finally, he signaled me with one of his economy nods. "If he'll talk to you, where will you be?"

Ever the optimist, I gave him my hotel and at that fortuitous instant, Jennifer came in to announce my time was up.

On the way out, I sensed she was in no mood for chitchat.

I sensed correctly. When I got back to my new hotel, two guys the size of Arizona were waiting for me. The efficiency of the mob. Who was it that said they should be running the United States government? Efficiency would shoot up by ten thousand percent.

Northern Arizona took a small step that placed him squarely in my path. "Tod Hanson?" he said. It was a question he knew the answer to.

Naïvely, with a touch of hope, I said, "Yes."

"Franco wants we should take you to him. Come with us." *That* was not a question. They *should* be running the government, I thought.

We went around the hotel to the parking garage in back, and into a dark corner where there stood a large, black, late model product of the gang at Ford Motor Co.

Instead of opening a door for me, Southern Arizona opened the trunk.

"Hop in," said Northern Arizona. He seemed to be the talker in the crowd.

I looked from one to the other of the Arizona boys. The fear in my eyes could not be hidden.

"Just a safety thing," Northern Arizona said. "Franco don't like nobody knowing where he is."

Before I could ask why not, Southern Arizona—a man of few words—hugged my waist, lifted me up, and deposited me in the trunk without noticeable fanfare.

The lid snapped shut and before I knew it, we were on our merry way.

It didn't take long for me to realize the trunk was not air-conditioned. Rather thoughtless, I thought, for people who used it as much as I suspected these the Arizona boys did. And I didn't think it was for ferrying chums to see Franco. With that thought, terror set in.

If you've never ridden in the trunk of a car, it is not a sport I would recommend.

All you can do back there in the dark is think. Under the circumstances, you don't think happy thoughts. Cold terror is more like it.

How brave would I be looking down the barrel of a gun, or feeling a rope tightening around my neck?

Even as I thought of brilliant (and not so brilliant) ploys to talk the Arizona boys out of rendering me into a piece of soap, I realized the futility.

Would I get to see Franco first? I doubted it. Recluses

are not so eager to see people they dispatch them with such lightening efficiency. That kind of maneuver is reserved for egregious, defensive gestures—like eliminating the enemy.

I don't know how long we drove or how many turns we made—either because the route dictated the moves or to confuse me so I would be unable to lead the police—probably beholden to Franco—to his hideaway—this thought was my fervent hope. I would gladly give up reprisals for a shot at talking to Franco, or so I thought. On further reflection I realized the only thing more remote than me getting an opportunity to talk to Franco was any cooperation coming out of it. "Sure, Tod, me boy," he would say, his Italian tongue turning to Irish brogue, "we'll cooperate fully with your defense of the blushingly innocent Cheryl Darling, and I'll even send the hit man to Angelton to confess on the witness stand. Bomber Hanson as Perry Mason."

My heart was still playing "Anvil Chorus" from *Aida* by Giuseppe Verdi—or Joe Green in translation—when the car pulled off the road and I felt it come to a gravelly stop.

Then nothing happened. No move was made to open the trunk and pop me between the eyebrows. I didn't even hear the car door open. Was someone to meet the Arizonas here with firepower? Or the hearse?

Perhaps they were waiting for a helicopter to whisk them away while the bomb went off in the car, blowing me into the Hoover Dam or some other popular tourist site. Maybe my remains would find their way into the concrete foundation of the next theme hotel built to look like the Watts Towers.

Then I heard a vehicle drive up and screech to a stop. The doors of my hearse opened and without discernible communication, other car doors opened and closed and I thought I was to be left in the trunk to die as a piece of petrified wood to be uncovered in the next millennium by some hiker who stumbled upon an old, rusty, internal combustion engine relic.

There was the gunning of the engine of the getaway car and I felt my doom sealed for all time.

Then in one sweet split second of a moment that I shall

remember for the rest of my life, I heard a popping sound and saw a sliver of light.

The other car roared off and was out of sight before I got the trunk lid lifted and drew hungrily on the fresh desert air. It took only a fraction of a second to realize I was nowhere. A dirt road that seemed to have no beginning or end. I stood on the ground just to prove to myself that I could. My first thought was maybe they left the keys to the car.

They were not in the ignition and a thorough search yielded nothing. Not surprising. Why would they give me a car?

I searched the glove compartment for any identification, but even as I was doing so, I realized how futile that was. I knew where these guys came from and they weren't sent by the tooth-fairy. I memorized the license plate anyway. Just in case there was any confusion about ownership.

There was still plenty of firepower left in the old sun as I made my way down the dirt road away from it. I had no idea which side of town I was on or where I was going. I was just looking for a real road with asphalt or concrete on it.

After a period of time elapsed roughly equivalent to forever, I got to the asphalt highway. Parched and hungry and threw out my thumb as though I was born to hitchhike, though I'm sure I did not hide my scant experience in this line.

Less than a half dozen cars went by before a lonely, garrulous trucker stopped and had a good chuckle when I asked if he was going in the direction of Las Vegas. He was, but I could just as easily have been on the side of the road that took me to Texas for all I knew.

He dropped me off within walking distance of the airport, which was fine with me.

I'd happily wait a week for a plane connection in that public environment.

I didn't return to my hotel. My former clothes were a bunch of ribbons anyway and who needed ribbons in my line of work?

I didn't bother with any communication with Bomber.

My experience in New Jersey that I modestly chronicled in *Phantom Virus* led me to the unshakeable belief that would be counter to my best interests.

In the airport waiting room, I kept my back to the wall. When my time came, I got on a plane, my back to the wall, and went home to Angelton and my darling Cheryl Darling.

21

Back in Angelton, I wanted to head straight for the women's prison, but decided political expediency dictated checking in with the man who pays my salary— penurious though it may be—the inimitable Bomber Hanson, dean of torts.

I found Bomber at his desk where I had left him, thumbing through some briefs on a medical malpractice matter. After a spare amount of pleasantries—an area in which Bomber did not excel, we got to the business at hand. I told him the whole story, breathlessly, stammering all the way. When I'd gotten it all out, I clinched it with, "So, obviously, we've got the c-culprit."

"Oh?" he said. "And who is that?"

I was astounded at his reaction. Hadn't he been listening to me? "F-Fr-Franco," I stuttered.

Bomber looked at me as though I'd lost it. "*Franco*," he boomed. "The mobster? He's going to put cyanide in the vitamin pills? After the party that he hasn't attended? Or wait, don't tell me, one of his henchmen screwed with the vitamins during the party—unnoticed by the kitchen crew or Aldo himself. Franco brought all of this off from Las Vegas and everyone involved hoped the pills would get in the right mouth? Gimme a break. The mob would send a good shot out to the house in the morning. When Aldo got into his car he'd get one between the eyes, and maybe a couple more for good measure. But they aren't going to mess around with pills with one hundred witnesses."

Talk about wind out of my sails—and my sales.

"And all this is some thirty-five years after some slight—and Aldo kept going back to Franco's hotel and gambled millions and nobody in all these thirty-five years thought to even punch Aldo in the nose? *Au contraire*, they all spoke highly of him."

"So," I sought for a shred of courage to carry me on, "why d-did they go after me like that?"

Bomber threw up his meaty shoulders. "Maybe there's something else they're afraid of. Maybe they just don't like snoops. Maybe they thought you were I.R.S. undercover—or F.B.I.—shall I go on?"

I shook my head. It was all I could manage.

As I left him with my tail between my legs, as they say, I vowed to redouble my efforts on Cheryl's behalf.

Bonnie Doone was in a mysteriously quiet mood as I passed through her reception area on my way to see Cheryl at the women's prison.

"Well, well, honeycakes—hit the jackpot in Vegas?"

It wasn't really a question. She was reading a magazine—*People* or a tabloid—something that matched her intellectual capabilities. She barely looked up.

Cheryl put up a good front in the visitor room at the lockup. It always tore at my heart seeing her there, but she was so brave with her dazzling smile. Was it, I wondered, a serene smile denoting if not contentment, then acceptance, or was it simply a smile honed by her years of professional demands?

I decided it didn't matter. Whatever it was, I loved it. But the longer I pursued the S.O.D.D.I. defense (some other dude did it), the harder it was to erase from my subconscious the fear that I was headed for a fall putting so much faith in Cheryl's innocence.

We did the small talk. Cheryl was much better at it than Bomber.

In spite of what Bomber had said, I couldn't give the Vegas mob angle up. Not yet. I asked Cheryl about it.

"Did Aldo ever say anything about Las Vegas—his trips there—a man named Franco? Can you think of anything strange or unusual Aldo might have mentioned?"

"Oh, I don't know," she said, then seemed to be

plunged deep into thought. "I can't...nothing comes to mind. I had no interest in gambling or in Vegas. I thought the shows were cheap prurience and so there was nothing there for me."

"Did Aldo tell you about Franco—the guy who owns the hotel he kept going back to?"

"I know the name," she said, her brows scrunched up. "There *was* something. You know, I'm no psychiatrist, but I always found this aspect of Aldo's character puzzling. Gambling was more than just a sport for him, it was part of his nature."

"Did he ever indicate it was a gamble just for him to go back to that hotel?"

"Franco's? I'm trying to think."

"Do you know the story?"

"Which story?"

"About Aldo and Franco. Franco gave him his start and Aldo cut him off. Not only cut him out of his business, but took his wife in the bargain."

"I may have heard some of that, but not from Aldo. I never paid too much attention to gossip. I know from my own experience how wrong it can be."

"But given that information, why do you think Aldo kept going back to Franco's hotel—*thirty-five years!* Franco, you understand, was organized crime—the kind of guy who could assign a dozen hits before breakfast. And Aldo kept stepping into his lair. Was he thumbing his nose at a crime boss? Was he atoning for past sins by dropping all that money there? Like Franco was no longer a partner, but Aldo was laundering a share of the business his way? Could he have been tied up with Franco some other way? Drug dealing? Laundering money from drug deals?"

"I don't think so. Aldo was not above a snort of coke now and then—maybe even more now than then—but he wasn't stupid enough to deal. Why should he? He was rich and successful beyond his imagination."

"Maybe to make it up to Franco. Maybe Franco had this hold over him. 'Okay, you shafted me out of your biz, now play ball in my biz or you're history.'"

"Doesn't sound like the Aldo I knew," she said.

I'll say this for Cheryl, she didn't jump at every opportunity to blame the murder on someone else. It was reassuring and distressing at the same time.

"Oh," she said, almost as an afterthought, "I do remember something strange Aldo said before a trip to Vegas."

"Yes?"

"See if I can get it right," she said. "It was something to the effect…I remember Aldo was laughing or chuckling like maybe he was a little nervous and excited at the same time. 'He can't touch me—' he said something like that. I thought he meant he was so rich and famous and so far ahead of the pack that no one could come anywhere near him. But if you're thinking revenge, it was like Aldo was flaunting his success to this mobster." She shook her head. "Why would he do that?"

"Exactly!" I said. "*Why?*"

She shook her head. "I have no idea," she said.

"Know anyone who might?"

She thought a moment. "Have you talked to Jeffrey Xavier?"

"Very briefly—at his spring show."

"He was Aldo's top designer. They were very close for a long time."

"What happened?"

"Falling out. Who knows what destroys long friendships? Some slight that is so slight in the scheme of things as to be ludicrous."

She wasn't disappointing me with her words. I just wondered what it all meant.

"He's got a studio in L.A. Maybe he can help you."

"Thanks," I said. "Oh, by the way, was Aldo's falling out with this Jeffrey important enough to end in murder?"

She bumped her pretty shoulders. "Ask Jeffrey."

22

After lunch I pointed my old jalopy south to the city of Angels—not to be confused with Angelton, my home town.

Traffic was reasonable, meaning my only slow up was getting on the 405 from the 101 and climbing that arduous hill to the Getty Museum and then down the hill to Westwood, Brentwood and swell places like that.

I didn't make an appointment with Jeffrey Xavier; I thought the surprise might be helpful. I did ascertain from a secretary type that he was in residence.

The place was like a warehouse. I didn't think the rent was breaking anybody. Dark, no windows to speak of. A partition set off his office, a row of unattended sewing machines were out on the floor, and this area between the machines and Jeffrey's office was well-lit and had banks of mirrors on three sides.

The moment I laid eyes on Jeffrey Xavier, *in* his *situ*, a light flashed in my head saying this was the killer. He looked much more creepy than at his show. He'd let his mouse colored hair down to shoulder-length, and had a droopy moustache to match. He wore a T-shirt with some irreverent slogan on it which I have mercifully forgotten, as well as a mangy pair of sawed-off jeans. An antifashion statement?

The contrast between this *milieu* and the fashion show was startling. It was as though that show was his last hurrah and now the money had run out.

Jeffrey Xavier was dressing a gorgeous brunette model with hair down to there. Though I know nothing about dress design and fitting, Jeffrey Xavier seemed clumsy to me. I kept getting flashes of the model's silken skin as well as her underwear that seemed fashioned out of the same silk.

I tried to concentrate on the scumbag while I spoke to him, but it was hard. I reintroduced myself and asked if he had any theories on the murder.

"Nah," he said, and even that one word again betrayed his origins in the Bronx. "The broad coulda done it—it don't look too good for her. She gettin' all that dough in the will he was changing the next day."

"How'd you hear that?" I asked, though I knew the answer.

"Tabloids full of it," he shrugged.

"Sorry to see Aldo gone?"

"Oh, yeah, well, man, there's the question. You know the history?"

"No, I—"

"Okay, so I'll tell ya." And he did with the most excruciatingly lurid, personal details, regaling me with the bizarre elements of his relationship with Aldo diCarlo.

"I was a male whore," he said, unabashedly, "and Aldo dialed me up and dat first night we just clicked. Incredible chemistry. Maybe our poor childhoods or somethin'. Anyway, he had me back again and again and by three or four weeks, I moved in. He had not had any male live-ins heretofore."

That "heretofore" was a lovely touch. He was probably a whiz at Scrabble.

"So I start helpin' him wid his business. I had no backgroun' in ladies dresses, beside da few I wore from time to time…"

The model tittered. Jeffrey paid no attention.

"I did stuff like window dressin' for his retail stores in New Yawk and L.A. He was nuts 'bout me. Led me do anythin' I wanted. When the regular window dresser complained I was musclin' in his territory, dat guy was history. Aldo always sided wid me. Face it, he *loved* me."

Quite a coup for a bum like Jeffrey, I thought. "How did you get your own business?"

"We had dis falling out," he said with a candor that

seemed so naïve it was refreshing. "I'd started helpin' him with his designs. A guy gets stale afta so many years. He needs new blood—a fresh eye. I was it. I was filling his needs at home and at work. 'His alter ego,' my shrink calls it. *Capisce?*"

I nodded.

"Anyway, more 'n mora my designs was gettin' into da shows and drawin' raves from da pundits, and natchly Aldo was gettin' a little uncomfortable, not to say jealous. I was satisfied awhile—I was learnin' from da mastah and I was gettin' a real kick out a it. Workin' side by side wid my lovah in da daytime, clubbin at night.

"In the beginnin', I was makin' suggestions for his designs. Den I was tinkerin' wid 'em. Then he was tinkerin' wid mine, an finally—pfft." He snapped his fingers and let his hand flutter above the model. "I was doin' everythin'. All I ask was a tiny, tiny acknowledgement of my contribution. Sure, I had ambitions ta go out on my own some day, but I nevah harbored no ideas of hurtin' him or his operation."

"But if you *were* his operation, how could you not hurt it by leaving?"

"Good question. Guess I didn't think dat way at the time. I thought he's stale, dry, lazy, whatever yah wanta call it, but I nevah thought he was kaput. An' he had othah designers workin' for him—"

I decided to throw Jeffrey a puffball. "Any as talented as you?"

"That'd be a stretch," he admitted with a charming self-affirmation.

"So what kind of credit did you ask for?"

"Only my due. Design credit. Well, he blew up, said he's da name—he made me—took me from da lowest rung in da whorehouse—da whole stinking bit. I'd a settled for a credit as a designin' assistant, anythin', but Aldo was adamant. He said, 'Ya want credit, open ya own shop.' And dat's what I did," he said looking around his inauspicious digs. I may have been mistaken, but I thought the model had a smirk on her face. The threads Jeffrey was pinning on her would not stop any traffic.

"Going all right, is it?" I asked.

"Can't complain," he said, but I detected some complaint in his tone. "Little early ta tell, natch."

"Would you mind telling me where you got your financial backing for this operation?"

"From Aldo," he answered without hesitation.

I must have flinched because Jeffrey continued to illuminate my darkness. "Oh, he was very generous ta everybody. He gave me money right ta da end. You know what he said to me when we parted?"

"What?"

"'I wish ya all da best. Go oud dere and knock 'em dead. I owe ya a lot. Ya was da best lover I evah had. Go on and upstage me. Get better notices dan I do. Sell more goods. I'm back in da game—wid ya gone I got no choice. It'll be good fa me. I'm lookin' forward to da competition.' Dat was Aldo, a competitor to da core."

"With him gone," I asked, "how will you stay afloat?"

"Got to sink or swim on my own now," he said.

Without his seeing it, the model rolled her eyes.

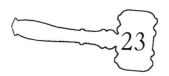

23

Was it because of my strong aversion to Jeffrey Xavier that I went back to see Cheryl Darling in her jailhouse visiting room, or was it because of the opposite feelings I harbored for Cheryl? I just know my feelings for her kept me hopping at a frantic pace. My visits to Cheryl were always overseen by an armed and burly guard, no doubt stationed by the door to see that I didn't pass her a hacksaw.

"Is it getting to you yet?" I asked when she brought her big smile into the room.

"I'm not letting it," she said. "Really, it could be a lot worse. The closer we come to trial, the closer I feel to you. And the more confidence I have we are going to win."

I looked at her pretty, yes, perfect face and felt a twinge of inadequacy jiggle my spine. "Every day I try harder to warrant your faith," I said. "I wish I could report I had a reason to share it. I just got back from a bizarre meeting with Jeffrey Xavier. Do you have a fix on him?"

"Oh, yes, Jeffrey. He was always an enigma. None of us around Aldo ever had a clue to what Aldo saw in Jeffrey."

"Carnality?"

"Obviously. But," she made a sour face, "he's so yucky. And, sure, for a couple of weeks, a year or two, but Jeffrey seems eternal."

"Any theories?"

"Lots. So many they have to be meaningless."

"Why did Aldo give him the money to go out on his own?"

"Love, at first."

"Then?"

"Blackmail. Jeffrey told everyone he was keeping a diary

to write a book—*My Life with Aldo Cabresi diCarlo* or something equally creative. Aldo did a lot of things he wasn't proud of—things he wasn't eager to get out."

"Such as?"

She laughed. "Jeffrey, for starters. Drugs—orgies, the usual. For a man so free with his appetites, Aldo was rather prudish about projecting his image." She laughed again. "He had this idea he'd go down as Albert Schweitzer and Joan of Arc rolled into one."

"Did Jeffrey have any design talent?" I asked.

Cheryl smirked. "Talent? I'm not sure I know what that is. Memory, maybe. In this business, everybody copies from everybody else. Jeffrey picked up the rudiments, but I don't see any originality or flair."

"Can he last in the business?"

"I doubt it. Unless he can use whatever attraction he had for Aldo and parlay it into some heavy backing."

"Was Jeffrey in the will somewhere?"

"I wouldn't be surprised, though I wasn't privy to Aldo's wills—including the one I am allegedly mentioned in."

"When did Jeffrey fit into Aldo's...ah, affection? Chronologically?"

"Years before me—maybe even during and slightly after."

"What do you know about Wissie Murray?"

"She was young. Pretty. I don't know much, really, except she succeeded me. She smiled. "I almost said, 'took my place.'"

"That would be impossible," I said like the smitten kitten I was.

"Thank you kind sir," she said with a slight bow of her pretty head. Prison duds, I decided, became her. But there was something elusive about her manner, something unusually distant. It made it difficult for me to go on.

"What did Aldo see in Wissie?"

She shrugged. "You met her?"

134

"Yes."

"What did you see?"

"A young, pretty kid, with very little truck in the real world."

"Accurate."

"So a worldly guy like Aldo? I mean, what do you suppose they talked about?"

"I don't think Aldo was looking for a conversation."

"But weren't you...hurt?"

"Sure, at first. Then I came to realize what Aldo was all about and I came to terms with it."

"What was he all about?"

"He was a creative dynamo. There are only a handful in this business at any time. They are special—unusual—people. Giant egos. Lust for success, adulation, approbation. Profound fear of failure. Twice a year with their spring and fall shows, they risk all their past successes with yet another attempt to be winningly creative. And face it, how much can you do with a woman's dress? You have two places for her arms to go though and one for her legs and one for her head. So, basically four holes. Then you need enough goods to cover her underwear. Buttons, bows, zippers—when you think about it, there has been an astonishing number of variations on a simple theme. Self-doubt is rampant. These superstar designers need constant reassurance and constant relief from the pressure. That's why so many use drugs."

"Aldo did?"

"Sure."

"Did you?"

"Oh, I went through a period. Models' problems are different—boredom, trying to look sexy when you don't feel it. But the fears are the same. Whatever magic touch you have could vanish. Wrinkles could suddenly appear on your face—photographers and couturiers and editors can be fickle—any day the phone might stop ringing."

"Cheryl," I said. "Would you mind going through that

last night again? I know you've done it one hundred times and probably can recite it in your sleep, but we're going to have to do it at the trial. Maybe this time something will click."

She sighed, but said, "OK—starting where?"

"How about when you got to the party?"

"I got there about an hour before it started."

"Why so early?"

"Aldo needed someone to lean on. I was a familiar face—like an old shoe."

"Didn't Gaiters run things?"

"Oh, yes, but he wasn't much for the emotional support. 'You look great, Aldo— what a great party you've thrown here, Aldo.' The simple buildup."

"He needed that? A guy as famous as he was?"

"You bet. And believe it or not, there aren't that many who can give it to a guy so big and important. They figure he knows how great he is without anyone telling him."

"But why would you build him up? I mean, he didn't exactly treat you well, did he?"

"Surprisingly, he did. Even the breakup was amicable. He did me a favor, he said, and he did."

"What do you mean?"

"The fling had run its course. He was an interesting guy, but he was a handful. Those ego demands were easier for me to meet if we weren't lovers."

"Like at the party?"

"Yes."

"Did you have any other function at the party?"

"I was sort of the hostess. Aldo thought it made a better appearance if he had a woman who could masquerade as his date."

"What about Lupe?"

"Discreet. He hung around in the beginning like one of Aldo's loyal retainers, which was what he was."

"Did he stay to the end?"

"I think he disappeared upstairs with Aldo before things

got going. Aldo came down alone, so I suppose Lupe stayed in bed."

"So what happens at parties like that?"

"Lot of people, lot of booze and drugs, lot of noise after everyone gets loosened up. Aldo had a band that played so loud you had to shout to be heard."

"So did people shout?"

"Some. Some gave up."

"How many people?"

"One hundred—more, maybe two hundred. Everybody I knew was there."

"Wissie?"

"And her mom."

"What's her mom like?"

"Weird."

"Was she okay with Aldo hitting on her sixteen-year-old?"

"I never asked her."

"Get a sense?"

"My sense was she was freaked out. Just a hunch. I don't think she found out right away. It didn't last long. I think mom stepped in. Aldo alluded to it, but it was none of my business, so I didn't press."

"Were there people you didn't recognize?"

"Oh, sure. Aldo's contacts were many and diverse."

"Would you recognize Franco from the hotel in Vegas?"

"Never laid eyes on him."

"Any other Vegas characters?"

She shook her head.

"Anyone suspicious looking?"

"You know, you're at a party like that, you never think the host is going to wind up dead at the end of it. Believe me, I've tried to think back and replay everything I remember in the hope of remembering something useful." She pursed her lips and shook her head. "No dice."

"Did you talk to any of the caterers?"

"Just to say, 'I'll have one of those, please.' Gaiters ran the staff."

"Remember the two who were left at the end?"

"Sort of. Two young girls cleaning up."

"They seem agitated, suspicious in any way?"

"Not really. Just the usual illegals trying to do what they're told and blend into the woodwork."

"See anybody unusual talking to them during the evening?"

"Nope."

"Jeffrey Xavier was there?"

"Oh, yes. He'd drive a thousand miles for a free drink."

"Any altercations with Aldo?"

"Not that I could see. They were lovey-dovey old chums. Kissy—so much it was a little distasteful."

"Remember who the last half dozen people to leave the party were?"

She tightened her brow in thought. "Jeffrey Xavier was last, I believe. Wissie and her mom stayed pretty long. They were in there somewhere. Then there was another couple I didn't know. Think they went way back with Aldo, but I didn't meet them."

"Would Gaiters know them?"

"Maybe if he saw them. But he'd gone to bed by then."

"So everybody is gone, and you're still there. Why?"

"I was helping to tidy up. Just a stupid habit of mine. Get everything neat and tidy so Aldo won't even know he had a party."

"But weren't the caterers doing that?"

"Sure, but I wanted to help. It was lonely at home. You know what they say—busy hands are happy hands."

"The pills?" I said, trying not to make it sound too ominous. "Where did they come from?"

"In a cabinet in the kitchen."

"You knew where they were?"

"Sure, I used to live there."

"How were they stored?"

"In a plastic box with sections for each day of the week."

"So Gaiters could have put poison in there?"

"Doubtful. Aldo wanted to control his own pills and set them in their little compartments every Sunday night. It was a ritual with him. Besides, Gaiters probably had the least motive of all of us."

"How many pills were there?"

"I think I counted seven—"

"He took seven every night?"

"I suppose. There were seven in the container, and I took seven into the dining room for him."

"Then what? Did you watch him take them?"

"No, I went back into the kitchen to tidy up some more."

"When were you going to leave the party?"

"When Aldo went to bed—or when I thought everything was tidy enough."

"Then you heard Aldo scream?"

"Yes. He was yelling for water. It was so shrill, I ran back to the dining room to see what was the matter. He was gagging. I thought he'd been shot the way he was rocking back and forth. He was gasping and begging for water. I filled his empty glass and he downed it in one gulp and croaked, 'More!' I brought him a pitcher, and that's when he said 'Hold me.'"

"What were the caterers doing?"

"Freaking out. When they saw him dead, they screamed."

"Could they have intercepted the pills in any way, any time?"

"I don't see how."

She wasn't helping me much. It only reinforced my belief in her innocence. A guilty person would have taken any opportunity to glom onto reasons to blame everybody else.

"So, with all the time you've had to think in here, what do you think? Who was most likely to have done it?"

"Me," she said, without laughing.

I didn't find it funny, either. It was demoralizing and I must have shown it, for Cheryl Darling said "I'm sorry, Tod, I'm disappointing you. I wish I could be better but I don't seem to have it in me."

Before I could ask if she was speaking professionally or personally, she reached over and cupped my face in her hands. "I cherish you," she said, as the guard lunged toward her.

"No touching!" he said, and I was devastated.

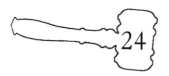

We were sitting around in Bomber's office trying to look intelligent. Bonnie Doone had wormed her way in there somehow, and trying to look intelligent put quite a strain on her.

"I don't like it," Bomber said. He wasn't usually given to understatement. Who *does* like it? I thought.

"Where are those caterer girls?"

"Back in M-Mexico, p-probably."

"Both of them? So soon on the heels of murder? Coincidence?"

"Probably scared to death they'd be implicated," Bonnie Doone graced us with the benefit of her wisdom.

"What if they *were* implicated?" Bomber asked no one in particular. It didn't seem to beg a response. From what I could piece together, I didn't see how they could have been involved.

"What kind of medicine was it?" Bomber asked me.

"Vitamins, I think. Maybe b-blood pressure."

"Uppers, downers?" Bomber asked like gunshot. "Manufacturers?"

"The Tylenol defense," Bonnie Doone said with a smirk. Bomber would never sit still for a smirk from me. Bonnie's beauty was skin deep, max, but as Bomber often said, that was deep enough for him.

What she meant in her simple minded way was we should prove someone put cyanide in the capsules at the drug store. Just how we'd go about proving that was an enormous question. The Tylenol trick had been pulled by a guy who wanted to kill his wife. So he put it in hers and another in the market just to be clever. Cost Johnson and Johnson a wad of dough to cut apart all their pills to look for more poison. Of course, they found none, but the idea amused our Bonnie.

Our court date was closing in on us. We'd pushed for an early date. It had the advantage of limiting the time for the D.A. to make his case. Of course, it limited our time, too, and put that much more pressure on me.

"Okay, Boy," Bomber said. "Get the pills. What they were and who made them. They don't have that much as far as I can see. Maybe I can convince the jury there is a *reasonable* doubt about her guilt."

"Yeah."

"I mean, all they have is motive and opportunity."

"What more do you need?" our resident Phi Beta Kappa chimed in.

For once, she was right on the money.

"Or how about the Twinkie defense?" Bonnie said.

Bomber arched an eyebrow at her, showing his patience with Bonnie Doone was not infinite. She was talking about the partially successful defense mounted by an ex-San Francisco supervisor in his trial for the murder of the mayor and another supervisor. He claimed he had eaten too much junkfood, especially the little cupcakes called Twinkies. He got only eight years for the two murders. I think he was out in five. Then he killed himself.

"How is that related?" I asked Bonnie Doone.

"Well, you could get some psychiatrists to say Cheryl Darling starved herself so she'd be thin enough to be a model and that threw off her balance. She got too thin and it affected her brain."

"So she killed her employer?" I asked, not bothering to mask my incredulity.

"Yes," she insisted. "You can probably find a dozen psychiatrists locally who would say so."

I groaned. Bomber seemed to be considering it.

I was scared. Admittedly, I had an unusual personal interest in the case and Bomber would never let me forget how ill-advised that was.

When you go into a criminal case, especially murder, it is comforting to have some alternate theory at hand. Something for the jury to think about during the testimony and during their deliberations. If Bomber had one, he didn't share it with me.

It was a no brainer that we wanted all the men we could get on the jury—and preferably no women who looked like Judge Emory. And the men should be young enough to include Cheryl in a fantasy or two. No missionaries need apply. Whatever sympathy vote we'd be able to garner would come from the men.

We got nine men—something of a triumph, I thought, because this jury pool, like a lot of others, was predominantly female. They seemed to represent the most available sex—those in jobs that could be missed for a couple of weeks in deference to the becalming of the civic conscience. They also seemed to hold jobs where their employers were honor bound to pay their salaries while they were gone—the school system, public utilities and the government.

The downside was the three women we got—after Bomber had exhausted his peremptory challenges—were not the ideal profile for the trial. If we had to have women, we wanted them young and good-looking, unthreatened by the witness' looks and success. I don't know how many of those were in the jury pool. I didn't see any. So we got stuck with a Bible thumper—not good, but perhaps not that bad. She might consider the dissolute, irreverent life of the victim and think he had it coming.

The second woman we thought might have been a lesbian. If so, our hope was she would fall in love with Cheryl Darling and vote to acquit. On the other hand—since the juror was rather coarse-looking, masculine, hirsute and generally unlovely, she might harbor the same jealousies as the straight women.

The third woman juror had one of those sucked-in, sour-lemon expressions on her face that connoted disapproval of any woman who wasn't home having babies and keeping the floors so clean you could eat off them.

Of course, not all the men were sure things. You never knew when you had a misogynist who felt used and abused by some woman, sometime, and resented *all* women as a result.

C'est la vie.

There was, as always, no substitute for the persuasive powers of counsel.

From the first day, I could tell D.A. Webster Arlington Grainger III was still smarting from Bomber's smart remarks to the reporters, as well as some of the ignoble defeats Bomber had handed him in the past. It was painfully apparent that he took these cases personally, and nothing would please him more than besting Bomber in one of these jousting contests. It was also pretty obvious that this time he was convinced he had a winner. I would have derived much comfort and pleasure if I could have argued with him.

As always, at the start of a trial, I cased the audience for familiar faces. I half expected to find Jeffrey Xavier there, but he wasn't. But Wissie's mom was. There was a handsome man sitting right next to her, and I noticed them chatting. I thought, she was doing all right for herself. He had dark, slicked-back hair, and a dainty black moustache—like one of those silent movie sheiks. There was no sign of Wissie herself.

The coroner and the cops said pretty much the same thing they said at the hearing, as did the pimple-faced lad who'd sold Cheryl the cyanide.

Bomber asked a few of what he called cementing questions of the coroner. "Could you tell when the cyanide was bought?"

"No."

"Or how old it was?"

"No."

"Or how it got into Mr. diCarlo's body?"

"No."

"It could have been in the pills or some other way?"

"I don't know."

144

He got the police to admit Cheryl seemed saddened by the death—she was crying when she called and again after they arrived. Her answers to their early questions did not raise any suspicions of guilt in them. It was only after they put all the pieces together that they decided to make an arrest.

"D.A. Webster Arlington Grainger III have any influence in that decision?"

"Yes, sir."

"Would you say he encouraged it?"

"Yes, sir."

"Even insisted on it?"

"Yes, sir—"

"No further questions."

Web got up and blustered about probable cause and got the cop to admit he did not argue or fight the arrest.

Still, he looked weak doing it. Sometimes lawyers will let their personal feelings color their behavior in court. This was one of those times. Bomber was grinning like a Cheshire cat. It was probably why Bomber said those outrageous things to the press about Web: to aggravate him by puncturing his thin-skinned sensitivity. To make him overcome the slights with his clouded judgment.

We had speculated whether or not Web would use attorney Pillburn with his recital of the new will. Perhaps he found some way to connect the will information to our client. If he hadn't, it was a chancy call.

When Web announced his next witness—Mr. Orban Pillburn—Bomber jumped up and asked to approach the bench. Judge Emory nodded and Web, Bomber and I went forward. It was a flattering bone Bomber threw me, allowing me to go with him for these off-the-record conferences with the Judge.

"Your Honor, you heard Attorney Pillburn testify at the preliminary hearing. I am, by the way, amused that the district attorney has him referred to as 'Mister' instead of 'Attorney,' such is the state of the reputation of lawyers—at any rate, unless he can connect this testimony to the defendant, I will object to hearing it as prejudicial, misleading, without foundation, inflammatory and irrelevant."

Bomber had given the judge a lot to chew on there, and she looked like she had indigestion from it.

"Will there be a connection, Mr. Grainger?" asked the Judge.

"Well, the most obvious connection is between the victim and the defendant. I can ask her under oath if he ever discussed this will with her."

"But she has no duty to testify," Bomber broke in. "I certainly would not entertain any notion of having her testify for the prosecution. And the testator is dead, so it is unlikely he could give intelligible testimony."

Judge Emory frowned. She didn't seem to appreciate Bomber's attempts at levity. That was not hard for me to understand. Humor was not one of Bomber's fortes.

Then I realized Bomber had switched gears on me. He was changing his tack with this judge. No bombast and bravado, just gentle deference. I saw in a flash his goal was to call attention to the judge's natural prejudice against the young beauty.

"I will also bring in, if need be," Web said, "others who were in Aldo's wills to testify that he delighted in lording this sometime generosity over them. They will also tell how Aldo diCarlo used these promises of fortune to have his way with them. The jury will be allowed to draw the inference that Cheryl Darling, the defendant, had the same knowledge."

Judge Emory looked at Bomber. "Mr. Hanson?"

"Your Honor is well aware of the pitfalls of that path. My argument stands. I don't feel I should take more of Your Honor's time. I will honor whatever decision you make."

Both Web and Judge Emory looked at Bomber in astonishment. The judge kept her mouth shut. The D.A.'s was agape with not only astonishment, but suspicion. Did Bomber have something up his sleeve? Web must have wondered.

I knew he did, and it came out on cross-examiniation. It added to the confusion factor, which should not be underrated in a criminal trial.

Lawyer Pillburn gave essentially the same recitation as he had given at the preliminary hearing, with the important difference that Web asked him the questions Bomber had before, usurping, and he hoped dissipating, the negatives. I knew Bomber better than to think he would let that fly. Bomber stood and moved easily toward the witness. Bomber had a smile on his face, not a smile of friendliness, but a smile of derision. Bomber's intimidation often began before he opened his mouth to speak.

"Attorney Pillburn," Bomber began. He would always address the witness as Attorney, as though Attorney Bomber Hanson delighted in the appelation's negative connotations. "You've testified you were Aldo diCarlo's attorney for a long time—from the beginning of his fashion business, I believe."

"Yes."

"And in that time, how many wills did you write for him?"

"Many."

"Can you be more specific?"

"I'm afraid I don't have the count in my head."

"So many you can't remember how many?"

"Yes."

"A hundred?"

"Oh, no."

"Ballpark?"

"Well, thirty or so."

"Fine. Can you tell us, in your professional opinion, why Aldo diCarlo wrote so many wills?"

Attorney Pillburn shrugged. "Well, he changed his mind."

"Apparently. So you write wills for other clients?"

"Yes."

"Have for many years?"

"Yes—I've been practicing almost forty years and I've written wills from the beginning."

"Good," Bomber said. "Approximately how many wills have you written?"

"Again, I don't have a figure."

"All right, can you estimate how many clients you wrote wills for?"

"No. Many."

"May we say between fifty and one hundred?"

"Close enough."

"All right. How many of them did you write thirty wills for?"

Attorney Pillburn smiled. "Just Aldo diCarlo."

"How many more than twenty?"

Attorney Pillburn shook his head. "None."

"More than ten?"

"None."

"So Aldo diCarlo was unusual in the number of wills he wrote?"

"Yes."

"All right. You testified that Aldo diCarlo changed his mind. That was why he wrote this unusual number of wills?"

"Yes."

"Can you be more specific? What essentially were the changes?"

"Well, the beneficiaries changed."

"Know why?"

"I guess some fell from favor, others he felt warranted his generosity."

"For what reason?"

"Objection," Web said. "Calls for speculation."

"If you know," Bomber said, making the question acceptable so the judge didn't have to rule.

"I don't think it would be professional for me to speculate."

"Lovers, Attorney Pillburn, were they his lovers?"

"They could have been. I'm afraid I'm treading on the attorney-client privilege here."

"Are you aware the Supreme Court has ruled that moot when the client is dead?"

"Well, that's an interpretation…"

"Then let me ask you if in this circumstance you don't think the interests of my client in this matter surmount the interests of a dead man."

"I'm not in a position to answer that."

"Perhaps we should turn this to the court, then. I respectfully petition Your Honor to direct Attorney Pillburn to answer the question."

It worked. She did what Bomber wanted.

"Yes, most of the changes concerned objects of his affection. They were put in the wills when they were in favor and dropped when his interest ceased."

"And this happened perhaps thirty times?"

"More or less."

"Cheryl Darling was hardly the only one to find herself in a will, then potentially out of it?"

"Correct."

"To your knowledge, how many of the others who were cut out of Aldo diCarlo's wills attempted to murder him?"

"None, to my knowledge."

"You testified you never told Cheryl Darling she was in or out of Aldo's will?"

"Correct."

"And know of no one who told her?"

"Not firsthand, no."

"Were there any other changes in the will in question? The one disinheriting Cheryl Darling?"

"Yes."

"What was that?"

"Lupe Espinal was added. Jeffrey Xavier was taken out."

"Jeffrey Xavier? He was in the will?"

"Yes."

"How much was he going to inherit?"

"Ten million—"

"Twice what Cheryl Darling stood to inherit?"

"Yes."

Bomber sank back on his elevator heels and made a great show of cogitating that answer. He bobbed his head several times.

"Are you finished, Mr. Hanson?" Judge Emory said.

"I'm sorry, Your Honor, it took me awhile to realize the importance of that answer, but I'll move on. Certainly. Sorry." Another long pause tickled the air in the court room. I could see Web getting antsy. He wanted to jump up and berate Bomber for his tactics, but he wasn't about to give Bomber *another* memorable moment. Judge Emory helped him out.

"Mr. Hanson..."

"Yes, yes, Your Honor, yes. Sorry. Now, ah, Attorney Pillburn, this, ah, ten million to Jeffrey Xavier, was it *ten* million?"

"Yes."

"Just so, ten million. I take it you had some discussion about that with Aldo diCarlo?"

"Of course."

"Would you tell the jury the nature of the discussion?"

"The nature?" It was a lawyer getting lawyerly with another lawyer.

"Shall I define *nature*, *Attorney* Pillburn?"

"We discussed the usual, I guess. Tax ramifications..."

"What were they?"

"Since Jeffrey Xavier was not a charitable institution, the estate would have to pay taxes on the bequest."

"Leaving how much for Jeffrey Xavier?"

"Oh, he would get the whole ten million."

"What would be the tax to Jeffrey Xavier in that event?"

"Oh, no tax on inheritance to the beneficiary."

"So, Jeffrey Xavier would have netted ten million?"

"Yes."

"Or rather, he will still get it?"

"I would assume. The will was the last one extant, as far as I know."

"In addition to the tax implications, I suppose you had some discussion about why he was giving so much money to another man?"

Web stood. "I object, Your Honor, this is hearsay evidence he is fishing for."

"It is *not*, Your Honor. A discussion between the parties is not hearsay. I didn't ask what Jeffrey Xavier said to someone out of attorney Pillburn's presence."

"Overruled."

"Please answer, Attorney Pillburn," Bomber said.

"What do you want me to answer? What Aldo said when he put him in the will or when he took him out?"

"Both, please."

"In which order?" It was as though Attorney Pillburn were grasping at straws to procrastinate.

"You pick," Bomber said with a magnanimous wave of an arm. I watched Cheryl throughout. She sat composed, unruffled and lovely as ever.

Attorney Pillburn cleared his throat. "When we put Jeffrey Xavier in the will, it was because Aldo said he, well, liked him a lot and appreciated what he was doing for him."

"And what was that?"

"I don't know," Attorney Pillburn answered softly.

"Did he say they were lovers?"

Web shot to his feet. "*Ob*-jec-tion," he virtually shouted. "Inflammatory, prejudicial, without foundation…"

"This *is* the foundation," Bomber broke in.

Judge Emory looked at Attorney Pillburn. "You may answer," she said.

"He might have," Attorney Pillburn said, still *sotto voce*.

"*Think*," Bomber boomed. "Yes or no?"

"I don't know if he was that broad—"

"But you understood Aldo to mean he and Jeffrey Xavier were lovers?"

"Yes."

"*Obj*ection," Web bleated, too late.

"I'll withdraw the question," Bomber said to smiles all around, even, if I'm not mistaken, from Judge Emory-board.

"And when Aldo diCarlo decided to write him out of the will," Bomber said, addressing the witness, "what did he say about that?"

"He was tired of him. Apparently, Mr. Xavier had gone off and set up a rival business."

Then Bomber asked the sinker. I was on the edge of my seat waiting for it—"Attorney Pillburn, under what circumstances might Jeffrey Xavier not get the ten million?"

"Well, if the estate didn't have sufficient assets to cover it."

"Was that, to your knowledge, a danger?"

"It was not."

"What other reason is there that could prevent Jeffrey Xavier from receiving his ten million?"

"Well...if he was complicit in the death of the testator."

Bomber smiled at the high falutin' language. Did Orban Pillburn really think Bomber would let it go at that?

"If I could try to put that in non-lawyers language, Attorney Pillburn, would it be fair to say Jeffrey Xavier would *not* be eligible for his ten million dollar bequest if he had some hand in Aldo Cabrisi diCarlo's death?"

"That is correct," Attorney Pillburn had to admit. I mean, Bomber left him no choice.

"Now if I may just clear up one other thing, Attorney Pillburn. The defendant here, Cheryl Darling, was in the will for five million, correct?"

"Correct."

"And she was to be cut out of the subsequent will the morning after Aldo diCarlo died?"

"Yes."

"If my math is correct, ten million dollars is double five million. Am I right about that?"

"Y…e…ss…" I could see Attorney Pillburn was trying to understand the trap he felt he was being led into.

"By the same token, wouldn't you expect Jeffrey Xavier to be *twice* as likely to murder Aldo Cabrisi diCarlo as Cheryl Darling would be?"

"Oh, I object," Web jumped up again. "That is so outrageous, I think Bomber should apologize for insulting all our intelligences."

Of course, it wasn't outrageous at all. Not the logic. It just wasn't a permissible question. It called for a conclusion which the witness just might be unable to give.

"Sustained," said the judge, and she didn't look happy with Bomber.

But Bomber was happy. He'd made his point. "I stand corrected," he said with that slightly *faux* bow.

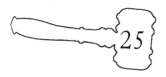

This case turned out to be a series of optimistic blips, each shot down in its turn by logic, reason and evidence. Usually there was none. Evidence against our client, Cheryl Darling, was scant and circumstantial, but it was preponderant, next to anyone else we could discern.

For instance, it was delightful to discover that Jeffrey Xavier was in the will that was being rewritten for double the amount Cheryl was. But it ended there. Somehow, we had to tie someone else to the fatal pill, and we didn't know how to do it. It would be nice to have those caterer's employees tell us they'd seen someone at the pills, but they weren't available.

At the break we met with Cheryl in a conference room off the court room. A ubiquitous guard stood outside the door. Bomber addressed our client.

"Cheryl Darling," he said, and I could tell he relished saying it—like her last name made them familiar buddies. "The big question is, do we put you on the stand in your own defense, or do we say it's not even necessary—the prosecution hasn't proven any kind of case. All they have is the poison purchase—to kill rats, you say—believable in that area. There are no witnesses to the contrary. And without you, they don't have first-hand evidence you gave him the pills. How many was it, by the way?"

"Seven," she said. "I think it was seven."

Bomber was testing her—my heart stopped, but Cheryl was consistent. Lucky seven.

"So let your imagination run wild. Say someone laced one pill with cyanide—it could have been done any time, couldn't it?"

"Yes."

154

"So a lot of people had access, didn't they?"

"I suppose. They weren't locked up or anything."

"Gaiters could have done it any time."

"True."

"Jeffrey Xavier could have slipped into the kitchen and pretended he was looking for a glass. Did he know you bought the cyanide?"

"I don't know. Aldo might have told him, though I don't think they were communicating much. I think Aldo was finally fed up with Jeffrey. He was a bit of an opportunist."

What a lovely word for a blackmailer, I thought.

"And Mrs. What's-her-name, Wissie's mom, could have done it before she left the party? Maybe that's why she comes to court every day—to make sure her secret is kept in the bottle.

"Was Wissie in a will, or was their affair too short?"

"I don't know about the wills," Cheryl said, remaining consistent.

"Tod, my boy, let's get copies of the wills."

"Better ask for them in c-court," I said. "I don't think they'll volunteer them t-to us."

"Yeah, okay, we will shout like holy blazes, but I expect we'll get them. He was apparently quite a will writer. Maybe we can learn something. We'll argue *any*body could have put the poison in the pills," Bomber went on, "all they have on you is you bought poison *like* it. We can call Gaiters, but I'm not sure he's your friend."

"What could he say?" I asked.

"That he used or caused to be used the poison on the rats, or the package was unopened, or he used or caused to be used all of it." Bomber turned to me. "Ask him."

"You were there when he died," Bomber said, turning back to Cheryl Darling, "but why would you hang around if you killed him?"

"Web will s-say to s-see he died," I contributed.

"Same reason Wissie's mom is in court," Bomber said. "Like the arsonist who watches the fire. It's a good argument.

Anybody's guess what the jury will buy. We have to do better than guess. This beautiful young woman's life is at stake."

When court was called to order, Bomber asked to approach the bench before the jury was brought in. Web seemed delighted for some reason, which became apparent after Bomber made his request.

"Your Honor, there are apparently many and varied last wills and testaments of the deceased Mr. Aldo Cabrisi diCarlo. The contents of these could be vital to my client's defense. I would respectfully ask to see copies of these. I think Attorney Pillburn will be able to supply them." Bomber looked at Web— so did Judge Estelle Emory. The D.A. was shaking his head. "Privileged and a fishing expedition. Irrelevant to the case."

"Your Honor," Bomber said. "We only want to see them. If there is nothing that might be helpful, no one else will see them. If we want to introduce evidence from a will, we will certainly petition this court before we do so."

Webster Arlington Grainger III, district attorney for Weller county, didn't give up his protest, but the judge, bless her heart, overruled him and Web was directed to have Attorney Pillburn produce all the wills he could in the morning.

Then Web dropped his bomb.

"Your Honor, since this case was opened—in the earliest stages of the police investigation—we have been searching high and low for the two caterer's employees who were in Aldo diCarlo's house with Cheryl Darling, the defendant, when Aldo died that miserable, wretched death."

"Save it for the jury," Bomber said.

"Yes," Web was flustered for only a moment. "By a stroke of good luck, we have found the two young women, and I would like to call them to testify now."

"Just a holy minute," Bomber said. "I don't see their names on the witness list you are required to give us before the trial. Did I miss them?"

"Were they on the list?" Judge Emory asked.

"No, Your Honor. I had given up hope of finding them.

I was told they went back to Mexico."

"Did they?" Judge Emory asked.

"I found them through a friend. I think they had gone on a trip—I'm not sure if it was Mexico or not."

"Fish market," Bomber said.

"Excuse me?" the judge said.

"It smells like very old fish to me. I'd like an offer of proof and a chance to question them before letting the jury hear what they say. And if the district attorney is pulling a fast one, and it very much looks like he is, I shall move for a mistrial, as well as his disbarment."

"I *resent* that inference," Web blustered. "It is *you* who pulls stunts like this all the time."

"So you're finally hoping to beat me, and this is what you had to resort to—"

"Gentlemen," Judge Emory said. "Calm down. Mr. Grainger, what will these young women offer in testimony?"

"The young women will testify they saw the defendant take the pills from the kitchen cabinet and take them to Aldo diCarlo in the dining room, set them on the table and return to the kitchen where she said to them, 'That should take care of him.'"

"Just a minute," Bomber said. "These women are fluent in English, are they?"

"They speak enough to recognize and remember those words."

"Perhaps you can tell the court where you were hiding these women all this time."

"Your Honor, I'd appreciate if you could tell Bomber to use some discretion, to think before he goes off on these unfounded, belittling accusation expeditions."

"Unfounded? Show me their names on the witness list!" Bomber said with expansive movements of his arms. Perhaps Your Honor got them on her list, they seem to be conspicuously absent from mine."

"Do you object to hearing them as witnesses?" Judge

Emory asked Bomber.

"Not with the proper notice."

"That seems to be moot," she said. "Do you want to file a brief?" Was she being facetious? Nobody would go through that rigmarole. "Surprise witnesses appear now and then, and usually they are heard." Bomber was making an opera out of it and the judge was calling his bluff.

Then I saw the familiar flicker in Bomber's eye that told me he had laid the groundwork and gotten advantage of the wronged party, and he would give in (kicking and screaming all the way, to be sure) in such a manner to leave the impression with the judge that he felt he had been roundly defeated.

He didn't press his request to question (voir dire) the girls out of the jury's hearing; I supposed he preferred to spring his intimidating self on them all at once—full blown—as a shock. He knew Web would tell him what a bully he was, but it wasn't the same as coming against him face-to-face.

When we sat down again to await the jury, Bomber leaned over and whispered, "When we ID the girls, stay with them. Find out where they are staying, who talks to them. Shadow—don't let them know it. Shouldn't be too hard, I doubt they're that sophisticated."

"Probably a p-policeman with them."

"Probably. So you're going to have to be smarter than a cop."

"Thanks," I said, realizing a cop could probably lose me. If nothing else his car would be a lot faster and more reliable. But even the attempt to shake me would tell us something.

"If you get caught, say you want to question the witnesses. Perfectly proper."

Easy for him to say.

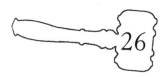

We didn't have to call Gaiters. The D.A. did it—but obviously not *for* us.

When Gaiters took the stand to testify he gave his name as Gaiters. District Attorney Grainger let it go. I knew Bomber wouldn't. The judge helped us out. "Is that your first or your last name?"

"Just Gaiters," he said.

"For the record," she said, "please state your full name."

"Gaiters is all I use."

"The name on your birth certificate. First name?"

Gaiters had a pained expression on his face. It wasn't going easy for him. Bomber was delighted. He liked nothing better than shaking up an enemy witness, except having the judge do it for him. Gaiters apparently recognized there was no escaping this disclosure. "Horace," he said under his breath, just loud enough to hear.

"And your last name?" Judge Emory asked. "Is it Gaiters?"

"No ma'm," he said softly.

"It is—?"

"—Glumschen."

Judge Emory couldn't hide her smile at the poor man's discomfort. "Would you spell it, please?" And he did with an eerie, halting, precision, hitting each letter as though it were a note on a glockenspiel.

"Does she dare ask for his middle name?" Bomber said, as usual, too loud to not be heard. As if on cue, Judge Emory asked Gaiters, "Do you have a middle name?" We all knew it was overkill, but took guilty pleasure in his discomfort, just the same.

Gaiters cleared his throat. His eyes darted left and right, then took a shot at the ceiling. "Archangelo."

"H.A.G., nice initials," Bomber said in that bogus stage whisper. "No wonder he wants to be called Gaiters. Gaiters!"

"Mr. Hanson, please," Judge Emory frowned at him.

"I stand corrected," Bomber said with his little I'm-so-sorry bow of the head.

"If the court please," Web said, "since Gaiters has lived most of his life as Gaiters, I should like to address him as such."

"Any objection, Mr. Hanson?"

Bomber stood up and waved his whole arm in a magnanimous gesture. "Gaiters it is, and Gaiters it shall be. I expect any one of us saddled with Horace Archangelo Glumschen for a name would do no less."

Web rolled his eyes but must have decided the less said the better.

"All right, Gaiters, please state your address and place of employ for the jury."

They got through the preliminaries all right, including his twenty-seven years of service to his master, Aldo Cabrisi diCarlo. Then the D.A. got down to the meat. "Gaiters, are you acquainted with Cheryl Darling?"

"Yes, sir, I am."

"In what capacity?"

"She was, I believe, a companion to Mr. diCarlo."

Bomber wrote the word "companion" on the yellow legal pad in front of him. Then he underscored it with two slashing strokes.

"Did she live in the Montelinda house with Mr. diCarlo while you worked there?"

"Yes, sir, she did."

"Do you remember the approximate dates?"

"That would be from April of last year to just after Thanksgiving…of last year, I believe."

"Did she move out then?"

"Yes, sir, she did."

"Did your employer, Aldo diCarlo, ever ask you to poison rats?"

"No, sir, he did not."

"Did your employer ever have any conversations with you about cyanide poisoning, specifically purchasing some?"

"No, sir, he did not."

"Did he ever tell you Cheryl Darling had been instructed by him to buy poison for that purpose?"

"No, sir, he did not."

I confess to being amused at the extra positive punch Gaiters gave to his answers. "No, sir," didn't do it for Gaiters, he had to add, "he did not."

"And as far as you know, Aldo diCarlo never mentioned buying cyanide poison for rats or any problem with rats to anyone?"

"No, sir, he did not."

"And who would have been the person to take care of such a poisoning operation had he cared to do it?"

"I would have been, sir. I would have been the one to direct the gardeners in that regard."

"Thank you. No further questions."

You could tell by the narrowing of Gaiter's already narrow eyes that he wasn't too pleased to see Bomber stalking toward him, towering through the courtesy of his elevator shoes.

"Mr. Glumschen, is it?" Bomber began, then, without waiting for an answer, consulted the tablet on his desk, making a one hundred and eighty degree turn to do so. "Yes," he said. "Glumschen. Mr. Glumschen, you testified you were in the employ of Aldo Cabrisi diCarlo for twenty-seven years, was it?"

D.A. Webster Arlington Grainger III stood up at his leisurely, nonchalant pace. "Your Honor, I thought we had agreement Gaiters would be referred to as Gaiters. Bomber seems to want to make a funny out of his name."

"Not at all," Bomber said. "I agreed *you* could address him as Garters if you wanted—"

"Gaiters."

"Just so. Whatever. For myself, I am a fossil of propriety. I am unaccustomed to using nicknames in court. Indeed, in most courts, in my experience, it is not allowed. Could it be they fear it is demeaning? At any rate, I merely said if the learned judge sees fit to permit this exception to our fine traditions, I have no objections. I did not understand this to be an *obligation* of the defense as well as an exception for the prosecution."

"Oh, Your Honor, Bomber is taking this to such exaggerated lengths—as he so often does. Can we move on?"

"Nothing would give me more pleasure," Bomber said. "*You* were the one who made the fuss."

"All right, Gentlemen," Judge Emory said. "Estelle is not a name I would have chosen for myself, yet I'm stuck with it. Mr. Hanson may use his real name. Proceed."

"Thank you, Your Honor," Bomber said with exaggerated gratitude. "Now, Mr. Glumschen, in your twenty-seven years as the manager of Aldo diCarlo's estate, did you have the opportunity to observe various 'companions,' as, I believe, you put it?"

"Yes, sir."

"Could you tell the jury how many?"

"Oh, no, sir. Not precisely, no."

"Why is that?"

"Because there were so many," Gaiters said, as though astonished, garnering a laugh he had not hoped to get.

"Ah, yes, so many. Could you give us a ballpark?"

Gaiters appeared to consider the question. "Oh, no, I couldn't really—"

"A thousand?"

"Oh, no."

"More or less?" Now Bomber got the laugh.

"Many less."

"Five hundred?"

"Less."

"More than one hundred?"

Gaiters frowned. "Well, it depends on the definition you

put on companion."

"It was your choice of words to describe Cheryl Darling. We'll settle for the criteria you used for her."

"Well, Cheryl actually lived in the house. There weren't many who did."

"How many?"

"There was Jeffrey Xavier and Lupe Espinal—"

"Both men?"

"Yes, sir."

"You classify them as 'companions'?"

"Yes, sir."

"Does the word 'companion' as you use it infer some sort of sexual intimacy?"

"I really couldn't say, sir. Not of firsthand knowledge, I couldn't."

"But that was your supposition in using the word?"

"I couldn't say, sir."

"So you don't know if there was any carnal knowledge between Cheryl Darling and Aldo diCarlo?"

"Not firsthand, no, sir."

"Could have been just platonic pals?"

Gaiters shrugged. "I didn't see anything of that nature."

"Not with any of the companions?"

"No, sir, it wasn't my business."

"Did you ever have any sexual intimacy with Aldo diCarlo?"

"Oh, sir, no, sir," Gaiters was visibly shaken. "That is a terrible accusation, sir."

"Not an accusation, Mr. Glumschen...just a question."

"The question itself puts an implication on it. The idea itself is unprofessional—just the thought that I would entertain such a notion is ludicrous. Beyond belief," he shook his head at the absurdity of the idea. "Really."

I glanced at Webster Arlington Grainger III. He was, as I expected, uncomfortable as the shift in his chair telegraphed to all.

In front of the witness, Bomber stared at the unfortunate butler, who looked back at him in a mixture of doubt and terror. Oh boy, I thought, the butler really did do it, and he was going to break down and confess any minute.

Web broke the spell. "Is counsel finished with his questions?"

Bomber continued to stare. Sure, it was theatrics for the jury. No one did it better.

"Mr. Hanson, do you have any further questions?" Judge Emory said from the bench.

"I'm waiting," Bomber said to the witness.

There was a merciful beat of confused silence. Before it was over, the witness— obviously a novice at the game—blurted out, "For what?"

Bomber didn't let a beat pass before he shot out, "For you to continue protesting your love affair with Aldo diCarlo too much."

Web was on his feet, outraged. The judge beat him to it. "That will be stricken from the record in its entirety. If you can't conduct yourself in a professional manner, you will be expelled from this courtroom and be cited for contempt. I won't warn you again. I simply will not stand for such outrageous, inappropriate behavior. Bullying a witness will not stand before me."

Now who was protesting too much, I thought. How did Bomber respond? You guessed it—with one step back and a duck of his head and an "I stand corrected."

But the damage was done, everybody knew it.

"Thank you, Your Honor," District Attorney Webster Arlington Grainger III said as he sat down, trying to pretend to some victory.

Judge Estelle Emory decided it was a good time to call a recess—probably to regain her composure.

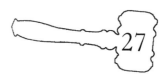

I actually feel sorry for some of the judges before whom Bomber tries cases. I wouldn't want to be one of them. He's always pushing, going right up to the line, stepping over as far as he can without being cited for contempt. It's tough for a judge. He or she doesn't want to overreact, or make it look like she can't control her own courtroom. And yet, restraint is always necessary with Bomber, lest he go hog wild. Usually, like today, the judge admonishes Bomber and he does his little "I-stand-corrected" dance and all is forgotten.

But the jury never forgets.

Horace Archangelo Glumschen was back on the stand after the recess. Just in case any juror forgot or missed the point of Bomber's prior questioning, the great advocate began, "Mr. Glumschen, I think I owe you an apology for my last comment before the recess. About any love affair you might or might not have had with the deceased Aldo diCarlo. I must add to my apology my confession that I have no firsthand knowledge of any carnal knowledge between you and Aldo diCarlo."

"Your Honor—" Web was bleating.

"That's enough, Mr. Hanson," the judge said. "Move on or sit down."

"Yes, Your Honor. Of course, Your Honor."

I waited for him to add "I stand corrected," but so did everyone else, so he said nothing.

"Now if I may turn your attention to the pills that your employer, Aldo diCarlo, took regularly, I believe—do you have knowledge of what they were?"

"Yes, sir," he answered. It was apparent Mr. Glumschen had not recovered from the bombardment he suffered before the break. He was both on the edge of his seat and on edge figuratively. It was also apparent Web had coached him to keep his answers brief and not volunteer anything.

"How did you acquire that knowledge?"

"I filled his prescriptions."

"What were the various pills he took?"

"Zoloft, Depakote and Lithium."

"What were they prescribed for?"

"Something to do with manic-depression, I believe."

"Aldo diCarlo was depressed?"

"If he didn't take his medicine."

"Did he take it?"

"I saw to it," he said, with a touch of pride.

"How did you do that?"

"He put his pills in a container that had seven compartments, each marked with a day of the week. I saw to it. Checked daily. I set his pills on a saucer with a glass of water in the morning and again in the evening, if he was in town, and if I was still up. I monitored the pills daily to see that they were taken."

"How could you do that?"

"I looked in the container."

"But if you didn't see him take them, how do you know he didn't dispose of them some other way? Perhaps down the toilet—or to poison rats?"

"I don't think Mr. diCarlo would do that."

"But you have no, as you say, firsthand knowledge that he didn't dispose of the pills without taking them?"

"No, sir."

"Or perhaps someone else intervened and disposed of the pills?"

"I have no knowledge of that."

"Either way—no knowledge that someone did and no knowledge someone did *not* dispose of them?"

"That is correct, sir." Gaiters was still unfailingly polite. Bred in the bone, the butler's butler.

"So Aldo diCarlo was sometimes depressed?"

"Yes, sir," Gaiters said. "He did exhibit some signs, though I am no psychiatrist."

"What were those signs?"

"General despondency. Lethargy. Lack of ambition."

"How often did you witness that behavior?"

"Oh, not often, sir. That's why I insisted on the pills so he would feel good all the time."

"All the time?" Bomber cocked an eyebrow.

"Well, of course, sir, no one is topnotch all the time."

"Was Aldo diCarlo?"

"With the medicine, he was in good spirits, yes."

"On the day he died? Did you find him in good spirits?"

"Lord, yes. He was on top of the world. He'd had this most gratifying triumph of his spring collection."

"And you saw him last at what time?"

"Just before midnight."

"And he was in good spirits?"

"Yes, sir."

"He died at what time?"

"I don't know firsthand," Gaiters said. "I was asleep."

"Ah, so you were. As far as you know—or have heard, it was several hours later, is that correct?"

"Yes, sir."

"And you didn't see Aldo diCarlo in the interim?"

"No, sir."

Bomber let it go at that. His goal, it seemed, was still to create doubt. Obfuscation. He was good at it.

Maintaining maximum secrecy until the last minute, our district attorney, Mr. Webster Arlington Grainger III called Rosa Gonzales to the stand. The doors in the back of the courtroom opened and a petite Hispanic young woman, who I pegged as still in her teens, walked in with a strange mixture of poise and self-consciousness. Her black hair had an enticing sheen to it. It was tied up in a bun in back—I'm sure at Web's instruction so as to be not too sexy—and the bangs fell over her forehead like vampire teeth.

If I had to use a word to describe Rosa on the stand it would be prim. She sat with her delicate hands folded in her lap, her head barely clearing the top rail of the witness box.

Web stood behind his table and addressed the witness.

"Miss Gonzales, you were employed by Queen Millie's Catering, is that correct?"

She said she was and gave the dates of her employment and the particulars of her work that evening which consisted of passing hors d'oeuvres and cleaning up. She and her friend, Mariá, were the last to leave the premises, after the police left.

"And Aldo diCarlo was dead by the time you left?"

"Yes."

"I direct your attention to the defense table. Do you recognize the woman seated there?"

"Yes—that's Cheryl Darling. She was at the house when Señor diCarlo died."

"Cheryl Darling was at the party after all the other guests had left?"

"Yes."

"What, if anything, did you observe her doing after the other guests left?"

"She got some pills from the cabinet in the kitchen," she said with her charming accent. "And took them to Señor diCarlo in the dining room."

"Then what happened?"

"She came back to the kitchen and washed her hands."

"She washed her hands?" Web said as though that were the most astonishing thing in the world. Obviously, he wanted to emphasize it so he could trot it out later. "Did she say anything?"

"Yes. She said, 'That will take care of him.'"

D.A. Webster Arlington Grainger III paused dramatically—though it must be noted his dramatic pauses had a stilted quality about them. He looked more awkward than alarmed. Was he trying to match Bomber? He came up short.

"No further questions," he said.

Bomber lifted himself up as though he had been listening to nonsense that he sought to rectify.

"Now, Miss Gonzales," he began. "How old are you?"

"Eighteen," she said.

"Were you born in Angelton?"

"No—in Mexico."

"How long have you been here?"

"Two years."

"Do you have a work permit?"

Web was on his feet. "Your Honor, I object to this line of questioning."

"What line?" Bomber said. "It's one question."

"It's immaterial, irrelevant, not covered on direct."

"Your Honor, I'm just trying to understand why this witness disappeared and was not on my witness list."

"Your Honor has already ruled on that," the district attorney said. "The witness is testifying. The rest is moot. The witness' whereabouts are immaterial to this charge."

"Then why are you fighting so hard?" Bomber said.

The judge banged her gavel. "That's enough."

"It's also prejudicial," Web added.

"I'm going to let her answer."

"No," the girl said.

"You have no work permit?"

"No."

"Citizenship papers?"

"No."

"Are you here legally?"

She hung her head, then tried to hide her glance at the D.A. from the rest of us. Of course, with that much scrutiny, that was impossible.

"Are you legal?" Bomber asked again. "Yes or no?"

"No," she whispered.

"No," Bomber boomed, scaring the poor girl into bouncing in her seat. "Can you tell us where you have been living since Aldo diCarlo died?"

"I was living with friends."

"What are their names?"

She seemed to search the ceiling. "I don't remember," she said.

"What *kind* of friends are they if you can't remember their names?"

"Not close friends," she said and got a laugh from the

audience, a smile from the jurors and very little from the D.A. "One is my friend María. We worked together at Queen Millie's Catering."

"She was with you the night of Aldo's death?"

"Yes."

"And you live with her?"

"Yes."

"And with some others whose names you can't remember?"

"Yes, maybe I should not call them friends. You have another word for people you know but are not friends?"

"Good enough," Bomber said. "How did you find this place to live?"

Web stood. "Objection, Your Honor. Bomber seems to be obfuscating again. Her living arrangements are totally irrelevant."

"Not so, Your Honor," Bomber said

"You plan to relate this to the witness and this case, Mr. Hanson?"

"Yes indeed." Bomber said.

"All right, she may answer—but let's get to the point."

Rosa didn't say anything. Bomber said—"Can you answer the question?"

"I don't remember."

"You don't remember the question or you don't remember who found the place?"

"I think my friend found it."

"Is this a friend whose name you remember?"

Web was seething, and I could see it took all his strength of character to keep his seat so it would stop looking as if he had something to hide.

"María Hermosillo."

"The girl you worked with?"

"Yes."

"How long were you there?"

"Since our first place."

Bomber smiled. "Yes. That makes sense. Where was the

place before the last place?"

"Fourteen Buchanan Street."

That was where I had looked for her.

"Why did you leave there?" Bomber asked.

She shrugged. "For a nicer place."

"Cost more?"

"Not really."

"Well, it cost more, less or the same? I don't understand 'not really.'"

"Less," she muttered in a way that made us all suspicious.

"Yet it was nicer?"

"Yes."

"How do you account for that?"

Web rose. "Your Honor, that calls for speculation on the part of a witness. It is outside her area of expertise. She's not a realtor. She got a better deal. How that reflects on the guilt or innocence of Cheryl Darling is beyond me."

"Maybe not so far beyond you," Bomber said.

"Your Honor," Web was exasperated. "He's at it again. Could we take a break?"

"You could use one," Bomber said in his too-loud-under-the-breath mode.

I half expected Bomber to slip in another zinger, but he apparently thought better of it when Web announced to the court he had received copies of the wills from Attorney Pillburn and was handing them to Bomber in open court, in front of the jury. Bomber noted, under his breath, Web was learning some showmanship.

Judge Emory said, "Well, then, I guess we'll all benefit from a break," and she called for a recess.

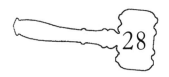

28

I was assigned to go over the copies of Aldo's wills to see if I could discover any helpful information.

There was the expected pattern of the loves of the moment getting their day in the sun. In for a year or so and out again.

With two exceptions. Jeffrey Xavier had been put in soon after Aldo met him, some four years before. Others had come and gone since, but he remained firm—his share increasing over the four years from one million to ten million. Cheryl was in for five million; both were to be taken out with the new will Aldo was to have signed the day after he died.

The big surprise was, Wissie Murray was in the will from the year she was born. Her mother, Gilda, also made a brief appearance around that time for one million. Mom's tenure in the will was for a little over a year. Wissie's money was to be held in a trust fund until she reached eighteen—still a few years off by my calculation. Her mother was her trustee.

I couldn't wait to bring the news to Bomber. When I told him in the hall outside the courtroom, he nodded. "I guessed as much," he said.

"You did?" That was astonishing news to me.

He tossed his head in the direction of the courtroom. "Why would that woman come to the trial everyday?"

"You think *she* did it?"

His head moved, not in the negative, rather in irresolution. "Love to hang the murder on her," he said. "I just can't figure how, yet."

He turned to Cheryl who stood like an angel beside him. "Any ideas?"

She shook her head. "I had *no* idea," she said. "I must

have been naïve."

Bomber gave me the assignment eye. "See if she'll talk to you," he said. "I've got to get to the bottom of these wetback witnesses."

Good old Bomber. Not only politically incorrect, politically impossible.

The recess was almost over. I ducked back into the courtroom and found Wissie's mom sitting quietly—I'd say almost morosely—in her seat in the back row. The dark, handsome man wasn't beside her. As I approached Gilda Murray, she seemed to withdraw further into herself. Instead of sitting beside her, I took a space in the row in front of her. Less intimidating, I thought. I sat and turned to face her.

"You read the wills, didn't you?" she said, making it rather easy for me. "It's not what you think," she said.

"Oh?" I said. "What is it, then?"

"It's nothing."

I nodded as though I accepted that.

"Aldo was a generous man. He felt sorry for me—getting in trouble like that."

I nodded again. "I've heard he was very generous," I said to encourage further sharing.

"He was."

"Nice," I said.

"Yes."

"So why are you here everyday?"

She started to tear up. "I loved him," she said.

"Yes—apparently others did, too—" I said with a note of sympathy in my voice. She just stared at me as though I had lost my mind. As though *she* were the only true love—so I plunged in the sword—

"Including, apparently, your daughter."

She cringed and did not respond. The recess was over, the man whose seat I had taken returned to claim it. In parting I said to Wissie's mom, "May I talk to you again? At lunch?"

"There's nothing more to say."

But I knew there was.

Bomber was so eager to resume the questioning of Rosa that he was dancing like a racehorse in a paddock.

When we were all in place, Bomber leaned toward Rosa Gonzales, the witness.

"Now, Ms. Gonzales, before our break, we were discussing your big break in housing. I believe you essentially said you got more for less. Correct me if I'm wrong, please. A bigger place for less money, is that right?"

"Yes."

"And the district attorney pointed out you are not a realtor; is *that* correct—you aren't a realtor?"

"No."

"How did you find your new place?"

Rosa looked blank, like a clean slate.

"Did you see an ad in the paper?" Bomber said as though helping her along.

"Nooo—"

"Did a realtor find it for you?"

"I...think...so—"

"Do you remember his or her name?"

"No."

"How about a physical description? Man or woman?"

"I don't know. I didn't do that part of it."

"Who did?"

Rosa stared straight ahead. Things weren't going well for her. "A friend," she finally muttered.

"Know his or her name?"

She shook her head.

"Speak for the record, please."

"No."

"Too much to hope, I suppose."

"Your Honor," Web blurted. "That is most unprofessional behavior."

"Yes, Mr. Hanson. Don't comment; save that for your summation."

"I stand corrected," Bomber said, humble as the day he was born. He turned again to the witness. "Can you tell me, Ms. Gonzales, how you can have so many friends without knowing their names?"

"No, I can't," she said. "I guess I'm not good at names."

Bomber let that sink in a moment. Then he asked, "Do you remember the district attorney's name?"

"Yes."

"What is it?"

"Webster Grainger."

"The third?" Bomber was having fun.

"I guess."

Bomber paused again. We could all see how nervous Rosa was in simply saying the D.A.'s name. We could also see the wheels turning in Bomber's head. They were the wheels of a dune buggy hitting pay dirt.

"Ms. Gonzales, was it District Attorney Grainger who found you that wonderful place to live?"

"No!" she answered too rapidly and too forcefully. You can suggest answers to a witness, even coach her, but some witnesses are more susceptible than others.

After another decent pause, Bomber asked the witness, "Ms. Gonzales, are you familiar with the quote, 'Methinks the lady doth protest too much'?"

She shook her head. "No," she said.

"Do you understand it?"

She shook her head again. "No."

"It means—"

"Objection, Your Honor—"

"Yes," Judge Emory said. "Sustained. Please limit your participation to questions, Mr. Hanson."

Bomber sauntered back to the defense table and leaned over to whisper to me, "I can get her to lie until we're all blue in the face. I'm going to ask her where she lives. As soon as she answers, you check it out. See if you can question the other Mexican."

175

Bomber turned back to the witness.

"Did anyone you know to be associated with the District Attorney help you to find the new, improved place to live?"

She didn't answer so quickly this time. "No," she said with just enough reserve to make me suspicious.

"No?" Bomber pressed.

"No," she said, more firmly.

"Oh, by the way," Bomber asked as a throwaway question, "Would you tell us again the address of your new place?"

She opened her mouth to answer when Web held up a hand like one of those road crew guys pressing their authority. "Don't answer that!" he snapped, a little too harshly for my taste.

"Your Honor, may we approach the bench?"

She nodded. "You may," and we all paraded up there. Whereupon District Attorney Webster Arlington Grainger III went into the strangest song and dance you ever heard.

"Your Honor, the prosecution is on its guard in this case. We've been outtricked once too often by the estimable Bomber Hanson. This witness is young and, you can see, inexperienced in the ways of the courtroom—"

"You mean she's not a smooth liar," Bomber interjected.

Web sighed. "See?" he said. "I am fearful they will visit this poor woman who has just driven the fatal nail in the defense's coffin, they will visit her, harass her, intimidate her, lie to her—do whatever it takes to shake her up so her effectiveness for the prosecution will be effectively nullified. She should have the standing of a protected witness."

"A catering waitress?" Bomber boomed and Judge Emory frowned. "Keep your voice down, counselor."

"Sorry." Bomber lowered his voice to the quietest whisper—so quiet we had to strain to understand him— "Fess up, Web. You stashed her away somewhere. Real nice place, apparently. One she could scarcely afford on her own. All in the interest of truth and justice, to be sure—as was, most assuredly, your oversight in not putting her on the witness list. What did you offer her? A green card? Citizenship—her pal, too, I expect? For what—testimony that Cheryl gave Aldo his pills? She didn't see her give him poison, nor put poison in pills—and she heard her say something about taking care of him. Nothing; he risked his case, reputation and license to practice law for a couple of lousy pieces of silver, which turned out to be tin."

"Bomber is getting carried away again with the sound of his own voice," Web said to the judge. "He may not realize it, but it is no more a disgrace to try to win a case for the prosecution than it is to try to win one for the defense."

"We're talking here about a serious breach of ethics," Bomber raised his voice just loud enough for the jury to have a good shot at hearing him.

Judge Emory frowned. "You're getting too loud again—this is not for the jury to hear."

"A-men," said Web.

"I stand corrected," Bomber said without a touch of irony or compassion. "All I'm asking for is her address. Obviously, a traditional, not to say, necessary component of the D.A.'s direct examination. Especially important in a case where the witness is liable to move often. Mr. Grainger neglected to ask the question. I am filling that void for him. Getting her address will not spur me to jeopardize my license by doing anything illegal. I leave that for the district attorney."

"Oh, Your Honor, Bomber is *so* outrageous!"

"All right, I've heard enough."

"Let the witness state her address to us," Bomber said. "Out of earshot of the jury."

Judge Emory was not happy with Bomber's interruption (all in the interests of my client, he would say, my duty calls for no less). The judge was especially perturbed because Bomber had stepped on her lines.

"The witness will write her address on a piece of paper and hand it to me for the record."

Both Bomber and I were astonished at the sound of that.

"We *will* get to see it?" Bomber asked.

"What?" Judge Emory asked, distracted. "Oh, yes, certainly. My courtroom will always be run in an evenhanded manner."

Doth the lady protest too much? I wondered.

When we saw the address, I memorized it.

Back at the defense table, Bomber said— "Check it out." Then he turned back to the witness stand. "Now Ms. Gonzales, were any promises made to you in exchange for you testimony here today?"

"No-o-oo-o—"

I left, knowing Bomber would get it out of her, one way or the other. I felt the eyes of District Attorney Grainger burning through my back.

29

The new abode of Rosa Gonzales and María Hermosillo was a quantum leap from the old. The old street had trees, also, but this one had decent tract houses also. It was in a pleasant, outlying edge of town.

Naturally there was a plain, unmarked law-enforcement looking car parked out front.

It was a one story house with gray asphalt shingles on the roof and pale beige stucco on the walls. The houses on either side expressed their individuality with a change of paint colors.

Getting in to talk to the other waitress didn't look promising. I parked down the block where I could see the front of the house and the car, a spot I hoped wouldn't be too obvious.

It seemed like forever. It gave me time to think. I formulated, and discarded, plan after plan. I had fantasies of the girl going for a walk alone, hopping into my car, and spilling, as they say, her guts. Some of my ideas were less fanciful, but almost as unlikely.

Finally, I decided it was bull-by-the-horns time. I walked over to the house and rang the door bell. If it was a cop I recognized, I'd lay it all out. If I thought I had a stranger, I was going to do the real estate appraisal routine.

The door opened. "How's it going, Tod?" he said. "We were wondering when you'd show up." He looked at his watch. "Not bad," he said with grudging admiration.

"Thanks, Sid," I said. I was looking at Sid Hardin, nice ex-cop who hired out for the occasional odd job and extra buck after he was knocked off his motorcycle by a drunken motorist. His spirits were still good but his back wasn't so hot. I could have done a lot worse.

"Where's María?" I asked.

He smiled his fatso smile—Sid wasn't fat—hefty, maybe—you couldn't see through him or anything—but his smile was fat. And jolly, and good natured. "Got her stashed in the attic"—his smile gave a twinkle to his eyes. "Bound and gagged so she won't talk to a certain attorney in town who gets his kicks making a fool out of a certain district attorney."

I heard the unmistakable sounds of a TV somewhere within.

"She's watching the telly," I said.

He shrugged. "Got to do something to pass the time."

"You watching with her?"

"You kidding? I don't do a lot of Spanish, *cómo está* is about it," he frowned. "Want to come in? Shoot the breeze?"

"Well, sure you've nothing better to do?" I said it as close to a serious question as I could make it, but Sid wasn't fooled.

He grinned, cracking up his whole face. "Yeah, it gets a little boring, I can tell you. But I figure, heck, not that much excitement at home, either."

He led me into the living room, which looked exactly like it had been furnished out of the D.A.'s petty cash fund.

The TV was barking away down the hall. I tossed my head in that direction.

"I imagine she's not much company?"

"Doesn't have much English. Why the other one's testifying."

I nodded sagely. I didn't want to ask to talk to her too soon, so I laid back—he offered me a beer, I declined, he had one, and we talked out of my depth about football and cars.

"Like working for Web?" I asked casually.

"It's a living," he said. "I don't have much to do with Web himself. He delegates."

I looked around the room as if I were in the real estate appraiser mode. "So this is Angelton's little witness protection hideaway?"

"Want to call it that."

"What do you suppose he's protecting the dame from?" I said, trying to talk like a cop.

"Told you—the Loose Cannon, Chief Bombardier of the U.S. Air force. She's not that swift—easily muddled's my guess."

"Yeah?" I said in disbelief. "What say I see for myself?"

Now his grin *really* ran away with him. "No can do, pal."

I shrugged. "Why not? You know I'm harmless."

"She puts the bug in someone's ear I let you do that, you wanna guess what my future is, jobwise, with the department?"

"So come over to Bomber's side. He could use a good man like you." I was shameless, but Sid wasn't stupid.

"Always liked Bomber—like his style—his guts, takes chances to win—anybody win more?" It wasn't really a question, because there was no question.

"Way I see it, you got to go to the john—you got to go. Can't be monitoring me every minute of every day."

"Wait, wait!" he said, holding his hand up like he did on the corner when the stoplight broke, "I get it—I'm constipated. Takes forever in there."

Now it was my turn to smile.

"Well," he said, clearing his throat, "they say the worst thing you can do with my condition is give up trying." He stood, stretched and moved with halting deliberation in the direction, I imagined, of the bathroom. I followed the TV noise. I was in the bedroom with the TV before I realized the program was in Spanish. I was looking at the back of a young girl's head—at the high gloss black hair that looked as though it had been combed with a steam iron.

I eased my way around to the side of her, then the front so as not to startle her. I startled her anyway. She fairly jumped out of her seat.

She looked younger and less sophisticated than Rosa, who was doing her best with Bomber's questions at that very moment. I could see immediately why Rosa was on the stand

and this girl was cooped up with an ex-cop in a safe haven. She was jumpy and did not exude any kind of confidence—she looked as though she were scared of her shadow.

"Hi, María," I said with an I'm-your-buddy smile, "*Hóla, Soy Tod*," I said, resurrecting my high school Spanish.

Her narrowing eyes told me she was afraid I was about to hurt her. So much for my killer smile.

"Rosa is on the witness stand now, testifying. *In corte*, we'd like you to be next. *¿Ud. también?*"

She looked like I'd asked her to jump off the courthouse roof.

"*Yo...no...*" she replied and began pecking at the English language. "I stay house. Rosa...*corte*."

"Yes, Rosa *corte*. She is in court, but you can have a chance, too."

"*No sé nada.*"

"That's *bueno*. Just tell me what nothing, *nada*, you know. Do you know who Cheryl Darling is? *¿Conoce Ud. a Cheryl Darling?*"

She nodded, her eyes now wide with fright—as though her worst fears were going to come true.

"Did you see her do anything while you were working at Aldo diCarlo's house? *¿Miró Ud. a ella hacer algo en la casa de Señor diCarlo después de la fiesta?*"

She shook her head.

"Anything with pills? *¿Algo con pastillas?*"

She shook her head again.

"Did you see anyone else do anything with pills? Just look at them—or maybe touch them? *¿Tocó otra persona las pastillas o las miró?*"

She didn't look at me. Her lips tightened. "*Ud. No puede hacer estas preguntas. No tengo que contestar. Ud. no es el D.A.*"

"Oh, but I *can* ask you these questions," I said, and I was right. I didn't bother to tell her she had the right to refuse to answer, but it looked like she was beginning to figure that out on her own.

"Can you tell me what the other person looked like? The one who got to Aldo's pills? ¿Como se miraba la persona que hizo algo con las pastillas?"

Stare. In that defiant stare, I saw pay dirt.

"María," I said. "Are you afraid? ¿Tiene miedo?"

She nodded before I had a chance to finish the sentence.

"About your papers? ¿De sus papeles?"

She nodded, less sure she should be responding to me.

"The district attorney promised you to get you papers so you could be a legal alien? ¿El D.A. le prometió papeles, no?"

She pursed her lips—the non-response—just as good as an affirmative to me.

"He isn't going to take that from you," I said. "As long as we know about it, he won't be able to go back on his promise. ¿Ud todavía va a conseguir las papeles." I looked at María to see if she could understand. My sense was she was getting the sense of it.

She said nothing. Web would have been proud.

"We would make it hard for him. Too much talking about it in the newspaper. Sería imposible por él no hacerlo—demasiada publicidad en los periodicos. ¿Comprenda Ud....chantaje?" (To ask her if she understood blackmail, I had to consult the pocket dictionary I'd brought along.) I asked with a smile. Those smiles of mine targeted to put her at ease weren't hitting the mark.

I asked my question again. "Who did you see at the pills? ¿Quién hizo algo con las medicinas del señor?" and "Did Web promise you a green card or citizenship? (¿Estaba prometida tarjetas verdes por Uds.?)" But María didn't answer. She was, as I said, scared but not stupid.

"Yo hablo con el Señor Grainger—si me permita hablar con Ud," she said, tightening her lips again as she told me she needed the district attorney's permission to talk to me. She was building some real musculature in those lips.

I patted her on the shoulder and smiled my non-muscular smile and had the sudden thought I would be accused of sexual harassment. I withdrew from the TV room with some guy blathering in *español*, and went searching for a telephone. I found it in the kitchen on the counter that separated the making of meals from the consumption of them.

I dialed Bonnie Doone, Miss Airhead of the Oughts. Mercifully, Sid was still playing Mr. Tight Bowels.

"Bonnie," I said with a quiet heartiness.

"Sweet meat!" she shouted in her least ladylike pose. "Miss America dancing in the streets, yet?"

"Will be if you do your bit."

"Ooooh, I'm going to save another case from certain failure."

"You'll be the heroine, Bonnie," I said.

"Ooooh." She was so easy to excite.

"Knock out a subpoena for María Hermosillo," I said, then filled in the details.

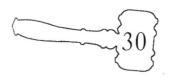

In my absence, District Attorney Webster Arlington Grainger III had wound down his case, and Bomber had made his usual pitch to throw out the charge because the D.A. had failed to establish a prima facie case. And, just as predictably, the judge had denied his motion.

After court was adjourned for the day, I gave Bomber my news. I could see he was happy and I leaned back waiting for him to shower the praise on me.

Drought. But he was beaming. "We'll wait till the morning. Web will scream bloody murder, accuse us of witness tampering and God knows what else." Obviously, Bomber relished the thought.

That night I had my first real burst of inspiration for my Cheryl Darling composition—a flurry of melodies, harmonies and rhythms were barging into my brain. After court, I couldn't wait to get home to pound it all out on my old upright piano. There would be a gentle, dreamy introduction—melody in low flutes with just the simplest string accompaniment below—sustained chords changing harmony while the flute sustained notes in its melody. Nothing makes me feel better—more euphoric— than when the creation of a composition is going well.

Next morning in court, I found myself at the judge's bench with Web and Bomber at a wrangling session a child could have predicted.

Web didn't think, predictably, it was such a hot idea for Bomber to call María as a defense witness—hostile or no. Unfortunately for Web, he was on very thin ice, his actions being quasi-legal at best. He was blathering on about how this was precisely the reason he felt the Latina girls needed witness protection.

"There's no telling what Bomber would do to a frightened, naïve young girl like that, especially one who barely comprehends English."

"I couldn't promise her a green card," Bomber said. "That's for sure. Takes a person deep in the bowels of the government to make such an offer. We can talk about bribing witnesses later."

"I resent that," Web snapped. Lucky for him the jury had not yet been called in, because he was mighty red in the face. Bomber was relaxed and confident, and Web knew he had a losing argument here—with my feeble knowledge of the law, I didn't see how he had a prayer.

Judge Emory couldn't see it either. "I'm afraid I can't deny the defense access to a witness. I'd be reversed on appeal in two minutes."

"Thank you, Your Honor," Bomber said with a courtly bow. He could get courtly when he won his point.

He was never, however, above rubbing it in. "We can wait the prescribed time if the D.A. so chooses, or she can be brought to court this morning. Since she passes her time watching television, I don't expect her coming now would create any meaningful hardship."

"Any objection, Mr. Grainger?"

Of course Web had an objection. He had to get to her first and "prep" her. If the court decided to do something so barbaric as call her in without the advice of counsel, blah blah blah.

"All right," Judge Emory said. "How about if we bring her in now and give you a half hour to 'advise' her."

"Oh, Your Honor, a half hour is hardly time. I myself need to look into several matters of law in connection with this request. It could take a day or so."

"Can you work around that, Mr. Hanson?"

"I don't mind taking a day off, if that's what you mean," Bomber said, knowing full well that was *not* what she meant.

"You can't put other witnesses on first?"

"Who I put on and when will have to be in response to what this witness testifies to. And," he added in his inimitable throw-away manner, "the longer Mr. Grainger has to coach her, the longer it will be to get the truth from her."

"I *resent* that."

"Sorry," Bomber said, but he wasn't sorry. "Get her in now, she's not a suspect. Let's just get the truth from her. Mr. Grainger and the state should never fear the truth."

And so Judge Emory ruled. María Hermosillo was to be brought to court by my buddy, Sid, and Web would have a half an hour to put the fear of God in her about all the quasi-legal things he promised her and her pal, Rosa.

I don't know what District Attorney Grainger told María in his half hour with her, but on the stand, she looked like a nervous wreck.

A court appointed interpreter was on hand to translate, deadpan, the questions and responses.

Bomber tried to put the witness at ease with friendly softball questions, but it didn't work. It looked as though Web had spent his entire half hour demonizing Bomber.

Finally, he asked her— "Are you frightened?"

She nodded. "*Sí*—yes."

"Did you kill Aldo diCarlo?"

"No—"

"Then you've nothing to be frightened of."

She didn't seem convinced.

"Did the district attorney tell you you should be frightened of something?"

She looked to Web for help. He blushed, but he didn't give her any.

"What did he tell you to be frightened of?" Bomber asked.

"*You,*" she blurted out and drew a respectable laugh. Even the staid judge cracked a smile.

"Do I frighten you?" Bomber asked—remember he was talking like an earnest suitor on a first date.

She shook her head. "No."

"The district attorney wasn't going to call you as a witness, was he?"

She glanced at Web—who merely smiled back. He knew all eyes were on him, not just the witness'.

"I don't think so. He wasn't sure."

"Did he tell you he was going to put you on the witness stand?"

"No."

"Do you know why not?"

"Objection," Web said, keeping his seat. "Calls for conclusion."

"I'll rephrase. As a result of any conversations you had with the district attorney about this trial, or with Rosa—did you form any conclusions about why you would not be called as a witness?"

Before the interpreter could complete the question, the district attorney broke in: "Objection," he said. "That is not her testimony. No foundation."

"Oh, I'll let her answer that if she can."

"I guess because Rosa is less scared than I."

"And?"

Web almost objected, but sank back, changing his mind.

"Rosa would say what helped his case."

"And you wouldn't?"

She shook her head, not sure her answer was correct.

"Say your answer for the record, please. So the stenographer can hear you."

"No," she said.

Web rose as a courtly gentleman. "Your Honor, I must interpose here—Ms. Hermosillo is doing her best with the English language, but it does not come easily to her. I'm afraid she may be misleading the jury with her answers. What she means is—"

"Just a minute," Bomber said, throwing out his hand. "Let the witness speak for herself. We have a court appointed interpreter and we don't need any interpretation from the prosecutor. He's not testifying—she is."

"Your Honor, Bomber is making a big thing about me not calling this witness. He's making it look like she has something to say about the case I don't like. I am merely trying to say—"

"Your Honor," Bomber cut in, "please don't let him testify."

"Yes, Mr. Grainger—I'm afraid Mr. Hanson is correct." She said it like she was surprised Bomber could be right. "You may certainly put your spin on her testimony in your closing argument—explain anything, anyway you want." She paused and frowned. "But you *know* that."

"Thank you, Your Honor," Bomber said, with a flourish.

"All right, Ms. Hermosillo, let me give you the opportunity to explain your last answer. What did you mean when you said what you would say would not help the prosecutor's case?"

"Just...that...I mean, his case is against Cheryl Darling and I did not see her do anything, or hear her say anything that would make her be guilty."

Bomber switched gears—to set her up.

"Did Mr. Grainger promise you anything, or Rosa anything to testify?"

"He didn't *promise* anything," she said in such a way Bomber slid in for the kill.

"Did he say he'd do something for you two girls if you cooperated with him?"

She looked blank. Her gut must have been flipping like Sunday morning pancakes.

"I don't think so," she said.

"Are you familiar with the perjury laws?"

"No," she said.

"If you lie under oath—you remember taking an oath to tell the truth?"

"Yes."

"And if you don't tell the truth you can be put in jail?"

Her eyes bulged.

"And then Web couldn't help you get a green card?"

"*Ob*-jection," Web bleated. "*No* foundation—not the slightest! Bomber should be ashamed of himself."

"Should I?" Bomber asked. "Did *I* offer her a green card or did you?"

"*Most* unprofessional conduct."

"*Yours*," Bomber said, "or mine?"

"All right, gentlemen—enough. Ask the proper question, Mr. Hanson."

"I stand corrected." There it was—another one. I'd lost count.

"All right, Ms. Hermosillo, do you realize if you lie in court you could go to jail?"

"I do now," she answered.

"And if you go to jail you can't get a green card?"

She nodded with a sheepish drop of her eyelids. "Yes," she muttered, barely loud enough to be heard.

"All right, so, what was your understanding that Mr. Grainger would do for you and Rosa if you testified?"

"He said he would help us get permanent visas and a green card and be citizens—but he couldn't promise—"

"Just that he would help you?"

"Yes," she said, and I saw Bomber kiss goodbye his leverage with Web. I figured she had got Web off the hook—no promises, just enough carrot to motivate.

"So tell us, what do you remember about that party at Aldo diCarlo's the night he died?"

"Vague and uncertain, Your Honor," Web said.

"Oh, all right. Did you see any pills that night?"

"Yes."

"Where?"

"I saw them on the table in front of Mr. diCarlo."

"Any other time?"

"I saw bottles of pills on the cupboard shelf when someone opened the door."

"You say you saw someone at the cupboard where you saw pills?"

"Yes."

"Man or woman?"

"Woman."

"Do you see her in this courtroom?" Bomber asked, and there was the question most lawyers would call him foolhardy for. Was he really sure of the answer she would give? If not, asking the question is a no-no. I don't know how he could have been sure—I wasn't sure.

María peered around. Her eyes settled on Cheryl Darling momentarily and my heart jumped up into my throat and I thought María was just about to sink the ship. Then her eyes drifted away, over the sea of faces until they settled on the back row.

"*Allí*," she said in Spanish, pointing. "There, the *señora atrás*. In the back row."

She was pointing at Wissie's mom, who looked not nervous, as you'd expect, but almost relieved, as though she had been waiting her whole life for this moment.

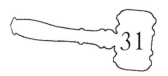

31

Bomber asked me to keep my eye on Gilda Murray, Wissie's mom, while we approached the bench. Bomber began— "I'd like to call Gilda Murray as a defense witness," he said. "But I'd like to talk to her first—perhaps we can save some time if you'll grant us a thirty minute recess."

"Thirty minutes!" Web exploded.

"Hey," Bomber said, "you got thirty minutes for a witness you'd already coached."

"I resent that—"

"Resent away. Thirty minutes is modest. I can put her on the stand, if you prefer, but that might prove embarrassing—"

"Threats?"

"My every thought is of your welfare," Bomber said, not entirely devoid of sarcasm. "Right next to the welfare of my client."

Judge Emory granted Bomber's request, I suppose, in the interests of truth, justice and mercy, not to mention expediency.

I'd kept my eye on Gilda Murray half-thinking she would bolt the courtroom. We had little legal grounds to restrain her if she took that notion in her head—but instead, she went like a lamb into the conference room off the front of the courtroom.

Cheryl was not allowed to join us, so she passed the interim in the company of her scintillating matron whose function was to see that Cheryl didn't flee. I guess we could be grateful they didn't have Cheryl in leg irons.

Gilda was moving on automatic pilot. But once I closed the door, something seemed to snap inside her and she became a wary, caged animal. Her eyes narrowed on Bomber, then turned to me, pleading, as though I held some sway in this case.

It was one of those rooms you experience in a nightmare—all essentials, but no windows to cheer it up and doors that looked like they would never open again.

"I think I should have a lawyer," she said, as though weighted down by a cast iron question mark.

Bomber turned so courtly it was almost an embarrassment. "Certainly," he said. "If you wish. I'm a lawyer, and I would be honored to represent you—Tod is also a lawyer. There will be no fee for today's consultation, and anything you say will be protected by the attorney-client privilege. That means I don't breathe a word of it to anybody."

"But..."

"You aren't being arrested. *Then* you would need a lawyer. I don't arrest people," he said. "I defend them. Much cleaner work."

"Will I be arrested?"

"I don't know. *I* won't arrest you. Have you done something that might warrant an arrest?"

"I don't think so—" she said in a fog.

"Did you look at Aldo's pills in his cupboard as the witness, María, said?"

She nodded her head.

"Did you—alter them in any way?"

"No."

"Why were you looking at them?"

"I just wanted to be sure Aldo was still taking them. That he was up to date."

"Was Wissie Aldo's child?"

She stared at Bomber, and I thought she was about to tremble. "Do I have to answer these questions?"

"Of course not," Bomber said ever so gently. It was fun to see him in his courtly gentleman mode. It was not a common occurrence. "I'm trying to help you—"

"You mean you're trying to help your client."

"That too," he said. "Do you see any reason why I

couldn't help you both?"

She pondered that but didn't produce an answer.

Bomber breached the silence. "I have two options," he said. "I can talk to you here and try to understand this crazy case, or I can simply put you on the stand in open court and fire away the questions. There, of course, I might be more aggressive. I thought you might prefer it this way. If I'm wrong, tell me, and we'll go the court route."

"No," she said, and looked away.

"All right, Mrs. Murray, if Wissie wasn't Aldo's child, who was her father?"

"She was a love child," she said, a tear working the corner of one eye.

"Another man?"

"Yes."

"Married?"

"Not to me." She was working her lungs like a bellows as though it would purify her memories.

"Did you know Aldo put Wissie in his will—soon after she was born, and that you were in that will too?"

"Yes. He told me."

"Why would he do that?"

"He had a big heart. He cared about me. I was one of his top models at the time."

"He ever do that for anyone else you know of?"

"I don't know."

"Would it surprise you to know Wissie was the only woman in Aldo's will for more than a couple of years?"

"No."

"Did you ever feel like killing Aldo?"

"Why would I do that?" I thought the idea startled her.

"How did you feel about Aldo dating your daughter?"

"Not good."

"Why not?"

"She was too young for him. She'd just turned sixteen. I didn't think his bisexuality was a good thing."

"Did you ever have an affair with Aldo?"

"I may have," she said as though she really didn't know. "Depends a lot—"

"On what?"

"Definitions."

"Well, I don't know what those definitions would be."

"I don't either," she said enigmatically.

Bomber didn't press. He wasn't in his court mode, he was rather attuned to confidence building.

"Do you know Cheryl Darling?"

"Slightly."

"What do you think of her?"

"She's all right," she shrugged. "The little I know."

"Used to date Aldo?"

"Yes."

"As you did?"

"Yes."

"And your daughter?"

(A labored sigh.) "Yes."

"I believe your daughter immediately succeeded Cheryl Darling in Aldo's affections."

"So I've heard."

"Think she was angry—Cheryl Darling?"

"I imagine."

"Enough to kill Aldo?"

"Apparently the police thought so."

"A year later? Isn't that a long spell for a crime committed in the heat of passion?"

"I wouldn't know."

"Wissie was supplanted by a young boy, I understand." She nodded.

"Not too long before Aldo was murdered?"

She shrugged again.

"Think that made Wissie angry?"

"I think she was better off because of it."

Bomber bobbed his head. "You think Wissie agreed?"

"I don't know. I doubt it. Separation hurts."

"Were you checking Aldo's pills to see if Wissie had messed with them?"

"No. Wissie had nothing to do with Aldo's murder. She's only sixteen."

Bomber nodded. "People are maturing faster," he said.

"No!" she almost shouted.

Bomber raised an eyebrow. "Oh? What else can you tell us?"

She fell silent again. I always thought it took a certain strength of character to remain silent in the face of interrogation. Questions always seemed to have a sense of urgency that demanded prompt responses. Many people found themselves in trouble for answering questions too quickly—and thoughtlessly.

"Well," Bomber said. "Allow me to recap your narrative. Please correct me if I misstate your version of events. You are a model—working for the rich and famous, celebrated Aldo Cabrisi diCarlo. You are dating him, yet find yourself inexplicably pregnant by another man—not your husband and not, so far as I can tell, even named. Aldo diCarlo was so overjoyed at this event, he put your progeny in his will. And the way you tell it, there was no blackmail involved—gosh, how could there be, the child wasn't his? Was he at all put out, by the way, that you had a child with another man while you were in a relationship with him?"

"I didn't say it was the same time."

"You didn't have to," Bomber said. "Lot of people these days can count to nine. The ubiquitous Gaiters, for example. Then, the great Aldo, celebrated on seven continents, has an affair with your daughter—virtually the minute she turns sixteen and clears the hurdle for statutory rape. No, I imagine if I were in your unenviable shoes and I'd had a relationship with Aldo sixteen years before, this could tick me off a bit."

"Well, yes," she cut in, "it did. I don't deny it."

"Ah, just so. And why *don't* you deny it? Could it be because, by the same token—putting myself in your place again—if it was not only *my* daughter, but *his* daughter as well, I think I'd want to kill him."

More silence from our guest of honor. Bomber decided to wait it out this time. There wasn't that much of our half hour left, but Bomber apparently thought passing it in silence with her at this juncture was a productive use of the time.

It worked. She spoke. "Do you think I could have a glass of water?"

"Certainly," Bomber said, and I was dispatched to bring it. I took my time, reasoning she might have wanted me out of there to speak more freely to Bomber alone. There is something inhibiting about these heart-to-hearts with a third person present. But I returned to the same silence. It was as though she were waiting for the water to loosen her up.

Being the dutiful son, I brought Bomber a glass, too. He even thanked me, but the gesture was, I suspected, more for the benefit of Wissie's mom. It was in Bomber's interest that she find him endearing.

After she took a healthy slug of the water, she sighed, paused for just a bit of further reflection, then said quietly: "What do you think happened?"

I know she was speaking generally, but Bomber took it as encouragement to give *his* version of her involvement.

"Thank you for asking," he said, and I could see the adrenalin shooting through him. "I'll tell you—but don't argue or interrupt until I'm finished." He looked to her for approval. She nodded—but barely.

"Here's the Reader's Digest version. If you need more details, just ask—when I'm finished.

"Number one. You had an affair with Aldo and he fathered the child. You had an agreement you would never name him in public—wouldn't file any paternity suits and such if he supported the child and put her in his will for, was it a million? A princely sum in those days, but had you sought my advice and counsel in the matter, I'd have tied it in to the consumer price index or Dow Jones or something, and it would be a lot more handsome today. I'd also have gotten you a nice piece of the action."

"I didn't…" she started to interrupt but Bomber cut her off.

"Remember our agreement," he said. "No interruptions."

She closed her mouth like a springing mousetrap.

"Oh, you can make an argument that too much unearned wealth can spoil a person, rob her of her self-determination and ambition, but we won't get into that—our time is fleeting.

"Aldo was happy to meet your terms. He is in a highly visible undertaking, and didn't care to risk a debilitating scandal. Though our tolerance for such things has inflated along with the stock market—in those days, disclosure wasn't worth the risk.

"I suppose all went well for sixteen years when, for some inexplicable reason, he wanted to have a taboo intimate relationship with his own daughter. Especially dastardly in your eyes—as well as mine—because his daughter wasn't aware of the paternity. You'd doubtless told her the same innocuous story you told me. You were, as anyone would have been—mortified—angry—furious, I don't think I can find a word to do your feelings justice. Now it gets a little murky for me. The simple answer is, you put some cyanide in one of his pills—put it in that night's dose and left the party early—knowing he would take them after you were gone—relieving you of suspicion. You probably had no idea Cheryl would still be there, so we can't hold that against you, though I ask you to consider her innocence and the future she faces in your deliberations."

Bomber was beginning to sound like he did addressing a jury.

"It all would have worked if that María from the caterers hadn't seen you fiddling with the pills. Did you know Cheryl Darling had bought cyanide? Did you find some of that or buy your own? You must have known the finger would point to her because of her purchase of the poison."

She stared straight ahead for a time.

Bomber said, "Close?"

She smiled a thin, self-satisfied smile. "Only close," she said, and there was a knock at the door.

"Time's up," a marshal said, when I answered the door.

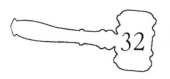

32

"Tod," Bomber said, "tell the judge we need fifteen more minutes."

I didn't see much chance of that, but I do as I'm told. I went to see the judge and made a fairly cohesive, if not eloquent, argument about Bomber being this far (indicating about an inch with my thumb and forefinger) from solving the case. The alternative was for him to dig it out of her with high drama on the witness chair, but that was more problematic, fraught with many hidden dangers, and could have been counterproductive to the prosecutor as well as the defense.

District Attorney Webster Arlington Grainger III, not eager to have Bomber pull another one out of his hat before his own startled eyes, generously and graciously agreed to the extra fifteen.

When I slipped unobtrusively back into the conference room, Mrs. Murray was in the midst of a painful narration. You could see the anguish in her face, sense it in her body—still the lithe body of a model.

"I haven't learned much in my mediocre life," she was saying, "but I know that no one is so big—so important—that he can ruin another's life for their own pleasure—to fill some need for constant variety and thrills. Like Aldo..." the name hung there in the air as though it were afraid to fall.

"Being a model isn't much of a training ground for real life," she said. "Standing around, trying to look sexy for no reason is no picnic, and it drains you. That's the funny thing. It drains you. You have a lot of time to think, but you can't think.

"And when the big, glamorous, handsome, sexy celebrity boss looks your way, you don't look away. Of course, you should look away—you know enough about him to send you running a three minute mile—but you don't. It's too flattering to ignore. You are the one that is going to make the difference for him."

"Impossible?" Bomber asked gently.

"Impossible," she said. "He's hardwired by his DNA to be what he is."

"And what was that?"

"Creative—some say a genius—I don't know. He sure could sell. But under all his genius and celebrity was this restless man. No triumph in his field was ever enough. I watched him—before, during, and after our fling. I obsessed about him, I'm not proud, I'm just stating the fact. He became my whole focus after having his child. And that was the turning point for him away from me. He said he hadn't the slightest aptitude for, or interest in, being a father. He gave me some money to go away and I took it. I will always be ashamed of that. He bought me. So many of us can be bought too easily. That was me—a sellout pushover. All I could think about was my baby and her welfare. I was destroyed when he told me he wanted nothing to do with our Wilhemina—that's what we called Wissie then."

She hung her head and repeated it, showing us some of the devastation she must have felt. "Destroyed!"

She looked off into space. "I still remember the hurt—still feel it over my whole body—when I realized he would have nothing to do with his own daughter. I so wanted a father for her. It's important for a girl to have a father."

She sighed. "When I finally came to terms with that..." she stopped dead in her tracks and started weeping quietly.

"He went after her," Bomber added. "Like a predator. Another experience for him—another notch on his gun. His own daughter."

She nodded.

"A momentary, demented thrill."

She nodded again and the floodgates opened.

Bomber and I sat helplessly by as Gilda got it out of her system. My stomach was doing flipflops at her revelations. This guy Aldo was a piece of work: soaring to the heights of his creative endeavors he plunged to the depths in his human endeavors. Celebrated and repulsive. When Gilda regained control, she said, "It's okay—I've come to terms with it. Sitting here, hearing all this. The world will miss him a lot more than they will miss me.

"It's all in how you look at things, whether you decide Aldo was a genius or a monster—or both. I made up my mind—I did what I had to do. I can't regret it. It isn't going to make Wissie whole, but it was all I could do—"

In that moment, Gilda Murray looked like a woman who felt she had done her bit, sang her song. "I'm ready to go," she said. "He wasn't worth it, but Wissie was."

"So, naturally, you had to kill him," Bomber suggested.

"No," she said, startling us.

"No?"

"No. Oh, I know I can't escape blame for it. He knew what he was. He couldn't control himself. Girls, boys, girls, boys again—Then…his own…" She couldn't complete the thought.

"Did he realize it?" Bomber asked.

"He did," she said. "It was part of his makeup. He did everything at top speed. Lived life on the edge. He was a bundle of nervous energy, and he was never able to rest on his laurels. Every triumph only made him want more. Every conquest set him thinking about the next one."

"Was that why he gambled?"

"*Yes!*" she exclaimed, coming to life. "His gambling was a double gamble. Not only did he throw money away in Vegas at the tables, but he deliberately went to his ex-partner's casino—flaunting his success in the face of a man he had done out of his share. In most cases, that would result in him sinking to the bottom of some lake with concrete shoes. But Aldo brought it off somehow. I'm sure the Vegas mob wanted to kill Aldo, but he just kept dumping money on them. Maybe it was to atone for cheating the mob in the first place. I think he was throwing it in their faces. And the irony is, they treated him like a king in Vegas. But losing money lost its fascination—the only thing that kept him going was the threat to his life. I think he'd come to the point where the only challenge left to him was to stay alive when the odds were against him. Well, they weren't against him, so he had to *make* them against him."

"How did he do that?"

"Going back to the mob's place again and again. Consorting with unsavories, picking lovers that put his life at risk. Jeffrey Xavier has AIDS, you know."

"I didn't," Bomber said, looking at me as though that was something I should have told him about.

She smiled the smile of sweet irony. "But Aldo continued to test negative. It disappointed him. He had a death wish, he did everything he could but jump out of a window, but he kept defeating the reaper. But being alive meant he had to continue to outdo himself. And every year that became harder. He lived in fear of failure so gigantic it would obliterate all the good he had done. That's why he agreed to my plan."

"What was your plan?"

"Russian Roulette. The most dangerous game in the world."

Bomber and I looked at each other simultaneously. "How would it work?" Bomber asked.

"He took three pills for depression and two vitamin pills each night. I added the poison and a placebo—so four of the pills looked like the vitamins. The idea was he'd take his five pills—out of the seven on the table. Three were distinguishable as depression drugs, the other four looked like each other. He was to take the three plus two of the vitamin look-alikes. That way his odds were four to one against getting the poison. It was a gamble and gambling excited him."

"How long had you been doing it?" Bomber asked.

"We'd talked about it for three months or so—right after he…"

"I know." Bomber said.

"It was going to be my punishment for him. I didn't want to kill him outright—well, I did, but I didn't want to go to jail for murder—" she stopped and swallowed air. "I guess I will, anyway—"

"Don't worry about that," Bomber said with a flag of the old bravura flapping. "I'm your attorney, if you want—Tod will tell you there is none finer."

"Oh," her eyes lifted, "he doesn't have to tell me—I've been in court."

"So when did the roulette begin?"

"The night of the party—I wasn't *checking* his pills, I was *adding* two as we agreed. I guess he got the poison."

"I guess he did," Bomber said.

"So what does that make me?" she asked, as though this were her first thought of the consequences.

"Good question. Perhaps an accomplice to suicide—suicide is illegal, you know—it's the only crime, if successfully committed, where the perpetrator is never prosecuted. But what it makes you depends on the intent of the dead man. Did he want to kill himself, or was he being blackmailed into it by you?"

"I'd hate to think of it as blackmail. Lets just say I gave him some moral alternatives. I could expose his incest—and as permissive as the attitudes in this country have become, you don't find much sympathy for an incestuous father. With Russian Roulette he had the thrill of a gamble and a fighting chance."

"Hmm," Bomber mused. "But sooner or later he was bound to get the poison. You could construe murder..."

"I *did* want to kill him after he went after our daughter. And I told him so."

"How did he react?"

"Contrite, like a little boy. He was always so charming. That was the thing about him. You wanted to kill him one minute and hug him the next. But he was out of control, and he knew it. I honestly think the next thrill he would have sought was the thrill of murdering someone himself."

"Would it have been you?"

"No—Jeffrey Xavier. What a shame he gets ten million

in Aldo's will instead. Another of life's ironies."

"And Wissie gets a paltry million."

"That's enough for a sixteen-year-old. She'll soon be making that much every year or so, thanks to Aldo launching her career. See what I mean about hugging and killing?"

"I see it," Bomber said.

I saw it, too.

Bomber turned to me. "Tod," he said, "how many pills were on the table when Aldo died? Was it three?"

"I think s-so."

"Let's verify it. Will the police still have them?"

"Hope so."

"Yeah—find out. Have them analyzed—what's in them—the ones he didn't take. If there were three left, they could have been the placebos. That would mean he took all his regular pills and the first one he came to was the poison."

"Or the pills could have b-been vitamins or anti-d-depressants."

"Exactly. Let's find out."

We were on our way back to court when the marshal came to tell us our time was up.

I walked beside Wissie's mom. "I'm glad things seem to be working out for you—"

She seemed surprised. "How?" she asked.

"Well, I see that handsome man you have beside you everyday in court."

"Oh," she said. "He's not mine."

Back in the courtroom, Bomber asked to approach the bench before the jury was brought back in.

He told the story of Gilda Murray with a touching and eloquent understatement. Then he asked the D.A. to drop the charges against Cheryl Darling (who I had secretly begun referring to in my mind as *my* darling).

Web said, "Is this a trick? Can he be serious? He wants me to drop a case based on his closed door sessions with a woman? No cross-examination? No nothing?"

Bomber smiled, "Yes," he said. "If I had displayed your suspicious lack of integrity with two cooped up witnesses, I'd be suspicious, too. I am extending this offer to save you further embarrassment."

"Embarrassment—counselor?" Judge Emory asked. "What sort of embarrassment?"

"We have a witness with exculpatory evidence—who the D.A. was hiding on the outskirts of town. There were no plans to hear from her, if I hadn't called her. Oh, we heard from the witness of the prosecutor's choice—the one that could do his flimsy case some good. Neither person was on the district attorney's witness list. Both were offered amnesty if they cooperated. I don't know how this learned court will view that, my own views have been made known. If the district attorney wants to drag this case on further, I will, of course, sing that song over and over to the jury—in all the keys."

It was a cute allusion on Bomber's part, but sheer hyperbole. He'd bore a jury to death repeating that bit twenty-four times—which was how many major and minor keys there were. Not to mention Bomber wasn't much of a singer.

Judge Emory said we'd hear this woman in camera in her chambers, and then she would decide if we would continue the case, or perhaps bind Wissie's mom for trial.

"We would also respectfully petition the court to subpoena the police evidence—that is, the pills that were on Aldo's table when he died—or, to be more accurate, when they arrived on the scene. I should like to have them analyzed by the police labs for content, if that hasn't already been done."

"Do you know if it has, Mr. Grainger?"

"I don't know. There didn't seem any need. The pill that killed him was already consumed."

"Do the police still have the evidence?"

"I hope so," he said, but I didn't believe him.

"If the pills are available, how long would it take to have them analyzed?"

"I don't know what the lab workload is."

"Can you have them rush it? We have a lot of people on hold here."

Web allowed as how he would do his best. Bomber whispered to me— "See that he does. If he gives you some cock and bull delaying story, follow it up."

We filed into the judge's chambers—Wissie's mom, Cheryl Darling, Bomber and I, and Wissie's mom told her story to Judge Estelle Emory, who barely blinked through the whole presentation. Gilda Murray had kept her daughter from the trial, in a belated effort to shelter Wissie's remaining sensibilities. When Wissie's mom was finished, Judge Emory looked at the D.A. "Well?" she said.

"If we are to accept the story on its face," District Attorney Grainger said, "I suppose I should bind her over for trial. Do you have an attorney, Ms. Murray?"

"Bomber is my attorney."

Web closed his eyes as though he had been struck with a stiff blow on his head. I could see his brain cells processing the information and looking for a place to dump it. Another case with Bomber he needed like a hole in the head.

We recessed and waited around the courthouse for word from the police lab. It didn't take long for the police to inform us they found the pills and were having them analyzed.

One of the wonderful things about Angelton was how close everything was to the courthouse. The police station was a block away, the lab another half block, our office three blocks. So we wouldn't have to wait for the Federal Express to deliver results from some remote metropolis.

Judge Emory told us she would take the lab technician's testimony on record with the jury present.

Cheryl Darling was in excellent spirits. Though Judge Emory said we should conclude the case before she released Cheryl from custody, it was all but over for her. Unless Web threw us a last minute hook, which I was sure he was fishing for.

I chatted with Cheryl in the hall and had a funny feeling about it. I couldn't put my finger on it, but I thought she seemed somewhat less interested in me. And conditions for dating and romance had not been ideal, what with me consumed with searching for evidence to clear her of charges and her being in jail. Could she have been faking the interest to get her through the trial? I did tell her I was working without charge on her behalf. Could she have been that mercenary? Unfortunately, I didn't have the nerve to ask her.

Bomber himself acted like Cheryl was home free, and he was shifting his efforts already to saving Wissie's mom from a murder charge.

Neither of us had any illusions that Web would go easy on Bomber's new client.

During the wait, I tried to talk to Cheryl, but the longer it dragged on, the more distant she seemed to become.

I asked her about it. "Is everything okay, Cheryl?"

"What?" she seemed distracted. "Oh, yes, thanks. Why?"

"You seem a little, well, distracted."

"I'm sorry," she said and put on one of her award winning smiles. "It's been an ordeal," she said. "Now I feel like I've been run over by a truck. I'm in limbo—my heart is pounding because it looks like we've won, but we're still on pins and needles waiting for yet another bit of evidence."

"There's nothing about that that should make you nervous, is there?"

"Oh, no, it's just—" she was on the verge of telling me something, then seemed to back off.

"What?"

She shook her head. "I can't," she said and clammed up. "You've been so wonderful," she said. "I don't know how I could have been so lucky. I'll never be able to thank you enough."

"Oh," I said, flirting shamelessly with batting eyes, "I think you will."

She seemed to shudder.

"What's the matter?" I asked.

"Oh, I think it's just hormones," she said, a theorem for which there is no rebuttal.

The chap from the lab showed up in his brown tweed jacket and askew knit tie. The jury was called in, and I could tell their patience had been stretched by the wait. Join the club.

Joseph Epstein was sworn in and he bounded to the stand as though he were behind schedule.

Bomber stood a good and unthreatening distance from Epstein and asked his questions gently—all the housekeeping stuff—where, when, how long, and the qualifications—thousands of chemical analyses, blah blah. The pills were given to him by officer so and so an hour and a half ago.

"Did you have a chance to analyze those pills?"

"Yes sir, I did."

"Can you tell us what you found?"

There were three pills given to me—which I was told were the three pills left on the table after the deceased Aldo Cabrisi diCarlo had taken the pill that killed him. The first pill, which I shall refer to as pill one, contained the element Lithium. Pill two was an anti-depressant, and pill three a mood stabilizer."

"Were there any placebos, or vitamins in the three pills you tested?"

"No, sir. There were not."

"No placebos?"

"No."

I looked back at Wissie's mom in the back row. The

dark, handsome stranger she said was not hers was hugging her.

Judge Emory was addressing the D.A. "Does the prosecution wish to make a motion at this time?"

Poor Web, he could have done the honorable thing and made a motion to dismiss—inevitable under the circumstances—without the prodding of the judge, but it just seemed to stick in his craw. Handing another victory to Bomber did not come easily to him. But he stood, and though he looked baffled by the request, he did manage to say, "Under the circumstances, the prosecution will move that the charges against Cheryl Darling be dropped. It would also appear that a case against Gilda Murray wouldn't hold water, as the apparent cause of Aldo diCarlo's death was suicide."

Web was referring to the evidence that Aldo took all four of the non-prescription pills, making sure he got the poison.

Web was a man who'd seen his great hope of beating Bomber melt on the living room carpet—he was not so morose from losing the case. He'd lost cases before. It was inevitable in his game (ours, too), but nothing made him salivate like the chance of beating Bomber. As often happens, a person has the fundamentals on his side, but he tries too hard. He lets his passion step on his reason.

Exculpatory evidence, they call it. Evidence which would clear from blame the accused. Web had it, and he hid it. Not the first D.A. to do so. Some say it is a gray area. The D.A.'s job is to win the case for the state. Let the defense attorney find the evidence helpful to his client. The district attorney can't be expected to try both sides of the case. It's the Vince Lombardi theory of gamesmanship—"Winning isn't everything, it's the only thing." It's an interesting argument. For myself, I can't see anybody wanting to convict a person who might be innocent. I know Bomber agrees with that. Whether or not he would subscribe to that if he were the D.A., I cannot say. But somehow, I doubt it.

When Judge Emory granted the district attorney's gracious motion, I jumped up and intercepted the slowly rising Cheryl Darling. We met in an excited embrace.

"You're free!" I said.

"*You* did it," she said.

Nervously, I reminded her of the autographed photo personally delivered, she owed Tiffany in Las Vegas. I don't know why I was so uncomfortable with her.

I heard footsteps approaching us and felt her grip loosening. She pulled her head away to look over my shoulder.

"Honey!" I heard a male voice exclaim—and it wasn't Bomber. I turned to see the sheik of Araby swim toward Cheryl with arms outstretched. They clashed head-on in a real embrace. The light from the window bounced off his shiny, slick hair, which was, no doubt, a metaphor for his slick soul.

I can't, or won't explain the depth of my despair at that moment. Count your blessings. But in those few moments, which I remember as my eternity, I tried to think of an instance where she had misled me about this movie sheik and I realized, to my horror, I couldn't think of any.

Forty-seven years later, when Cheryl Darling and the sheik came apart, she said, "Oh, Freddie, this is Tod. Tod, this is my fiancé, Freddie Haajib."

"Nice to meet you," he said.

I said nothing. For some stupid reason, all I could think of at that moment was how disappointed Mom would be.

"Tod saved my life, Freddie," she said. Then she turned to me. "We're going to be married in Vegas, so I can give that little Tiffany my picture. You made it possible. We'd like you to be our best man."

I was flustered. That didn't light any fires. I thought it was a cruel consolation. I should have been large spirited about it, but I just said, "Thanks. Very nice. May I let you know?"

"Sure."

I didn't, and the offer was not repeated.

Freddie raised an eyebrow as though he didn't believe it. Freddie, I found out later, was the richest man this side of Bill Gates.

When I came to my senses, I saw Wissie's mom hugging Bomber who looked like he'd seen a cockroach in his Coke.

He was not a man to suffer a hug gladly. I expected that hug would cost her a handsome fee that might otherwise be waived. But one thing I learned through it all was that models weren't poor, being too thin could make you too rich, or whatever.

When Bomber, in full understanding of the circumstances between Cheryl Darling and me, asked for my advice on the fee, I said he should pour the coals on. At a thousand an hour, Cheryl Darling had run up quite a tab, but she should be happy to pay it.

"I guess there's no senior citizen discount?" Bomber probed.

"No," I said without a trace of a stutter.

"And I guess the family discount is out."

"Yes."

"Doesn't really qualify for *Pro Bono*, not with that sheik on her arm—her thou an hour will be petty cash in that operation."

As I recall, it took me several days to realize that in Bomber's deep seated reticence where personal matters were concerned, his oblique comments about his fee were inadvertently indicative of his inner deep feelings for me. That was as close as he would come to verbalizing his empathy for my wounded feelings.

When I got home from court, I took out my musical sketches for my Cheryl Darling composition. I looked at the notes but they didn't make sense to me now. I realized I'd have to change the whole piece. I decided a minor key would be best—more in tune with my mood. E minor was my favorite minor key, but I also like C minor—C for Cheryl. And though it was hardly a compatible key, I'd work in a modulation to D minor for the finale. I'd call it "Darling." Or maybe not.

I never did finish that piece. Some things are better left undone.

The following are excerpts from other
David Champion books:
Bomber Hanson Mysteries
Phantom Virus
Celebrity Trouble
Nobody Roots for Goliath
The Mountain Massacres

The Snatch

Excerpts from *Phantom Virus*
A Bomber Hanson Mystery
by David Champion

I went back to the The Three Bears bar at slack time—
around dinner. Sam was behind the bar polishing glasses again.
It seemed to me that was all he did when he wasn't serving
drinks. And now that I think of it, I believe he had to keep his
hands moving so he wouldn't go nuts.

He seemed to stiffen when he saw me. I could tell what
was going through his mind—I told you no, kid, and I mean
no.

I didn't say anything, but nodded in the direction of the
piano.

He fixed me with his meanest stare. (He was really a
pussycat. How could he have been anything else, still selling
booze after his daughter was run down by a drunken driver?)
He held that stare for a long time while polishing the life out of
the glass at hand. I could tell he wanted to make me sweat, but I
don't think he realized how easily that was accomplished.

He finally let his head bob, but not without telegraphing
his feelings of disgust.

I went to the piano and started with some gentle Chopin

preludes. I didn't look up. The corner of my eye caught Sam at the bar polishing away, making a Herculean effort to look insouciant.

I swung into Mozart's twelve variations on *Twinkle, Twinkle Little Star*, then his popular C Major Sonata. On to Mendelssohn's E Minor *Rondo Capriccioso*. A few snippets from Bach's Well Tempered Clavichord, Book One—all the while trying to divine what moved Sam. I decided I had to get more romantic. I switched to Schumann: The *Träumerei*, the *Aufschwung*, opus 12.

The place was filling up when I hit him with Debussy's *Clair de Lune* again and *Arabesque*.

I thought I heard him draw a breath, or perhaps sniffle during the schmaltz. So, I continued it with some Brahms, Liszt and Rachmaninoff. The schmaltzier I got, the more affected Sam seemed to be.

By this time I was at the keyboard about three hours, and I vowed to stay there until (1) they closed, (2) he threw me out or (3) he agreed to testify. I felt that was about the order of likelihood.

For a change, I did a few Bartok and Prokofiev simple pieces. I'm not a great pianist—I couldn't make my living on the concert stage, but that night something came over me, and I don't believe I ever played better. It was as though I had a cause and that cause was Merilee Scioria, and I felt things coming out of me I didn't know were there.

I made a point of not looking at Sam. But I was just as careful to steal the sidelong glances that told me whether or not my music was striking a chord.

I had been holding back on *Für Elise*, but I wanted to play it as well as Sam thought his daughter played it, and who knew how that might have been. It was a piece so many played—often mechanically—often pitifully, but I wanted to pack it full of all the pathos, delicacy and gusto Beethoven must have thought he was putting in it.

When I began the single notes that started the piece, I

felt an adrenaline rush that almost knocked me off the bench. I had neither the energy nor the opportunity to check Sam at the bar. The place had thinned out and Sam was not extra busy, but I had been transported, and the notes flowed out my fingers as though drawn by the goddess of music.

Those main theme notes just floated on air as Beethoven (and I) returned to them again and again. The arpeggios of 16th notes swept along with a soulful sweetness I had never imagined.

As I arrived at the end, I closed my eyes for the theme and closing. I was so emotionally spent, I didn't think I ever wanted to open them.

When I finally did open my eyes, I saw Sam standing over my right shoulder. His gaze was straight ahead and steady—as though he were visualizing an apparition.

It seemed like I could have replayed the whole program before he spoke.

"You win," was all he said.

Excerpts from *Celebrity Trouble*
A Bomber Hanson Mystery
by David Champion

James stared straight ahead. I looked at his profile.
What a lousy spot for a kid to be in, I thought. Pleasing his
father (which must not have been a lead-pipe cinch) and telling
the truth to a stranger. His mother would have encouraged him
to tell the truth, of course, but it had always been so hard to
please his father.

"Did he offer to give you some money—or buy you
something if Steven gave you money?"

"Said I could have a bike."

"You don't have a bike?"

He shook his head. "Stolen," he said.

I had a sudden despicable thought (and I *am* ashamed
of it) that dad stole the bike and hocked it. "Would you like me
to get you a new bike?"

There was a sudden movement beside me, and there
was no more profile, it was face front. "Would you?" he said, in a
sense of hope but disbelief.

"Yes, James, I would, and I will. But first you must do
something for me."

He sank back, deflated. I got the profile again. "What?"
he said with the dullest inflection.

"Easy," I said. "Just tell me the truth about what happened at Steven's house, when you were in bed with him."

I could feel him cringe. From the look on his suddenly
pale face, I wasn't sure I wanted the truth.

His eleven-year-old mind was working, but I couldn't
tell if it was working for us or against us. I had complicated the
mix by throwing in the bicycle offer. How did he know which
truth I would find acceptable?

"Can you just tell me this: Did anything happen before
you went to sleep?"

"We just talked, like I told you."

"Was he touching you at all?"

"I told you, he was holding my hand."

"Nothing else?"

"No."

"So then you went to sleep?

"Yes."

I paused, hoping he would volunteer the rest. He didn't.

"After you went to sleep, what was your first next memory?"

James paused a long time. We were at the crux and he knew it. He probably also thought his father would kill him if he told me—but I had nullified one of the big convincers, I had offered him a bike, too. As if to verify my sincerity, he looked over at me again, before he gave me the profile again.

"It was morning when I got up," he said so softly I almost didn't hear him.

"Where was Steven?"

"Already up—"

"Then what happened?"

"He came back in the room and said he was sorry he left me alone, was I okay?"

"Were you?"

He nodded.

"Then?"

"I got dressed and we had breakfast and went outside and I drove the cars and the planes and rode on the merry-go-round."

"And nothing bad happened?"

He shook his head.

"Did you tell this to your father?"

He nodded.

"What did he say?"

"He said you never knew what could happen when you were asleep. He said Steven was a fag and those fags were all alike. He wouldn't trust a naked fag in bed with a little boy further than he could throw him, including the bed and the little boy."

James was still in profile, but he was crying—I reached out and put my arm around him.

"You don't like him calling you a little boy do you?"

He shook his head.

His mother came in. She'd heard the sobbing. "Oh, James, what's wrong?" she asked him, then looked to me for the answer.

"James just told me the truth. It wasn't easy. There are a lot of conflicts. He doesn't want to displease his father."

She looked me in the eye. "Then everything's fine?" she asked.

I nodded.

She seemed flooded with relief. She had been so sure, and yet—

"Well, young man," I said, "you've earned your bike. What kind do you want?" It wasn't until I said that that I realized he could ask for an Italian racing model in the thousands. I hoped and prayed Bomber would be good for it, but couldn't be sure. Making decisions based on economic considerations were not his thing. He could have easily overlooked the triumph for the client and say, "You made the promise; you deliver the goods."

But, no, it was a modest bike as new bikes go. We'd get out of the shop for under two hundred. There was this model in the window and it was a metallic-silver paint, and he had been looking at it every day going to and from school, hoping it wouldn't be sold until his father got the money from Steven as he assured James he would.

"Was it still there today?"

He stopped crying to say, "Yes!"

I took his mom aside and told her what to expect. I thanked her profusely for her help and offered to do anything to help them if the going got rough.

"Just to be safe," I said, "I wouldn't tell his dad about

this talk—or the bicycle."

On my way out, I shook James's hand. "You were a soldier," I said, not realizing that that line probably works better on a five-year old. Then I added a gratuitous platitude: "The truth never hurts as much as a lie, does it?"

He looked at me as though he didn't understand the question or I wouldn't understand the answer.

On my way back to the office, I stopped at the bike shop, and there was the coveted bike in the window as advertised.

I was pleasantly surprised at the reasonable price and the small gratuity it took to have it delivered right at closing time.

"Little kid been coming here ever'day," the store owner said, "drooling over this bike." He shook his head. "He's gonna be mighty sad it's gone."

I smiled so much it hurt. "No he won't," I said.

Excerpts from *Nobody Roots for Goliath*
A Bomber Hanson Mystery
by David Champion

She was driving so damn fast I didn't know what was going to give first, the engine mounts of the old pick-up or my liver.

It was probably nerves that gave her the lead foot on the gas. Her nerves. My nerves were already shot.

Carrie Zepf was her name, short for "Carol" she had told me. She was strongly built with dishwater blond hair that was sheered off above her shoulders, by one of her sisters from the look of it. She was old enough to vote, but way too young to drive. She had written the letter that got me into this death trap in the first place. It was a beguiling letter—poignant and engaging—about her blind father on his last legs from lung cancer and her institutionalized mother with twelve girls at home. I had pictured the sender as younger, less worldly—not someone who would pilot a hundred-year-old Ford pickup on these rutted-country dirt roads at a million miles an hour.

"Carrie!" I yelped, my hands braced on what was left of the dashboard. "If I don't get there alive, I guarantee we won't take the case."

"Sissy," she said, taking a corner so fast I was thrown against her. She giggled, "Not my fault your plane was late. Dinner be gettin' cold by now."

"I'm not hungry," I said.

"I am," she said.

My father had flipped out this time—sending me across the United States to look into the feasibility of taking a smoking case on a contingency. It was a loser for sure, and I was against it from the beginning.

It was a harebrained idea. Of course, that is not a sentiment I would have the nerve to express in Bomber's presence. I didn't say "Boo" to my father, Bomber Hanson, who claims to be the leading trial lawyer in the country—and he doesn't get much argument. Not many people have the nerve to say "Boo!" to Bomber Hanson, except a few judges who are appointed for life.

I am unable to explain how we arrived at the Zepf farm without any structural damage. My nervous system, I was sure, was irreparable. And when I saw the flock of hens in their Sunday-go-to-meeting dresses fly at me from every angle, I got a lump in my throat as big as that battered pick-up I was just stepping out of. And, believe me, the earth never felt better under my feet.

*   *   *

I adored the way she talked; earnestly, intelligently, her eyes so alive and probing. She had the aura of honesty, decency and goodwill. I not only hired Shauna, I fell in love with her.

Of course, I didn't tell Bomber how I felt. When I told him I had hired our researcher, he asked, "What's his name?"

"Shauna McKinley," I said.

He paused for a moment. "Isn't that a girl's name? He's no pansy is he? I'm not keen on pansies, you know."

"He is a she," I cut him off before he got deeper into his Neanderthal prejudices.

"A she? Jesus Jenny Tod, a *she*! You hired a *girl* lawyer?"

"Woman," I corrected him.

"How old?"

"Twenty-five."

"Jesus Jenny, oh my God in heaven. I should have known you couldn't be trusted. Weren't there any men available? There must have been."

"I interviewed two b-b-boys." I said. "She was j-just so much b-b-better."

"Oh, my God!" Then he seemed to pause for reflection. "Say, you aren't sweet on her are you?"

"How could I be?" I lied. "I just met her."

"Well, get her started," he said with a sigh.

"We are not talking penny-ante crime here, we are talking the crime of the century. Up to about three mil a year in deaths now, isn't it?"

He winced. I wasn't sure what could be said for Don Powell at this stage, but he was sensitive to the daily disaster he helped bring about.

"You are one of the most important industrial manufacturers in the world," I said, laying it on. He shifted only slightly. "I am just a kid lawyer doing legwork. But my father is Bomber Hanson and, if you've ever read a newspaper or looked at a TV news show, I don't have to tell you who *he* is."

He gave me a small nod.

"Bomber doesn't take cases to harass people. He's a big-picture man—and where is there a bigger picture?"

"Nowhere," he muttered in agreement.

"He wants me to offer you two first-class tickets to the coast. Limousines both ways from L.A. to Angelton. You pick the time and the duration. He'd like to have an hour or two with you, but he'll settle for half that."

"What do I have to do in return?"

"Just listen to his story."

He smirked. "Like one of those condos-in-the-Bahamas scams?"

"I wouldn't know about that," I said. "This is no scam."

"You mean, if I'm not convinced, I don't have any obligation?"

You'll be convinced, I thought, but I said, "That's right."

"Besides a free vacation," he said, "what's in it for me?"

"I don't know," I said. "A clearer conscience maybe." I was throwing darts I had not intended and they were hitting the target.

"And all I have to do is sell my lifelong friends down the river," Don Powell said.

"Bomber would probably prefer to look at it as saving lives."

His head bobbed as though it were Jell-O on springs.

"But before we put either one of you to the trouble, I am obligated to get a few things straight. One thing always comes up hazy in discussions about cigarette manufacturing—at least to me. When you refine the tobacco, I understand you take all the nicotine out?"

He nodded. "Temporarily."

"Then you put it back?"

He nodded again.

"Do you sometimes put back more than you take out?"

He shrugged as though I had asked how the roast beef sandwich was. "It's possible."

"Why don't you just leave it out?"

"The taste," he said. "People don't like the taste."

"Isn't it the nicotine that makes the cigarettes addictive?"

"So they say."

"But you don't know? Is this another case of you not believing the studies because that's your employer's conceit, or do you genuinely not know?"

"I'm not a scientist." He started to say he was just a manufacturer, but I cut him off.

"And Eichman was a geneticist."

His cheek twitched. "Low blow," he said, but I didn't apologize.

"But is it so remote? You'd need a lot more gas chambers than the Nazis had to do the job you are doing."

"People smoke by choice," he said, trotting out the company wisdom. "Relaxes them. Like a drink of liquor. Booze will kill too, if you overdo it."

"So we have some three-million a year who smoke too much."

He started to nod, but he got only halfway.

"Well," I said, "it's up to you. We can call you as a friendly witness or subpoena you as a hostile witness. From my experience, when you are facing Bomber Hanson, you are much better off in the friendly category."

He stared straight ahead. No more pretense of reading

the newspaper. "I'd be finished in this town," he said. "No question. No job, no reputation, no friends. Everything gone."

"You have anything put away?" I asked, being practical.

He gave a short laugh. "I have a good pension coming, unless I screw up. I've got a lot of company stock in options and bonuses."

"Sell it," I said.

"Not so easy," he said. "I'm an officer of the company. I have to report any substantial changes. I blow the whistle, what do you think happens to my stock?"

"Hard to outguess the stock market," I offered without much conviction.

"It won't make the stock go up," he told me.

"Do you have any other assets?"

"House."

"Is it clear?"

"No, there's a small mortgage. These places aren't worth what they are in California, you know. I have about two hundred equity in the house, I guess. Of course, if you *are* successful and it starts a chain reaction, the house won't be worth anything either."

"Sell it," I said. I was full of advice.

"Think anyone would wonder why?"

"Who has to know?"

It was that hopeless snort again. "In this town, a secret lasts about five minutes until everybody knows it."

I was going to ask if he knew his wife's secret, but I refrained.

"Think about it," I said.

"I'll think about it," he said.

"Fair enough," I said, putting out my hand for a shake. "Your wife has my number."

That smirk was on his lips again.

"Everybody has your number," he said, and I watched his back shamble out of the park.

Excerpts from *The Mountain Massacres*
A Bomber Hanson Mystery
By David Champion

"Now, I believe you gave testimony that you told Mr. O'Neil he might want to get a lawyer."

"I might have."

"And did you suspect him of killing his own dogs?"

"No, I..."

"Or of any other crime?"

"Not at the time, no."

"Just so. But still you suggested a lawyer."

"Only if he wanted to file a civil action."

"Did he?" Bomber asked. Yankus looked like he didn't understand the question. "Did he bring up the civil suit, or did you?"

"I don't know. It was only a suggestion."

"A suggestion, or a put-off?"

Web was up again. "Your Honor, how much of this do we have to put up with? The officer made the report. Let him ask if he has it. What it says. We can jaw forever about this trivia. We can take this case into the next century. This is the guy who took the report. He *took* it! It's in the records. The rest is window dressing. And Mr. Hanson knows full well, he..."

"Mr. Grainger, is there an objection in there somewhere?"

"Yes, sir..."

"Sustained," the judge grumbled, adding, "sounds like a speech to me."

The D.A. sat down.

"All right," Bomber said to the witness, "you took the report?"

"Yes."

"May I just clarify the sequence of events then? Mr. O'Neil came to you at the desk of the police station on Newport Street?"

"Yes."

"He asked you to make a police report?"

"Yes. Told me his dogs were shot."

"Had a suspect?"

"Yes." Officer Yankus referred to the report. "Alf Ritchie."

"Thanks for that gratuitous answer. I didn't ask for it. Then you told him he should see a lawyer?"

"I may have."

"*Before* you made the report?"

"I don't remember."

"Is it possible?"

"I guess."

"Why would you suggest a civil action?"

"For retribution. For remuneration..."

"Not to save you writing the report?"

"Objection."

"Oh, let him answer," Judge Murdoch said.

"No, sir. I took the report."

"Eventually, you did. I just want you to know we can fill this courtroom with people who think you've discouraged them from making police reports."

"Objection, Your Honor. He doesn't have to badger this officer."

"Yes, lay off, Mr. Hanson."

"I stand corrected."

I realize, listening to Bomber go, that he has these remarkable qualities that I lack. I am more passive, like my mother. I get no thrill from besting my fellow man. I have no bloodlust. No killer instinct. I probably would have lasted two seconds in the jungle where Bomber would have been king.

But, I was satisfied. I had my music. Writing music was not combative. I could create a perfect world of sound to be reproduced by a musical ensemble where the prerequisite for participation was the ability to harmonize with each other—to work together toward a common goal. Power trips and temper tantrums were the purview of prima donnas, the conductors, the soloists. The soldiers in the pit hewed a line of their own understanding. They were the indispensable music makers.

And so was I.

"Two more questions, if I may?" Bomber said.

The judge waved his hand for Bomber to proceed.

"Is it possible Mr. O'Neil got the impression you didn't want to file the report?"

"I guess anything's possible."

"In his position: Your two collies have been shot, you think a policeman doesn't want to bother with you—might you be angry?"

"I suppose so."

"Mad as hell?"

"Maybe."

"That's *three*," Webster Grainger muttered.

"So sorry," Bomber said.

The judge waved the D.A. off.

"Okay, this is the end," Bomber said, smiling at the witness, who smiled back in obvious relief as he started to rise. Bomber put his hand up. "One more thing," he said, "if you don't mind." Yankus sat down, dejected.

I saw the zinger coming a mile away.

"Did you make any recommendations as far as hiring any particular attorney went?"

Officer Yankus smiled sheepishly. I guess he was relieved the question didn't reflect on his gold-bricking.

"I may have."

"And what did you tell him?"

"I may have told him he should hire you—if he wanted to win."

The sheepish smile was now a big grin.

"Oh my God," the D.A. groaned.

Excepts from *The Snatch*
By David Champion

The big doors opened on the stroke of two. As though they didn't want to keep Badeye a moment longer than was necessary.

Coming toward Harry, Badeye was the cock of the walk, a man who had faced down the gas chamber for killing a cop.

When Badeye reached the corner of the city park–elevated above the detritus of its everyday life–Harry fell in behind him. Badeye turned suddenly and exclaimed, "Horseshid," and started running up the steps to the park.

He was no match for Harry, who made a religion of keeping himself in shape–he easily tackled Badeye on the grass.

As the wily con's nose sank into the moist green grass, he decided he liked the smell. Where he came from, nothing smelled like damp grass.

Harry snapped a nice new pair of handcuffs on one wrist behind Badeye's back, then the other.

Badeye wanted to put up more of a fight, but there wasn't that much fight left in him.

Holding Badeye's arm, Harry directed him to his Volkswagen Bug, sat him inside, none too gently, on his cuffed hands–then shut the door as if on a date.

In the driver's seat, he smiled at Badeye and gave him a playful wink. Badeye spoke first as Harry started the engine.

"Fukkin' sewing machine," Badeye sneered. "Fuzz on the take like you oughtta have a big-assed car."

"Now, now, Badeye, mustn't judge others like they were you."

"So what do you want, hotshot? You gonna waste me, get it over with."

"Hey, would I do that? I'm a policeman."

Badeye snorted, but seemed to relax.

Harry shifted gears and climbed the on-ramp to the

Harbor Freeway.

"This thing's a piece of shit," Badeye snorted.

"I notice you were walking," Harry said. "Let's just rap a little about the meaning of life and stuff like that. I'm speaking, of course, of the late Charlie Rubenstein–a prince, Badeye–and you will admit you are a punk–and next to Charlie your stature is something between a wart and a festering boil."

"Hey, get off my case, man, I wasn't even indicted," Badeye snorted. "Shitty police work." He seemed amused.

"Ah yes, my boy, the system." Traffic was light on the freeway. Harry was in the right lane, the speedometer needle frozen on fifty-five. "It's a system that lets a punk like you take the life of the prince of the police force and get away with it on some flimsy technicality. Now, Badeye–you boys don't seem to spend a lot of time worrying about the law of the land, and I'm just speculating on how you would handle the thing if you were in my shoes."

"Charlie was gettin' too close to the boys..."

"He was trying to show the ten- to twelve-year-olds there was more to life than killing each other. So where's the beef?"

"Not his business."

"Rather have cops on your case all the time? Better than trying to work with you–give you an alternative to the streets?"

"She-it, you don't know nothin' 'bout the street. We ain't gettin' outta here nohow. There ain't no opportunity out there for the brothers."

"Yeah? Tell that to the black mayor–tell that to the black police commissioner, tell that to all the blacks on the city council. Charlie Rubenstein wanted to help, so you killed him."

"Hey, man, I ain't had nothin' to do wid it. I mean, man, I incarcerated, or I free as a bird?"

Harry nodded vigorously, "You is free as a bird."

"Then get these goddamn cuffs offa me. They's killing me."

Harry headed the car down the Century Boulevard off-ramp. Badeye felt another twinge of relief. He was going home.

The car stopped outside an isolated deserted building that served as a warehouse in happier times. Before the brothers took it in their heads to burn the neighborhood back in '65. Though this building employed fourteen local men, the owners threw in the towel after it had been looted and burned.

"This is where we get out, Earnest," Harry said, waving his pistol in the direction of the burned-out warehouse.

"We? Hey, man, you a policeman, remember—you no executioner." Badeye's good eye was starting to twitch. "You said you wasn't gonna waste me."

They were inside the charred building, with the blackened bricks and the steel beams still intact.

"Now you just stand there, Earnest, nice and quiet like, and give me the details of how you gave it to Charlie."

Badeye stared dumbly at Harry. "You *is* gonna waste me."

"No, no, I hope not. Certainly not if you cooperate."

"Cooperate? What I gotta do?"

"Tell me about Charlie, for starters—how did you get the brainstorm to pull out his fingernails? Was that your idea—Whistler says it was—or was he really the genius behind that?"

"Stop jerking me off, Horseshid—I know my rights backwards and forwards. You get me a lawyer, you wanna ax all these personal questions."

"A lawyer? Why, what a good idea! But, geez, lawyers go with indictments, and we wouldn't want that," Harry said. "And the teeth, Earnest, you broke all his teeth with a hammer. This was the best friend your boys ever had. He was a guy who cared about them. He wasn't a cop, he was an optimistic social worker. You cut him down before he had a chance to get jaded. Hey, you know I've had a little trouble keeping partners—I never had one like Charlie. Here was a guy more interested in his duty than a free lunch. And the cuts, Earnest—the cuts all over his body and the ants—if you are in that line of work, I suppose that would be considered artful."

"I don't know nothin'."

Harry sighed.

"Now I'm walkin' outta here, man. I ain't takin' no more a your shid."

"Ah, Earnest. You wouldn't want me to have to shoot you for resisting arrest."

"Hey, man, you said you wasn't gonna waste me."

Harry was beginning to smell the perspiration. "Satisfy my curiosity," Harry said. "How did Charlie take it? I mean, was he stoic—you know, brave—or did he cry like a baby?"

"Oh, man, you know it weren't pleasant—took it a hell of a lot better'n you woulda..."

"I appreciate that, Earnest..."

"Hey, but I had nothin' to do wid it. I was just watchin'."

"Yeah, watchin'." Harry drew a breath. "Okay, Earnest, here's what I'm offering you..." He backed away from Badeye, keeping the pistol pointed at his forehead. Harry reached into his back pocket for his handkerchief, then drew another pistol from the side pocket and wiped it clean of his fingerprints.

"Here," he said, "I brought your piece from Frisco. I even put a bullet in it." He laid it on the floor a few paces from Badeye. "I thought a long time about this, Earnest. My first choice was to give you the exact treatment you gave Charlie. An eye for an eye. Then I realized Charlie would never have gone for it—woulda said we gotta treat you better 'cause we had more advantages. I never, myself, bought into that philosophy, but in Charlie's memory—I'm going to make it easy on you."

"You said you wouldn't..."

"Earnest, you got three choices. One, you run for it like a coward." Harry smacked his hand against the gun. "History. Put your prints on the piece. Two, you take yourself out like a man. Eye for an eye sort of thing." Harry stopped.

"You said three."

"Very good, Earnest. You got a good memory, and on top of that you can count as high as three." Harry shook his head. "You'da made it in the real world, Earnest. What a terrible waste. But, hey, I thought your third option was obvious. You try to get that bullet in me before I get one in you."

"How I gonna do that? You already got the piece pointed at me."

Harry smiled. "Won't be easy."

"Man, you said you wouldn't..."

Harry unlocked Badeye's cuffs, then walked around to face him, keeping his gun pointed at Badeye's gut.

Badeye looked at the gun down near his feet. The lazy mind was working, calculating his chances.

"Where's the bullet?" he asked.

"First chamber."

"How I know?"

"Pick it up an' look at it, stupid."

"You'll shoot."

"Yes, unless you shoot yourself, that's the plan."

Badeye Iler licked his lips. He had to admit he enjoyed more giving Charlie his.

Slowly, Badeye picked up the gun and gently turned it to look in the chamber. Harry told the truth, there was one bullet in the first chamber, ready to go off.

Badeye whipped the gun around, but Harry got him—Badeye's went off, but he was already on his way down.

Harry looked down at his adversary in the last throes of life. What a rip-off, he thought. An unfair trade, a sacrifice of a punk for a prince.

Badeye's eyes were open. The last thing he saw was Officer Harry Schlacter, LAPD, looking down at him. The huge, blond, lily-white policeman was crying.

Also Available from Allen A. Knoll, Publishers
Books for Intelligent People Who Read for Fun

The Snatch
By David Champion
Two cops whose methods are polar opposites—in love with the same kidnapped woman—race against time and each other to save her. From Los Angeles' lowlands to its highest mountain, *The Snatch* races at breakneck speed to a crashing climax. $19.95

The Mountain Massacres: A Bomber Hanson Mystery
By David Champion
In this riveting, edge-of-your-seat suspense drama, world-famous attorney Bomber Hanson and his engaging son Tod explore perplexing and mysterious deaths in a remote mountain community. $14.95

Nobody Roots for Goliath: A Bomber Hanson Mystery
By David Champion
Mega-lawyer Bomber Hanson and his son Tod take on the big guns—the tobacco industry. Is it responsible for killing their client? $22.95

Celebrity Trouble: A Bomber Hanson Mystery
By David Champion
Unspeakable acts of child molestation against mega-star Steven Shag prompt him to call Bomber Hanson. Courtroom theatrics abound as the nature of man unfolds in this continuation of the accalimed series. $20

Phantom Virus: A Bomber Hanson Mystery
By David Champion
Did the cure for the disease kill the patient? Was her diagnosed virus a Phantom Virus? $23.00

Ship Shapely: A Gil Yates Private Investigator Novel
By Alistair Boyle
Did the five gorgeous women who sailed the pacific with their lusty captain have a hand in his disappearance? $20

Bluebeards Last Stand: A Gil Yates Private Investigator Novel
By Alistair Boyle
A rich widow, a gold-digging boyfriend and a luxury cruise to New Zealand is Gil Yates's latest escapade. $20

The Unlucky Seven: A Gil Yates Private Investigator Novel
By Alistair Boyle
Do seven powerful people rule the world? Control all of our actions? Someone thinks so, and is systematically sending bombs to kill each of these seven wealthy and influential men. Three are dead already by the time mega-priced, contingency private investigator Gil Yates arrives on the scene. $20

The Con: A Gil Yates Private Investigator Novel
By Alistair Boyle
Gil Yates is at it again—this time in the high-stakes art world, bringing the danger, romance and humor that Boyle's fans love. $19.95

The Missing Link: A Gil Yates Private Investigator Novel
By Alistair Boyle
A desperate and ruthless father demands that Gil bring him his missing daughter. The game quickly turns deadly with each unburied secret, until Gil's own life hangs by a thread. $19.95

Order from your bookstore, library, or from Allen A. Knoll, Publishers at (800) 777-7623. Or send a check for the amount of the book, plus $3.00 shipping and handling for the first book, $1.50 for each additional book, (plus 7 ¾% tax for California residents) to: Allen A. Knoll, Publishers, 200 West Victoria Street, Santa Barbara, Ca 93101. Credit Cards accepted. Please call if you have any questions—(800) 777-7623 or email bookinfo@knollpublishers.com.